THEORY
OF WAR

THEORY OF WAR

JOAN BRADY

ALFRED A. KNOPF

NEW YORK

1993

THIS IS A BORZOI BOOK
PUBLISHED BY ALFRED A. KNOPF, INC.

Copyright © 1993 by Joan Brady
All rights reserved under International and Pan-American
Copyright Conventions. Published in the United States by
Alfred A. Knopf, Inc., New York.
Distributed by Random House, Inc., New York. Originally
published in Great Britain by André Deutsch, London.

Library of Congress Cataloging-in-Publication Data

Brady, Joan.
Theory of war / by Joan Brady. — 1st American ed.
p.   cm.
ISBN 0-679-41966-7
1. United States—History—1865– —Fiction.   2. Slavery—
Middle West—Fiction.   I. Title.
PS3552.R2432T47   1993
813′.54—dc20   92-24236
CIP

Manufactured in the United States of America
Published April 19, 1993
Second Printing Before Publication

*This novel was supported by a grant from the
National Endowment for the Arts.*

For

ALEXANDER BRADY

and his children
and his children's children

ACKNOWLEDGMENTS

This book has been in the works so long that I have lost track of most of the sources found for me by the resourceful and endlessly patient staff of the Totnes Library. I do remember Percy French's memoir *Railroadman,* though; I couldn't have written the book without it. Nor could I have managed without Dr. J. Morrison Brady and Mrs. Esther Arnold, both of whom answered all my questions about their father more fully than any interviewer could dare to hope. I also owe a great deal to Ruth Mathewson, Michael Wood and Alexander Masters for early readings and suggestions. As for Al and Jo Hart, who gave me courage to go on, the simple thanks I have to offer could never repay the debt I feel. Nor can I ever repay James Hale and Mary Siepmann, without whose generosity of spirit this novel would still be just a manuscript. And then there's Dexter Masters, who taught me all I know about writing, who encouraged, debated, suggested, edited—all to the immeasurable benefit of these and other pages— and who himself supplied what is, in my opinion, the best line in this book.

CONTENTS

PART 1

TUESDAY:
RECONNAISSANCE

1

HOW STUPID the young are. When I was twenty-one I enrolled in philosophy at Columbia University. I wanted to find truth. I hired helpers to wheel me to it. My professors said, "Truth exists. It's real and absolute. But the only place it has any meaning is in questions like 'Is it going to rain tomorrow?' Wait until tomorrow and see. Then—hey, presto—you've got the truth." Well, what the hell good is that to me? I live down here, deep down in this wheelchair. I need more.

I'll start in Sweetbrier. I hate the Midwest, and Sweetbrier never was up to much, anyway. Today it's no more than a smattering of shacks tossed down along one of those roads that score the cornfields. Cars don't stop here. Farmers go elsewhere to shop and socialize. You can still make out Benbow Wikin's name over his grocery store if you really want to, but there's hardly anything on the shelves inside. The few patrons that come and go are as creaky and barren as the aged toad of a man who sleeps behind the counter.

Here lie the beginnings of truth.

Sweetbrier started to fall apart in 1923. The Midwest Pacific decided to close the line through the town, which had become not much more than a water stop on the way from Topeka to Jefferson City. This wasn't the way the townspeople looked at it, of course, but people do kid themselves so. The news first appeared in the *Overland Sentinel*. Most everybody refused to believe it until Senator George Stoke—the great windbag himself—told them it was true. History calls this windbag a "fearless liberal." Encyclopedias talk about his reformation of the Senate rules, his campaign against the First World War, his denunciation of the Treaty of Versailles, his federal power projects—one so famous I'm afraid to mention it—and all those farm relief measures. John F. Kennedy wrote him into *Profiles in Courage.* Even so I say he was a windbag. Worse than that, he was a first-class shit, and the end he came to was too good for him—way too good for him. I'll get to it.

Anyhow, he'd formed anti-railroad committees before anybody else had even absorbed the news. The *Overland Sentinel* suggested a picnic lunch on the lawns of his mansion, where at this late date in his career, the senator was still growing power as his main crop, manuring it well with money and years of patronage, planting in spring, flourishing in summer, ready for harvest by November and election time, for the festivals, the cider, the corn dollies—the win, the kill—and then plowing under in preparation for years to come. The senator lived just out of town. "We'll run a full-page ad, Senator, sir," the gangly young journalist said to him. "Course we will." And the senator's eyebrows slithered around on his face like live bait in a fishing bucket.

It would certainly help if I knew what truth is. At Columbia they said they taught a powerful technique for making successive approximations to it; the phrasing is theirs, not mine. Like calculus, they said. But calculus produces something solid, slope of a tangent, orbit of a planet. Ask the philosophers what they produce, and all you get is drivel about weather reports and rain today. Well, as I say, it isn't good enough. Besides, I'll bet truth (whatever it is) is sometimes truer when you make it up. Like that first Saturday in June of 1923, out on the senator's lawn. I wasn't there. I wasn't even born. But I can *see* the wives of local worthies setting up tables on the grass. I can *see* the senator's Greek-columned portico, asquat above rolling lawns like a tourist caught out with diarrhea alongside a golf course. Tablecloths flap in the breeze. Wicker baskets disgorge hams, salads, pies, cakes, lemonade, ice cream. The women gossip while they work. Hats bob. Dresses billow. My uncle Atlas knew most of these women. He told me about them years ago, when I was young, before the tumor in my spine began to grow too big for its bony enclosure. They had names like Hattie and Maude, Gertrude, Carrie and Hope.

At eleven-thirty, guests from all over the state of Kansas begin to arrive. Men in Sunday suits take out hip flasks and add gin to the lemonade. It would have been bootleg gin, wouldn't it? The twenties were Prohibition years, weren't they? Not that it matters. Boys in knickerbocker pants and girls with hoops. Barking dogs. A banner says SIGN AND GIVE TO SAVE SWEETBRIER and snaps in the breeze. Or perhaps the day was windless. This doesn't matter, either. At twelve, the dancing begins. At one, the senator's vast bulk irons down the grass across the lawn on the way to his speech. "Timing's everything," the senator used to say. "Get the timing right and you got your public fucked before you lay down a penny." He stops here to shake a hand and there to bend his public smile over a lady's glove. He makes a perilous stoop from the waist to accept ice cream from a girl in ringlets.

Photographs of Senator George Stoke at the age of sixty-two are not pretty. Some fat men look well contained. Not George Stoke. He oozed. His lower eyelids gaped; they exposed their angry red interiors, which showed not red but black in the grainy black-and-white newsprint of the time; they seeped. The flesh hung over his starched collar as moist and flaccid as rotting pork. He carried a walking stick that ended in an open-mouthed snake with real snake's teeth and pearls for eyes. He wore a frock coat, shiny at the elbows and cut to a pattern that had gone out of style nearly thirty years before. This frock coat was important to him—and it's important to me and to what goes on hereafter. He'd worn one like it throughout his career. Everybody knew George Stoke's frock coat. Everybody knew his monumental vulgarity, too; he worked hard at it. He jiggled with glee when he shocked the straightlaced and the starched. "See this litmus paper?" he'd ask one such. "I'm gonna put it up to your face just like this, right? And by the"—oh, what a deliciously hideous, famous, favorite phrase: oh, how long in my life I've wanted to use it and never, never once, found just the right meeting of opportunity and, well, what? courage? confidence?—"And," said George Stoke, Democrat of the State of Kansas, essential bit of plumbing in the United States Senate for more years than anybody could remember, "by the quivering cunt of the unfucked mother of Christ, it's gonna tell me whose ass you had your nose stuck up last night."

But it was more than words. This Senator Stoke was a cobra of a politician. He knew what he wanted; he knew what was right for the people who voted him in, and he saw no reason to modify it for anything or anybody at all. He lulled his enemies into comfort, then squeezed them dry and threw away the husk. He'd survived in politics for a long time. He'd been re-elected again and again according to laws that in any civilized society would have ruled him out to begin with. But then there aren't any civilized societies, are there?

2

MY GRANDFATHER knew George Stoke well. They grew up together, but there couldn't be any two men less alike, at least to look at. Where George was suet, my grandfather was fire. He reminds me of the steelworks at Cardiff that lie alongside the major artery from Wales into England, where I live the life of a resident alien. They're a vast landscape of foundries, furnaces, rolling mills, chimneys. At night the area for miles around glows red from the fires inside. This is hell on earth, a shroud of fiery smoke, a lowering, breathing, glowing miasma that pollutes the night as surely as it pollutes the air and the waters of the Bristol Channel—as surely as my grandfather's fury pollutes my life, even though the man was dead before I was born. He was all teeth and claws, as the uncrowned king of Arabia said of himself. This is why I went to Columbia to seek truth: to find out what my grandfather's life means. I have a right to know; I bear his curse.

My father told me stories about him when I was small. But it was Atlas's stories I remembered: Atlas's stories that I felt, that I dreamed about while I was growing up. "When Dad first laid eyes on George Stoke—" and I could feel myself straining to get the focus clear, straining to see that first sight of George as my grandfather's eyes took it in; not to reproduce the memory, not just that: I coveted my grandfather's memories in the biblical sense, sinfully, secretly, and I strained to do the actual remembering itself, to colonize these fleeting intimacies inside my mind, steal them from him wholesale with all the rights to ownership that go with them. Atlas once said, "He rode that first train across the Rockies—" And the clackety-clack: Do I remember it? Do I? Dare I? If you turn your head quick enough you can kiss your own lips. Sometimes when I'm alone, I can— Well, almost anyway, just for a second. My head buzzes with the effort, but when the horizon clears, I'm back where I started, just plain old me again. Of course the idea's absurd. How could I remember my grandfather's life? I never even met him.

This man, my grandfather, was called Jonathan Carrick. He was about two years younger than the senator. My uncle Atlas said nobody ever did find out precisely how much younger. There isn't a record of his birth anywhere. At the time of the senator's party he was somewhere in the region of sixty, which is one age in a greasy old senator and quite another in such as Jonathan. There's kinship here even so; not only a shared past, deeper than that: the kinship of old enemies, the kinship of war.

A war between two people is not all that different from a war between two countries. To begin with the surface of things, the troops must have a flag, a banner, colors, and so they do in the war between my grandfather and the senator. Jonathan Carrick wore a frock coat, just as the senator did; his was out of date, too, just like the senator's: the cockade of the frock coat, and no sillier than the roses, ribbons, feathers that make up national cockades, either. My grandfather looked good in his frock coat with a velvet collar, but then the good-looking look good in anything; there's an ease to the body, a sureness to the gestures that ordinary-looking people never show. My grandfather's gestures were remarkable. Sometimes he answered with his hands alone, and you were left in no doubt as to what he was saying. Atlas explained this to me. It was a captivating talent, discordant, unexpected in so permanently angry a person, yet so graceful, so magical in its accuracy, so oddly moving that it aroused maternal feelings in women for miles around in the county where he lived—just as the boiling undercurrent in him aroused feelings of a less respectable nature. There is always much speculation after a man like this becomes a widower.

People said he'd taken his wife's death too hard. They said he should get on with life. But what is there to get on with? What is the point? When he went shopping he stopped sometimes midstride in the streets with a look of anguish on his face. "His heart," said the gossips. But it was his war, not his heart, that caught at him: that look came over him when he suddenly realized that some flank lay exposed. At night, he paced back and forth in the dark of his empty house, studying the psychology of the enemy. "Does it have meaning?" he would say. "Or is this meaningless, too? If this is meaningless, then— But it can't be. Because if it is— No, goddamn you! No, you go too far. I won't have it. Do you hear? No!"

To go a little deeper into the subject of war, it is a cardinal rule of strategy, an axiom set forth by that great philosopher of the subject, Karl von Clausewitz, that whoever really knows what he wants has the edge. Jonathan tested for fixed points. How about this? Did he really want it? No, dammit. How about that? No! It looked like the options were down to one: George Stoke. My grandfather read about the lawn party in the Seattle *Intelligencer;* he worked a farm near a tiny town called Hannaville up in the mud and pine trees of Washington State, half a continent away from Sweetbrier and the senator's party. He read about the party on the same day—the very same day—that he read about the annual Methodist Congress, which that year was to be held in Topeka. Topeka is only fifty miles from Senator Stoke's mansion. Clausewitz says war is a wonderful trinity of emotion, reason and chance, and here in the Seattle *Intelligencer,* a paper as relentlessly dull as the *Overland Sentinel* of Sweetbrier, my grandfather finds himself on the right side of "that play of probabilities"—these are Clausewitz's very words—"which make war a free activity of the soul."

My grandfather didn't finish reading about the lawn

party. He threw the paper down, ran out into the yard and began overhauling his elderly Saxon to make it ready for the trip. A week later he was nursing it over the dirt roads that wound through the Northwest, over the rutted tracks of the Rockies, out onto the straight gravel runs across the cornfields of Colorado and Kansas.

3

WHEN JONATHAN parked his car on the sweeping curve of the driveway into the senator's property, he couldn't see George. I know that. I went to Sweetbrier and surveyed the land myself. He would have seen only the crowd with the ladies' skirts billowing and their hats bobbing. He couldn't even hear George until he was halfway across the lawn. All the national papers ran George's speech. It wasn't anything special, but because of what happened afterwards, it got the kind of coverage few senators manage even when they pay out in hard cash.

As I play the scene for myself, Jonathan began to hear the words just as George was saying, ". . . and what are these fancy bosses in their button-up suits tellin' us? Eh? 'Sacrifice this little town of Sweetbrier for the greater good of the nation.' That it?"

When I was small, my two sisters and I spent a year at an elegant boarding school far away from home. My father and mother did a lot of wild quarreling; sometimes it was best to have us children out of the line of fire. Three little maids at school: there were banks of rhododendrons at the edge of the school's lawn, and to this day the scent of rhododendron brings back the peculiar unhappiness of that place and that time in my life with a force not even my most vivid memories can evoke. It was much like this for Jonathan, hearing George's voice for the first time in more than forty years.

"Got us licked? The Midwest Pacific? Us? Lemme hear what you say to that, friends."

Jonathan took in his breath and began his report to the generals at base camp in Topeka, where the Methodist Congress was just getting under way. "The salesman's smoothness: it rules everything—always did, of course, but there's real power in it now. And money. Then what? There's something—what is it?—something that's askew. Why are the eyes dull? Is it greed? Fear?"

George had become a traveling salesman at the age of fifteen when times were hard for his family. He was big for his age even then. They called them drummers in those days— some ten years after the Civil War was over—and George drummed up trade for Sweetbrier Chewing Tobacco in First Chance, Dixon, Nirvana and all the other little towns, dozens of them, that are still spotted here and there over the Midwest like mold on damp linen. Jonathan hadn't seen George in the flesh for nearly half a century, although he'd watched him grow older and fatter in newsprint: the papers carried many pictures of the great senator. It was such an illustrious career. Even so, when Jonathan thought of George, he thought of the boy who practiced his salesman's spiel, elbow on makeshift table, black eyes shining: "Set 'em up, friend. Bourbon for me."

Youth is merciless, feral, but age? There aren't words terrible enough. Look at the fat old grotesque perched on that top step. Whatever happened to the shiny-eyed boy? Look at the mountainous thighs that touch even though the stance is splayfooted. When George got his first frock coat, frock coats were fashionable. He'd got it to sell in, because a drummer has to dress well or the suckers won't buy. It had come from Sears Roebuck; it had a satin lining and shell buttons. Thinking of these things, Jonathan swayed and caught himself, the look of anguish appearing on his face as it did in Hannaville when some weakness opened up in the war-torn principality of his mind.

"Are you all right, sir?"

He peered down at the owner of one of those billowing skirts and bobbing hats.

"You don't look well," she said. There were bows on her shoes. "Would it help to get out of the sun? You're a stranger here, aren't you?"

Why the hell do people interfere? By what right? He was unaware that this sudden gust of anger flickered in his eyes, but he knew it would show in his voice, so he gestured with those beautiful hands of his that he was fine, that he didn't want to cause her any trouble.

"Oh!" she cried in delight (intrigued, too, as people always are by evidence of emotion suppressed). "You don't need words at all, do you? How did you learn to do that?" But then she rushed on. "It's no trouble. Really. I live here."

He stared down at her, unbelieving, unable to believe—which made him even more uncertain of his voice. He used his hands again, and his meaning was so clear that she laughed out loud with pleasure.

"Yes," she said. "You're right. The senator's my father. Come on, let me help you."

She guided him around the crowd toward the back of the mansion. The grass crunched dreamlike under his shoes as though it were still frozen in midwinter while the rest of the world had moved on to this summery day. She urged him through a door and along a hallway. Black and white squares of marble on the floor, then carpet, then wood, then another carpet.

"Sit down here," she said. "I'll get you a glass of water."

Books lined three walls. On the fourth, eaglehead candelabra stood on either side of a battle scene from the Revolution where flags flew, horses reared, mud everywhere, except near the dead man in the center, immaculate in cream-colored tights and satin coat, a pretty trickle of blood at his throat. Jonathan eyed the dead man in disgust; he had a puritanical aversion to sham. People crap their cream-colored tights when they die. Their mouths yawn; you have to tie the lower jaw up as Ichabod Crane tied his or it stays gaped wide, a detail missing from the actors who play dead people on television screens every night just as it's missing from elegiac pictures of war like this one of George Stoke's.

The young woman appeared with a glass of water. Beyond her, Jonathan could see an ornate desk. On its surface stood a silver-framed daguerreotype. He knew at once what the picture would show: what it had to be.

"You go to college, I suppose," he said abruptly.

She plumped herself down next to him with enthusiasm. "You *can* speak. I thought you were mute. Wellesley. I go to Wellesley. I major in French. I'm leaving for Paris next week. Paris! Isn't that wonderful? Do you suppose they talk any English there?"

"With your father?"

"Oh, don't worry," she laughed, misunderstanding. She had the shiny black eyes her father had once had (but had, so it seemed, no more). "He wouldn't let Sweetbrier down in its hour of need. Anyhow, Europe is bad for the image." She laughed again. "Daddy's image is the most important thing in American civilization. No, Mother's taking me. He's going to be all on his own for two whole months."

When she left him she told him to rest indoors as long as he liked.

Usually a spy's job is slow and tedious, but in all professions there are windfalls. Sometimes God bestirs Himself in His majestic boredom and smiles. So it was with Jonathan;

the answers dropped into his lap without the slightest effort on his part. He knew the layout of the house. He knew George was going to be in it. So he approached the silver-framed picture on the desk. He shut his eyes as he sat down. When he opened them again he was staring, as he'd known he would be, into the face of Alvah Stoke himself.

PART 2

WEDNESDAY MORNING: REVOLUTION

4

IT WAS PAINFULLY APT, that painting of the American Revolution on George's wall. Immaculate cream-colored tights and a fairy-tale battlefield: these don't matter, not really. What does matter is that Jonathan Carrick's first war in life, like his country's, was revolutionary. Alvah Stoke was a major force in the *ancien régime* he fought, the infantry, you might say, if not the Republican guard. Alvah was one of Sweetbrier's first settlers, not the very first—an honor that rests with Benbow Wikin, whose store lies moldering alongside the road to this very day. There was a time, starting just before 1850, when "Benbow Wikin's General Store & Post Office" was all there was to Sweetbrier. My story begins fifteen years later, just months after the Civil War ended. By this time, the town had grown into a proper town: saloons, undertaker, lawyer's office, barber, and rival grocery that imported cheese from New York. The *Overland Sentinel,* the same old grab bag that proposed a party on Senator Stoke's lawn, opened its offices then. Farmers and their wives came to town every Saturday morning. The boardwalk bustled: calico dresses, pigs, horses, chickens, and even some of the Indians who managed to survive the massacres going on in the countryside nearby.

One Saturday in September of 1865, Alvah Stoke sought out Benbow Wikin in the back room of his general store.

"I want to buy a boy," Alvah said.

This is the beginning of all that follows.

"What for?" Benbow asked.

"Want to work him."

Benbow, who sold practically anything anyone might want, shifted some goods around on his counter. "That'll cost you money," he said.

Alvah said nothing.

"Prices for boys ain't strictly official," Benbow went on. "No harm in starting low."

Alvah said nothing.

"You got to let people know, though," Benbow said, nodding. "I'll give you a hand with the ad."

The *Overland Sentinel* was already the typical small-town newspaper that it remained for its entire lifetime: crude type, cheap paper, headlines that scream the resolutions of ladies' clubs and the nuptials of local clods, she with heavy jaw and dull eyes, he with pimples and sloping brow. When gossip was slim, only then, only to plump itself out in a bad week, the *Overland Sentinel* touched on the Indian wars and sometimes on the spread of the railroads, although this was long before the Midwest Pacific even planned its route through Sweetbrier.

Here is the advertisement it carried:

WANTED: Boy, age six to eight years old. Good home 'til twenty-one years old. Payment twenty dollars depending. Apply B. Wikin's General Store & Post Office at 3 o'clock this Saturday afternoon.

Black slaves were out of the question: the Civil War was over. Besides, black slaves had been expensive—a thousand dollars for no more than a little girl. But all wars leave poor widows and hungry children; wars tend to leave out-of-work soldiers, too, who can't feed the children they have and, in those days, didn't know how to keep from fathering more. The result after the Civil War was a crop of kids nobody wanted.

A farmer could pick one up cheap, and a boy at that, as long as the boy wasn't black. Lots of people did it. They called it "bounding out." Alvah didn't really think he could find a boy for twenty dollars. He was figuring on thirty at least—and a saddle probably, when (and if, of course) the kid finally made it to twenty-one.

"But deals are possible," Benbow said, rubbing his hands together. "Deals are always possible."

5

I'D FLOWN the northern route over the pole from London to Washington State, over thousands of miles of dead white landscape, to take down what my uncle Atlas could tell me about Jonathan, my grandfather. It was all very spur of the moment. I'd been reading a book about paradoxes and run across this one of Lichtenberg's: "The thing that astonished him was that cats should have two holes cut in their coat exactly at the place where their eyes are." The moment I read this, I could hardly believe I hadn't thought of talking to Atlas before, and having thought of it couldn't bear to wait any longer. Atlas was dangerously old: if I wasn't quick I might never find out where the holes in that cat's coat belonged. Suppose he died on me: who else was there? The rest were already dead. There's an attachment for a portable phone on my wheelchair, which was made for me by the very same man in Cambridge who built the great Professor Hawking his chair. I punched in Atlas's number, forgetting in my excitement about such details as time

changes; it turned out to be one o'clock in the morning on the
West Coast of the United States, some six thousand miles away
from my little Devon village, where the morning was just beginning—milkman, postman, newspaper. At first Atlas was
less than pleased; as we talked, though, he came to seem as
anxious to tell me about Jonathan as I was to hear about him—
or almost, anyway.

"I got to go into the hospital Friday," he said and then
rushed on. "Nothing much, but you wouldn't be able to get
here for a month or more, anyway, would you? I'll be in good
shape again by then. When were you thinking of coming?"

I didn't ask about the hospital—some sort of surgery, I
gathered—but his mention of it put the fear of God into me.
"It's Tuesday," I said. "I think I can be in Washington this
very evening, maybe eight, maybe ten o'clock your time. Can
you pick me up?" Within hours, I was aloft over that frozen
wasteland. The airlines are superb with wheelchair cases like
me, especially when you excite them with the thought of some
miraculous new medical treatment. A pity Atlas had none to
offer me.

We'd always been close, Atlas and I, despite the sepa-
ration two continents enforce on two lousy letter writers. When
I was small he used to say I was "astute." It was his warmth
I liked. He met me at the airport in one of those huge, soft
American cars that drive as though they were negotiating bowls
of Jell-O. It was late, dark, on the ride to his house—mile upon
mile of the stippled two-stripe that makes up highways at night,
red taillights on one side, white headlights on the other, a pretty
sight—on that ride, we decided to spend a day taping and the
next day looking at Hannaville, my grandfather's town, which
was a hundred miles upstate from Atlas's house.

It seemed a hard schedule for somebody who was pushing
eighty, as Atlas was, especially somebody preparing to be
carved up in a few days, but what choice was there? Besides,
he was still hale, solid, hairy, still big enough and strong

enough to lift me in and out of the car all on his own, and still practicing medicine. He'd been various kinds of doctor in his life, usually with a whiff of the shady about it: medical director to the Tobacco Institute Research Corporation in New York, for example. In his dotage he'd manipulated himself into the post of geriatrician to one of those American old-age ghettos, all coarse grass and motel architecture, no dogs, no children, this one run by somebody who had the impudence to call himself Dr. Youngballs. On the bedside table in the room where I slept—arrangements for the old serve me very well—lay a magazine called *Senior Society;* on the cover, a piece of elderly cheesecake showing off pulpy thighs and hoisted bosom in a one-piece suit from years ago.

I'd never met Atlas's present wife. She was a fiercely efficient woman, not as old as Atlas but not so far from it, either. Atlas introduced us over cornflakes.

"This is Claire," he said to me.

"I'm so sorry I wasn't able to greet you last night," Claire said, fetching milk from the refrigerator. She had one of those faces that are purely American. Even at whatever ancient age she'd reached, there was nothing in the skin, nothing in the eyes, nothing around the mouth to betray a single thought or a single experience; all was as hygienic as an unwrapped roll of toilet paper, no hint whatever that anybody had ever lived there: a safe house rather than a face. "I've got such a heavy day ahead of me. Did he tell you?"

"No," I said.

"Well, it's my French dinner party. We have a club. It's to spread culture. Sounds silly, I know, provincial and all that, but it isn't, at least it isn't necessarily silly, and this time it's my turn."

"I didn't know. I'm afraid it's an awful imposition I'm putting on you."

"I'll manage," she said, a trifle sourly. "Seven around the table is the problem."

"What problem?" Atlas said.

"We only have six chairs—"

"Jesus Christ, Claire. You think a mess like that"—he indicated me—"could make use of a dining room chair even if we had one?" Some able-bodied people, Atlas is one, can say things worse even than this without offense. Quite the contrary: it's as though you're in it together somehow, no longer an outsider.

Claire sniffed. "This party is just the thing for you, Nate," she said. Atlas is a family name for my uncle. The brass plate outside his house reads DR. NATHANIEL CARRICK in elegant Times Roman. Claire doesn't like the sound of Atlas; she says sibilants at the end of a name are ugly. Myself, I think Nate sounds kind of ugly. Anyhow, she turned all her attention, mischievous now, girlish, in his direction. "We're going to have five wines."

"Five? What do you want five for?"

"It's French."

"What's French? Having five wines?"

"It says so in the book. Right here. *Reader's Digest International Cookbook.* Five wines."

"Jesus, Claire, these stupid bastards don't know wine from hog piss," he said. "What the hell are they going to make of five of the fucking things?"

"Precisely," she said.

She urged us off into his study soon after breakfast. We took our coffee with us, settled ourselves and began to record on tape what Atlas could remember about his father.

My father was Atlas's brother, Jonathan Carrick's oldest son. When I was small, he told me stories about Jonathan, frightening stories, and I came to fear my grandfather the way other children fear the bogeyman. I could see him, can see him now as I saw him then, clothed (for some unknown, childhood reason) in black—black hat, black coat—bringing with him a cloud of black that engulfed anybody and anything who got close enough, swallowed them up, never to be seen again. It wasn't his anger that frightened me then; I knew nothing of his anger until Atlas told me about it, nothing of the fire in him, nothing of his resemblance to the steelworks outside Cardiff. I'd always seen him through my father's eyes, and my father saw him as icy cold—how could two brothers see their own father so differently?—the embodiment of a meaningless and yet implacable justice: whatever sin you sinned was to be rooted out and punished without mercy, whether you sinned knowing or not knowing. I am a born, bred and wholly convinced atheist—an orthodox atheist, you might say—and yet I have, I think, a religious temperament. I fear my sins, all of them, known and unknown. My father called my grandfather "the old man." If a stair creaked in the dark, it was the old man come to get me. If I awoke suddenly in the night, it was the old man come to get me. If there was a rustle at the window . . .

Atlas began my introduction to my grandfather's fire by telling me what he knew about Alvah Stoke.

Alvah was weeding full-time on a tobacco farm in New Hampshire when he was only eight years old. At twenty-six he was pulling in two dollars a day for dawn-to-dusk hard labor on the same farm. He'd have tried practically anything, and he listened carefully to Jason Yoxall, a traveling medicine man with a large daughter: Jason was newly married to a rich widow who wanted no part of her husband's offspring.

"You ever think about going west?" Jason said.

"Why should I?" Alvah said.

"You know, Alvah, my Dotter cooks and spins and keeps chickens—a fine woman, Alvah. What a wife she'd make, eh?"

"What's her name?"

"Name's Dotter. Like I said."

"That ain't a name," Alvah said in disgust.

"Well, what else am I going to call her? When she gets married, she gets called Wife. Ain't that enough?"

"She can't read," Alvah said. Alvah had no education to speak of, but even he could read a little.

"What does a woman want with reading, you ass? Her mother left her three hundred dollars. You marry her, it's yours."

Alvah and Jason fashioned themselves on the he-man of the 1850s. Take away Hollywood's sanitized version and this much-loved hero was as brutish a creature as the pit of hell ever spewed forth: a humorless, ruthless, benumbed half-wit, at home with dogs, cows, horses, rifles and rotgut liquor: proud of feeding habits that belonged in a zoo, of a face as expressionless as his backside, of an unrivaled imbecility at conversation, friendship, love, courtship, copulation, family life, all art, all music, all learning, all words. Reading was for women: you despised the accomplishment in yourself, but you wanted it for your wife. Besides, Dotter's lumpen inertia oppressed Alvah. Her face was glutinous, like uncooked rolls on a baking tin; she smoked a clay pipe. The money was real enough, but a man needed something like five hundred dollars to set up in the West—plows, tools, animals, that kind of thing. Where was a man like Alvah to get the two hundred dollars extra?

"Dotter, come here," Jason said. Dotter lifted her apron and hid her face in it. "Look at that back, Alvah. With a back like that a man don't need a horse. Just take a look at those hips. The hips of mother earth. Think of the children to come from hips like those."

Women often pulled plows. It was customary. Kids were for hoeing the rows; if they were lazy you beat the shit out of them. Dotter smiled—she was of her time, too, and at that, only a woman who couldn't read. Her mouth curled into a Cupid's bow, and the pipe rolled across her teeth, scattering sparks and ashes. It *was* a strong back, no doubt about it. Alvah's heart beat a little faster, but he said nothing.

"Tell you what," Jason said. "I'll toss in a pouch of tobacco seed."

"What kind?"

"Colory—the best."

"Two pouches," said Alvah.

The marriage took place a week later. Alvah and Wife— or Wify, as Dotter became known on her wedding day— worked their way across the country, hiring out to farmers while the warm weather lasted and to railroad builders through the winter. When they reached Sweetbrier the next summer, Benbow Wikin's General Store & Post Office already carried most anything people wanted. Not that anybody wanted much—salt, honey, cream of tartar, molasses, vinegar and the occasional whole codfish, salted and dried, over which flies swarmed as thick and hungry as any newcomer's passion for land. Benbow was the local land agent for the government; he helped Alvah find ground to squat on. Alvah, true to his chosen kind, was no man of vision. He dreamed of one day growing tobacco worth nine cents a pound down at New Orleans; he dreamed of one day living in a house made of wood—no more. Wify dreamed of nothing at all. She was too tired to dream. She swept, cooked, spun, wove, washed, kept chickens, grew vegetables, had babies—and pulled the plow.

Alyoshus came first, then Cathern less than a year later; then several stillbirths. The third child who lived was George, the future Senator Stoke himself. After he was born, Wify's great hips ceased to deliver. But she would not give up. Nor would Alvah: he serviced her from the rear because it was faster and because the genes that made her youngest son hideous in old age showed themselves early in her. No more babies came of it. Wify wept. Alvah showed no reaction. Was he a he-man of his time or was he not? But it rankled. It was breach of contract, this unexpected barrenness, and a breach of contract has to be punished.

So it was as much revenge as the need for extra labor that led him to advertise in the *Overland Sentinel* for a boy that wanted buying.

6

TWO TINY BOYS waited at Benbow Wikin's that Saturday afternoon in September of 1865 after the ad appeared. As soon as Alvah arrived, Benbow drew him aside.

"You don't want that one, Alvah." Benbow gestured toward a scrawny child with fever spots on his cheeks. Alvah nodded agreement.

The second boy had black hair that curled over his collar and blue eyes that looked out eagerly at everything around him. This is conjecture: this is what I was like as a child—or so I've been told anyway. The child chattered to himself, swinging back and forth at the end of a bearded man's arm.

"That's your boy," Benbow said.

"Wikin Store. Wikins Tor," the child chattered. "Rudabega and Potata—"

"What's he talking about?" Alvah asked Benbow.

"Don't know—always going on like that. Don't mean anything."

The child skipped in a small circle around the bearded man, who turned in a circle himself to keep hold of the child's hand. "No, no. No tomato. Bega, tata, no tomata—"

The bearded man's ragged uniform and battered army boots told Alvah most of what he wanted to know. He knelt down beside the child.

"Mama makes a baked potata—Mama bakes—"

"Quiet," Alvah said, laying his head against the bib of the child's overall. The little boy held still. Alvah thumped him on the chest and then on the back.

"Kinda small," Alvah said. He pressed open the child's mouth and peered at his teeth. "Ain't no six years old. Four at most."

The veteran said nothing.

Alvah got to his feet. "Fifteen dollars," he said.

The veteran looked down at the child, up at Alvah and back to the child again. Then he nodded.

Benbow drew a sheet of paper out from under his till and bent down to write. The veteran watched without moving. The little boy danced around, peeking into sacks, squeezing himself between barrels, chattering as before. Then Benbow said, "What this document says is this: 'For a payment of $15 to Daniel Carrick, Private, U.S. Army, the boy Jonathan Carrick is bound out to Alvah Stoke until the boy is age 21 years.' " Benbow glanced at each of the men in turn. " 'When 21 years, he gets $25 and a saddle. Signed Alvah Stoke and Daniel Carrick.' Acceptable?"

Both men nodded.

"Well, then, that's official. Sign here, Alvah." Alvah lettered his name. "And here, Daniel Carrick." The soldier drew a cross.

So it was that my grandfather was sold and bought as a slave, and so it is that I, who am as white as they come, can lay claim to kinship with most American blacks. There are many others like me; bounding out—although comfortably forgotten these days—was a common practice in its time. There's more than just the fact of slavery, too: my family tree stops short at this deed of purchase. Nobody ever located the bearded man again. Nobody even knows for sure that Daniel Carrick was his name.

Alvah took his new acquisition out to the wagon. As he drove away he found doubts forming. Why had the veteran been so willing? The more he thought the more it seemed to him that the veteran might have taken ten dollars, maybe even less. He certainly needn't have committed himself to that saddle. He began to feel he'd been cheated.

Jonathan sat in the back of the wagon, arranging and rearranging a few bits of stray hay in front of him. "Clip, clop, wagon hop," he sang. "Hip, hop—"

"Shut up," Alvah said.

Jonathan fell silent, but a few minutes later he began again softly. "Never stop. Never, never—never, never—"

Alvah's children didn't chatter that way. Not Alyoshus or Cathern or George. Suppose the boy was unhinged. Weak-minded. Alvah had read stories about boys who set fire to haystacks and did no work.

"Shut up," he shouted, turning from his reins to clout the child across the ear. He slipped as he turned, and the blow was harder than he'd intended. Jonathan let out a yelp and began to bleed from the mouth.

"Shut up!"

The child shut up.

7

"I'VE GOT HIS DIARIES in the attic," Atlas said in the middle of a sentence about something else. "Would you like to see them?"

"Diaries? Your father wrote diaries? You have them? You're not— I never heard about any such thing. Are you sure?"

"Sure I'm sure. I've had them for years. There was a whole load of junk—didn't know what to do with it. So I just put it up in the—"

"Are they complete? His whole life, or what? God, I'd love to— They're really here? Right here in this house?"

Atlas shrugged. "Yeah. I didn't know whether you'd be interested or not. See, that's one of the funny things—they're in code. I always figured I'd get down to cracking it one day, but somehow—"

"Code? Really? Why'd he do that?"

Atlas shrugged again. He'd been a handsome man once, my uncle Atlas. "I was so good-looking," he said to me, "it gives me shivers to think about it." Even pushing eighty, with jowls and trifocals, he had the air of an old-time movie idol.

"Atlas, go get them. I've got to see them. I can't wait another minute."

He pulled his bulk out of his chair and disappeared. His office was a mess, a heap of papers trailing over the edge of his desk, old files open and strewn over the examining table. It drove the efficient Claire mad. Atlas was a much-married man.

"She's nothing but a white-haired old lady," said my aunt Ruth in disgust when Atlas announced his decision to take on Claire. Ruth was Atlas's only surviving sister at the time (dead now, too, like the rest). "What'd he possibly want to marry a white-haired old lady for?"

He returned with an armload of books. There were five volumes of diaries. Five! In Babylonian times, five was the secret of the universe. Five was in fact the number of Atlas's wives and the number of Claire's wines, too, as exclusively prescribed by *Reader's Digest*. Five is the number of the Pentagon in Washington: the number of war. Five is the pentagram, and out of the pentagram you conjure the devil, which was most assuredly what I hoped to do. Fairly thick volumes, in clean condition, not matching, no attempt even to try for a match. The first—each had a date on the spine—was a ledger, bound in horsehide. The middle three were various sizes of cloth-bound. The last, the greatest treasure of them all, was a paper-backed school exercise book from Wool-worth's.

My grandfather's hand was not an easy one: angular, jerky, letters written at high speed, often not wholly formed, as though the thoughts had flown by him so fast that he'd never had time to reflect on them. But the code was simple. I could see that at a glance. I've always been interested in codes: I like secrets. Back in England in front of my computer—a week after this day of taping that has just be-gun—it took me under half an hour to crack it. The earli-est entries, plainly written many years afterwards, have to do with that afternoon in Wikin's store and the first week with the Stokes. Even when Jonathan strained with all his might to remember, he says he could bring to mind nothing of his life before he became a slave, not a face or a voice or a room, not a single image. He'd gone willingly to the spring wagon, though. He'd even delighted in the prospect of a ride in it. When Alvah hit out at him for his babbling, he'd been more puzzled than anything else. It was nearly six o'clock when Alvah reined in the horse and jerked his head in the direction of the lean-to that served the homestead as a barn.

"Do you live in a shack?" Jonathan said, climbing down to the ground. "Why do—"

"Quiet, boy." Alvah led Jonathan to the door of the soddy.

When Alvah and Wify had arrived in Kansas years before, there was grass from one horizon to the next, no big trees, no rocks, no adobe, nothing to build a house with, only a few caves—and these already occupied. They'd built the sod hut themselves. Wify pulled the plow with a special device attached; Alvah sliced the surface from an entire acre of ground to make the hut. The walls were solid dirt bricks, weighing a hundred, two hundred pounds each, and heaved into place without tools or levers. The roof was cottonwood and more sod. Inside the hut, Alvah, Wify, the children, a pig, the mice, the bugs, the damp, the weeds that straggled from the ceiling—all lived together.

"You live in a little square hill," Jonathan said, "with a little square door—"

"Quiet!"

There was one tiny window: the room was dim even though it was still bright outside. Wify was an enormous, draped figure, bent over a kettle that hung above the coals in the fireplace. There was a cloud of steam. The figure turned, revealing its unbaked dough of a face lit up by the red from the fire.

"What a big lady!" Jonathan cried and then clapped his hand over his mouth, remembering that he wasn't supposed to talk.

"This the boy?" Wify said irritably.

She was even bigger face-on than from the rear; huge shoulders, huge breasts, huge hands. She maneuvered the great bones inside her body as though she were still straining at the yoke. She'd borne her children alone; she'd dug the graves for the stillborn herself. The vast shoulders shivered with resentment.

"Don't see no point in a boy," she said, turning back to her kettle. "Could have got a calf—or another pig . . ." Her voice faded into a querulous mutter. Jonathan tightened his grasp on Alvah's hand.

"Let go," Alvah said.

In the middle of the room stood a large dry-goods box, turned upside down to make a table. Alvah seated himself on a crate next to the box, held a newspaper up toward the window and started to read. Old newspapers, rotting from damp and age, covered the walls and gave off a sour reek. A boy about Jonathan's own age crept out from a corner of the room.

"What's he called?" the boy said.

This was George Stoke, the senator-to-be himself, eyes aglitter as he flicked them over Jonathan, who was at once enchanted by what he saw. Childhood pictures of George show a plump, animated little boy with little round legs and little round eyes, shiny and black.

"What's he called?" George asked again.

"Jonathan Carrick," Alvah said.

George circled Jonathan, who held very still for the moment of judgment.

"Carrick Darrick Farrick!" George said at last. Then he poked Jonathan's nose.

The most angelic of children sustain passions that would kill their elders; only physical weakness—though fortunately they're also inept—keeps them from acting out what they feel. And George was not one of the most angelic. The blow was nothing, but Jonathan, after the wild-animal fashion of his kind, had caught a whiff of George's soul. He turned and dashed toward the door.

Alvah reached out and swung him back.

"This is our house," George crowed. "Never yours! Ours!"

"Food's on," Wify said.

George climbed onto one of the crates that served as benches for the box table. Alyoshus and Cathern appeared from behind a bed. Cathern had red pigtails; Alyoshus was round all over. Wify doled out stew onto tin plates, and the family shoveled it down as fast as they could. Jonathan stood silent and watched.

"What's the matter?" Wify demanded. A gobbet of stew flew out of her mouth and arced across the room in Jonathan's direction. "Food not good enough for him?"

"Eat, boy," Alvah said.

Almost before he knew what was happening, Jonathan was at the door again. This time he kicked and scratched when they tried to stop him. Wify caught both his wrists in one of her great hands and both his ankles in the other. She trussed him with a rope; when she let go, his thrashings were so violent that they bounced him across the tiny room.

"Switch, George," Alvah said.

At the first blow Jonathan stopped his struggles to stare at Alvah. Even as he watched Alvah's arm lift into the air for a second blow, he couldn't believe it. When the switch hit the third time, he cried out.

Alvah nodded and put the switch away.

The next day, after Alvah and the Stoke children went out to the fields, Jonathan lunged for the door whenever Wify took her eyes off him. He beat at the dirt walls with his fists. Before she went out into the fields herself, she drove a stake into the floor of the soddy and tied him to that with the halter she'd hoped she might be using to tether a calf instead. He remained tied up for the rest of the week. He drank because he did not know how to resist the liquids they poured down his throat, but he would not eat. Every day he fought the halter. Every day Alvah beat him.

At the end of the week, on a blustery afternoon when the Stokes were out in the fields, he managed to jiggle the stake out of the ground. Outside the door, a track disappeared into the grass. He dashed along it, trailing stake and halter behind him. The grass was higher than his head on both sides; it swung back and forth in great billows, and he lost the track. When he found it again, he ran down it—only to find himself back at the door of the sod hut where Alvah stood, switch in hand.

The following day Alvah took him to Sweetbrier and Benbow Wikin's store.

"Tell him about his ma," Alvah said, depositing Jonathan (who was still trussed up in the halter) on the counter.

"You don't got to tie him up, Alvah," Benbow said. He was a small man with a pouter pigeon chest. "It ain't official, tying boys up."

"He's mine, ain't he?"

"Well, yes, course he is, but—"

"Tell him."

"You go out while I tell him." Alvah didn't move. "I ain't saying nothing while you're here."

"I want to go home, Mr. Wikin," Jonathan said as soon as Alvah left.

"Oh, dear—" Benbow began to loosen Jonathan's hands. "It's sort of complicated. See, I didn't rightly know your ma. She come to town only on her own, sort of, a week or so before you come here to, uh, meet Alvah. Nobody'd ever seen her before. I don't even rightly know how she got here. No horse or buggy or nothing. Just appeared that day. Out of nowhere."

"Where is she?"

Benbow went to work on the rope that bound Jonathan's feet. "You been with Alvah most of a week now, ain't that right? Well, uh— She didn't know what was to become of you. I'm not even sure—" He broke off.

"Where is she, Mr. Wikin?"

"See, Jonathan, I ain't even sure Carrick was her name. Or yours. I got the feeling, sort of, that she and him just made it up. I mean, it's a good name, and that's official, but—" He broke off again.

"Where's that man?"

"What man? Alvah?"

"The man! The man!" Jonathan insisted.

"You mean your pa? If he was your— I don't know. Only time I ever saw him was when he came here with you. Gone west, I suspect. California probably. That's where most of them go."

"Where's my mama? Where is she? Where is she?"

"Well, Jonathan, see, that's the thing. How can I find your people if I don't even know your right name?"

"I'm Jonathan," Jonathan said, fears momentarily giving way to the abrupt anger that was to mark his character all his life. "Where is my mama?"

"Oh, dear, oh, dear— But Jonathan what? What's your last name? Can you tell me?"

"Jonathan! Jonathan!"

"That's all you can remember?"

"Jonathan!"

"See? You're too little to know things like that, and— Remember how she coughed? Consumption, that's—"

"What's consumption?"

"It's—well, it's a sickness—sort of—"

"My mama's sick?"

"Well, no, not exactly."

Jonathan stared at the broken veins in Benbow's cheeks. "Dead?" was all he could whisper.

"Ain't you going to cry none?" Benbow said. "I won't tell."

When Alvah returned, Jonathan was sitting on a barrel, holding himself as still as he'd held himself for George's inspection. Alvah jerked his head in the direction of the door. Jonathan followed him out once more to the spring wagon, climbed up into it and sat there as still as he had sat before.

Teeth and claws must learn patience.

8

LICORICE AND SPICES boiled in the iron pot over the fire all winter long. Tobacco hung on racks to dry. In the dank, damp half-light Alvah taught Jonathan to strip leaves, knead them into plugs for chewing, compact them in a screw press, and wrap them in blue paper: Sweetbrier Chewing Tobacco. Jonathan was too little to run away; the grass was too high; he'd learned this lesson. Every night, even though he didn't have any gods to pray to, he prayed to grow bigger. Every day, his mind wrestled with the tactics of escape while his hands worked on tobacco. From time to time he looked up to see George's round, shiny eyes on him.

When the snows melted in April, Alvah sowed seed and George threw himself exultantly into a war of attrition against this boughten boy. He leapt from behind bushes. He laid tripwires across paths. He teased, tweaked, scoffed, poked, giggled, punched, slandered. Jonathan marshaled what forces he had, a pitiful supply, no allies, no weapons but his wits; tiny as he was, he came quickly to the conclusion that in battle a loser must be seen to lose if a victor is to be seen as victorious.

So began the first, tentative probings into what was to become his life's strategy: absolute control over himself. He set out to stifle the chattering child he had been—to stifle any show of soft underbelly: that quick anger of his as well as his ingenuousness, his humor, his gaiety. Nothing was to go free, not the slightest errant thought, not the faintest twitch of an eye.

In May Alvah pricked out. George intensified his campaign; Jonathan hardened his resolve. In June Alvah constructed hills for the young tobacco. The children weeded the ground by hand, and at night their knees were so raw they couldn't touch them with their fingers. In July the worms came—and with them Jonathan's first dark hint that there were massed legions behind the spearhead of the Stokes.

In the evening the tobacco field was calm, silent, harmonious, blowing in the wind, profoundly vegetable: just as a field should be. The next day, without any warning whatsoever, the boundary between vegetable and animal was gone. Everything looked the same, and yet there was a grinding, discordant, intensely animal sound of chewing, as though the plants had sprouted jaws and were frantically eating away at their own insides. When a snake swallows its own tail, what happens in the end? When the eating's over, who's won? The paradox is old. How can the jaws eat the jaws? how can the stomach digest itself? But what was a tiny child to make of it except unadulterated terror?

Alvah knelt, opened the leaves of a tobacco plant, and beckoned to the children.

"Tobacco worms are bigger than other worms," Atlas said into my tape recorder. "About like this"—he held up his index finger. "Jesus, they're ugly bastards, green, no real shape, no head, no eyes, insentient and insatiable. They're digesting machines, efficient as hell: jaws at the near end, stomach in the middle, waste disposal unit at the far end." He curled and uncurled his finger, still holding it up to the light. "Kind of like my patients—you know, the ones in the Medi-

care rooms—ever seen one of those places? No? They got four
rooms set apart in the nursing home here, three beds each,
awful smell, you can't even tell the sex of the poor bastards:
fetal positions, heads back, mouths open, faces gray, tubes in,
tubes out, no brain—life reduced to its essentials. Makes a lot
of rich guys an awful lot of money. Anyhow, tobacco worms
curl up in the axils of the leaves and eat and crap, and that's
all they do."

Alvah picked the worm off the plant and spurted it open
between his fingers. Jonathan bolted.

"They had no chemical insecticides, see?" Atlas went on.
"So what could you do? You had to pick them off by hand—"

"How often?" I asked.

"Once a week. Wednesdays. Dad was always at his
touchiest on Wednesdays—all his life—it never left him. The
second time Alvah had to beat him to get him into the field."

But later on that day, in the sod hut after supper, Jonathan proved what a valuable chattel he was. He hinged together two blocks of wood with a leather thong to be hooked
over the thumb like a castanet. Alvah watched and did not
interfere. He was no fool; he knew a good thing when he saw
it. The Wednesday after that, Jonathan picked and squashed
faster than any of the others.

"Make one apiece of them," Alvah said that night.

"What for?" George said, glaring at Jonathan.

"Works, don't it?" Alvah said, and he gave Jonathan the
materials he needed.

George turned his shiny eyes on his father, only half taking in the meaning of this. "Ain't no boughten boy gonna make
me a squasher," he said. "I'll make my own."

"Nope," said Alvah, the man who was no fool. "You ain't
no good at that."

George kept vampires deep down in his soul; when they
weren't out seeking blood on the front lines, they ravened and
drooled; so he set them to suck dry the people he loved with

as much ferocity as they sucked dry his enemies. And George loved his father. Jonathan understood this—which is why, years later, sitting in the opulence of the senator's living room, he knew that the silver-framed daguerreotype had to be Alvah: the bald head, the fringe of hair, red in life, black in the picture, the deeply lined face that despite its lines was as pure an American face as my aunt Claire's: a face that expressed nothing, not age, not pain, not evil, not good, nothing at all. In the sod hut, the child George gawped at Alvah, his beloved father; the vampires clanked in their chains, stunned, hungering, adrift. How could this beloved father—how could the object of such unrestrained devotion tell him he wasn't good at what a boughten boy was good at? He? George? Not as good—? He grabbed the pieces of board and leather out of Jonathan's hands and hurled them at Alvah, then threw himself after them. Alvah fended him off. George fell to the ground in a faint.

He lay sick in bed for several days. Even when he was well enough to go back out to work he could not shake off his father's betrayal. Alvah was quick and sure in everything he did, economical, and economy made him graceful. George was animated. He had shiny black eyes. But he was clumsy like his mother. He was fat like her. Before his illness, he hadn't noticed these things. Where did they leave him? He couldn't figure it out. Who was he to be? From time to time he stopped in the middle of his weeding, sat back to study his father's grace, far off in the field. Then slowly, deliberately, brow furrowed with puzzlement, he turned his gaze on Jonathan, already a slender, economical figure himself, even more graceful in his small size.

9

ONE EVENING in late August of Jonathan's second summer
at the homestead, a schoolteacher walked up to the door of
the sod hut. Her name was Miss Emelina McClanahan and
she came from Cincinnati, Ohio; she wore a wide-brimmed
hat with a ribbon on it and leather shoes that buttoned up.
She announced herself and waited for Wify or Alvah to ask
her in.

Nobody said anything. The children stared.

"I'm opening a school for boys and girls around Sweetbrier," Miss Emelina started off in a rush. "I'd like to talk to
you about that."

Nobody said a word.

Miss Emelina's fingers fluttered nervously over the row
of buttons that secured her bodice. She was very young, as
pink-cheeked as a porcelain milkmaid, tiny rosebud of a
mouth, wee little teeth inside, big eyes as unreflective as a
teddy bear's, but—plainly, plainly, Jonathan could see it, hear
it, almost taste it—a spirit as pure as any Stoke spirit was
besmirched. It was an impressive mound of bodice, too: whatever would Alvah have made of it? and of her petticoats? Jonathan couldn't take his eyes off her. "Education is vital to your
children's advancement—" she began.

"I got to work 'em," Alvah said, eyes glued (I'm sure of
it) to that bodice.

"Oh, I quite understand," she said. "As soon as planting
begins, school ends—"

"You ain't charging nothing, are you?"

"Well, yes, I—"

"We ain't paying," Wify interrupted.

Alvah swung around. "Shut up," he said.

But Wify had no sense. "We ain't even got a calf, Alvah," she whined.

"Shut up!" he said again. He often resented Wify. He wanted vengeance against her for all kinds of things, most of them wholly out of her control. So to spite her, he turned to Miss Emelina, to her impressive bodice and her clean petticoats and said (while Wify began to sob, huge shoulders ashudder like a washing machine with an unbalanced load), "How much?"

"Well, for four children—"

"Three. A boughten boy don't need learning."

Just as we reached this point in Jonathan's life—it was about half past nine in the morning—Atlas's one patient of the day showed up at the door. He'd put off all the others in my honor, but he hadn't been able to reach this one. He wheeled me into the living room to meet her.

"This is Malory Carrick, my niece," he said. "She's come all the way from England to see me. Malory, this is Mrs.—" He scrambled around in his head for her name. "Oh, Christ, I'm sorry," he said then, "but I've forgotten—Just read the damn thing, too. Begins with a B, doesn't it? Mrs. Blake? Am I right?"

"Miss Pemberton, Dr. Carrick," she said. She was frail and very thin; she wore a man's watch that slid down over the bones of her wrist as she shook my hand.

"I'm an old fool," he said to her. "I do apologize. We've known each other for years, haven't we?" Then he said to me, "Let me introduce Miss Peeberton."

"Pemberton," she said.

He didn't spend long with her. "You ever get her name right?" I asked him when he'd shown her out and taken me back into his office. He'd only spent a few minutes with her.

"Happens all the time," he said. I said nothing, and he

laughed. "Well, Christ, these guys are all so goddamned old they don't rightly remember who I am, either. You could make out it's a bond between us."

But the fact is, it wasn't age, or not just age: not in Atlas's case, anyway. Even as a young man he drank too much; by the time I taped my daylong interview with him he'd been drinking for fifty years solid. He had holes in his head big enough to swallow up any misery he wanted to, any misery in his own life, that is. But he couldn't seem to lose his father's misery with such ease; talking about Miss Emelina hurt him. He went out to the living room, fetched an almost empty whiskey bottle and poured it out into the coffee left over from breakfast, now cold and forming a dark ring around the cup; but whiskey or no whiskey, his voice trembled. As for Jonathan, his version in the diaries is simple reportage. I came to see that when he was most upset, he was at his most straightforward—no adjectives, short sentences, the control pulled as tight (even though he was a grown man by the time he wrote this section) as Miss Emelina's stays. He took the denial of school very hard.

After lessons started in November he spent the days in silence with Alvah and Wify and the drying tobacco leaves. In the evenings after dinner, while the others studied by candlelight, he wrapped tobacco plugs and watched the excitement of book-learning replace the sense of betrayal that had come to George with his illness.

" 'A is for ax.' " George read out the line in early January and then handed the book to Cathern.

" 'B is—' " Cathern began. She bent over the picture. Her red pigtails fell onto the page. " 'B is for,' uh—"

" 'Box.' It's 'box,' you dummy," George said irritably.

Alyoshus took the book and squinted down at the page. " 'C is for puss,' " he announced.

George grabbed the book away. " 'C is for cat. D is for dog. E is for—' "

By February he managed to read out a passage with all the words joined together. " 'O Ned! Watch me toss my ball. See how high it goes! Do you not love to play a game of ball!' "

Jonathan felt a sudden chill. There is a moment when the tide stands still, just that one moment, and then reverses its direction. Stout Cortez stares out at the Pacific in wild surmise, silent upon a peak in Darien. Jonathan—strong-hearted, too—did not know what an ocean was but stared, too, in wild surmise, too, silent upon a dry-goods box in Kansas. It doesn't matter if it's Chapman's Homer or a McGuffey reader; it's the clean cut of the salt air: that's what counts.

"Just grow up as fast as you can," Benbow had said to him. "Shut your eyes and grow."

When Cathern's turn came, Jonathan craned his neck to see over her shoulder.

"Get that boy out of there," George cried.

She started to pull the book away, but George had not yet learned (as my father, who became a professor of economics, used to say in the stuffy, professorial way he sometimes played with) how "to affirm that the rewards of an endeavor are commensurate with the risk entailed." George teased Cathern at school; he pulled her red pigtails; when she peed behind the fence, he poked at her from the other side with a twig. She scanned him, cocked her head, ruffled her shoulders and held the book so Jonathan could see. In the evenings after that, Jonathan followed her finger along the words. Working on tobacco plugs with Alvah and Wify, he reconstructed whole pages in his mind. Before the year was out, he was whispering answers in Cathern's ear. School finished for the summer. The McGuffey reader—its purpose served—was thrown away, and so became Jonathan's.

"You don't understand," my uncle Atlas said, eyes dry but red-rimmed, coffee cup of whiskey already empty. "This was the very first thing he ever owned." It is true. I don't understand. I'm a child of the intellectual middle classes who whimpered when my heap of presents under the Christmas tree looked smaller than the heaps coveted by either of my sisters. "He didn't have his own bed," Atlas said. "He slept on the dirt floor like the pig. He didn't have his own clothes. No mother. No father. No brothers and sisters. Nobody that was his. He had open sores on his legs. He didn't have any shoes. He wasn't even sure he had his own name. Then all of a sudden he's the owner of *McGuffey's Eclectic First Reader, Progressive Lessons in Reading and Spelling Mostly in Easy Words of One and Two Syllables.* Can you blame the poor bastard for what he became?"

AS I SAY, the young are stupid. They think they can escape. Worse, they know it. They are immortal and, in their essence, invulnerable: it's enough to make you weep. One evening in the following year Alvah came back from Sweetbrier and jerked his head toward the west, "New town out there." As soon as it was dark everybody climbed up to the roof of the soddy. A faint line of light flickered below the evening star.

"How far away is it?" George said.

"Mebbe fifteen miles."

That very night my grandfather crept away. He'd grown big enough to see over the grass; it tickled his nose as he forced his way through it. But he couldn't see the town from the ground, so—like some lone bearer of frankincense to the Christ child—he scrambled toward the evening star until it set. He slept the rest of the night by a stream. In the morning, the horizon showed nothing but grass, no town at all. He played all day in the water, a magical day for a child never allowed to play. That night again he followed the star. He spent another day playing. On the third night he heard the tinkle of pianos, followed his ears, found a dozen dance halls and dashed through the swinging door of the nearest one. There were kerosene lamps and a haze of smoke. Hurdy girls danced with men in hats. A man pumped a player piano. People at the bar laughed. Dogs barked. Gamblers gambled. Jonathan burst into tears, and the love of whores he found that evening stayed with him all his life.

"Look," one of them shouted, discovering him, "we got us a wee john."

You couldn't really call them whores, though. Most of them were farm girls running from work that would reduce them to hags at forty and kill them at fifty—big girls in dirty calico skirts like Wify's, with strong backs, great shoulders and powerful arms. What passed for dancing among them wasn't much more than clumping around in heavy boots, but they were young—and all the young (while stupid) are beautiful. The hurdy girl who discovered Jonathan had tiny sequin-eyes that peeped out from above mountainous flanks of cheek. "How'd you get here, little johnny?" she demanded. "You gonna be my johnny, ain't you?"

"Oh yes!" he cried.

She set him on her shoulders, hooked her skirt up under her belt, and galloped from one end of the room to the other. Jonathan bobbed up and down atop her in ecstasy. Toward morning everybody slept. Alvah found his boughten boy curled up in a chair like a house cat.

Until winter closed in that year, Jonathan's hands stayed tied behind his back every night, an ankle tethered as before to the stake in the sod hut's floor. As soon as spring came he ran away again. But Alvah had promised two dollars reward for the return of his boughten boy: Jonathan was bundled back to the homestead in handcuffs. The next year—the year of Alvah's big crop—he stayed put. In October Alvah's final shipment went overland to Kansas City, from there to St. Louis and on down the Mississippi to New Orleans, where tobacco was selling at nine cents a pound. Nine cents a pound! The American dream come true! Alvah's expressionless face showed the faintest hint, the most remote shadow of a smile. Wify's vast hunch unhunched a quarter of an inch. Payment came back in the form of a wooden box with thirty gold pieces in it. Alvah bought a cow, two pigs and a piebald mare, and when spring came he and Jonathan hitched up the mare and drove into Sweetbrier. Time had come to build the wood house that was the capstone and the mighty fulfillment of the Stokes' ambitions in life.

Jonathan was eleven or so by this time, still small, fine-boned and narrow-faced; his hair was black and his eyes were blue. He'd designed the new barn and worked out a ventilating system that could be adjusted according to the weather. This is why Alvah took him along to town to look at houses even though the blue-eyed face, young as it was, already glowed with hate; and Alvah knew in his bones that the boy wasn't to be trusted.

"Which one?" Jonathan asked.

Alvah pointed at a narrow, two-story structure with a porch out in front. A woman of about twenty-five in a crisp, clean apron answered Alvah's knock. She wore a tea towel over her shoulder.

"Who sold you them roof tiles, Bessie?" Alvah said.

"Mr. Finster made them," she said.

"Then I'll make mine. Who made the stairs?"

"Mr. Finster." Alvah nodded. "So you're going to make your house like this one, are you?" Alvah nodded again. "Well, then, you start with the foundation." She told them how much cement Mr. Finster had used, how much gravel, how many buckets per cubic foot.

Jonathan paced off the walls. "You got it?" Alvah asked.
"Enough for now," Jonathan said.

Alvah turned to leave. There was tsk-tsking in Sweet-brier about the Stokes and their boughten boy: "Suffer the little children," they said and shook their heads; "poor little mite," they said. Bessie put her hands on her hips. "You let this Jonathan of yours have a biscuit or you can't look at my house anymore."

In the kitchen sat a man with muttonchops. "Mr. Conductor Finster of the Pennsylvania Railroad," she said, "this here's Alvah Stoke."

"Good morning, Alvah Stoke," said Mr. Finster, rising from his chair. "It's a pleasure to make your acquaintance."

"How'd you make them shingles?" Alvah said.

That night, while George, Cathern and Alyoshus studied, Alvah cleared a space on the dirt floor and Jonathan began to draw lines with a stick.

"What's that?" George said.

"House," Alvah said. "Foundation."

"Our house?" George said. Alvah nodded. "You letting that boy design—"

"Shut up."

"Ain't you got no shame, Pa? You can't let no boughten boy—"

Alvah raised his hand in threat.

By this time George knew that school provided the wherewithal of something important; he didn't know just what, but he knew—he *knew*—that there was real power there. He says so in his autobiography; everybody remembers the endearing modesty of his sentence "One dirt-poor, barefoot kid felt the future stirring in him." He's understandably vague about Jonathan, "an orphan," as he says, "whom my parents were kind enough to take in"; most people don't remember even this mention. Why should they? He gives it no importance. "Hey, boughten boy," George said.

"I told you—" Alvah began, swinging around.

"I just want to read him a story. Ain't nothing wrong in that, is there? 'Once upon a time there was a boy named Johnny, and when he was ten he went to work for a merchant.' " There was no such story in the Third Reader, or in any of the other readers. Jonathan knew that. He could read as well as George. Alyoshus began to giggle. " 'This boy worked very hard, and by the time he was grown up he wore a frock coat and—' "

Alyoshus hooted and doubled up laughing. So did George. Alvah glowered. Jonathan trembled with the indignation that was always so near the surface of him; but no word, no sign, not even the flicker of an eye escaped his iron control to betray him. He rubbed out a line with his foot and redrew it.

The next afternoon George cornered Jonathan in the curing shed. "There wasn't no story about Johnny in my book," he said. "There ain't no Johnnys in any books. Not a single, solitary one. You just got to make up Johnnys."

Jonathan waited; he could hear rats scramble across the floor of George's dungeonlike personality.

"You get in my way, know that?" George's voice slid into rage. "You're a tobacco worm in my field, see? A man got to squash worms. I don't care how long it takes—or what it takes, but I'm bigger than you and I'm better than you—every which way you look at it—and I'm going to destroy you. Get me?"

The work on the house continued. They cleared a piece of land upstream. They dug the cellar, mixed and poured the concrete. They split shingles and tiled the roof. They built the staircase. Early the following summer, they piled pots, pans, blankets and bedding straw into the old crate that served them as a table, lugged it over the ground, and installed themselves in the new house.

It was understood that Jonathan was not part of this ceremony. A slave is a slave: when the gentry becomes gentry, a slave lives in slave quarters. Jonathan ate supper at the wooden

house, worked there afterwards on tobacco plugs, sitting beside Cathern to study with her; but when the Stokes went to
bed, he went out to the old sod hut alone. He tried to make
out to himself that he had become the owner of a house, but
he couldn't hang on to the idea for long—not sharing the dirt
floor with the animals like that. The animals lowed, chewed,
farted, shat and let loose sudden hot torrents of urine. He
made himself a bed of hay and carved a small box to keep the
McGuffey's First Reader safe from the filth around him, and
doubtless to keep it safe from the intensity of his own hatreds,
too. He himself was thin—the Stokes didn't feed him enough—
but his hatreds were fat; without gods to back him, he fed his
prayers on these hatreds: prayers of stature, dark, forbidding,
encrusted with the power of a powerful imagination that had
no other outlet. Night after night he prayed as fervently as
Moses in Egypt for a plague, his own plague this time, not
worms, something new, some horror so great that the very
thought of it would blister the skin—a plague to come and
wipe out the lot of them. He would bear it himself, and joy-
fully, just to hear the Stokes scream in agony.

11

WHY BOTHER with a special plague? Life itself is a plague—
"a sexually transmitted disease with a hundred percent mor-
tality," as R. D. Laing put it in a television interview not long
before his own death. All Jonathan had to do was wait, and
he'd have had the pleasure of watching Alvah and Wify suffer

the tortures of the damned: this is what old age and the far edges of life are all about. But what could he have known of things like this? What do any of the young know? Death for them—when they think of it at all—is a box-office hit of a tragedy, elegantly plotted, somberly choreographed, with the world weeping in the stalls. No wonder we worship them; they're so magically blind. My uncle Atlas's telephone rang periodically throughout our morning's taping; a geriatrician gets more calls than any other kind of specialist. I forgot to turn off the recorder once. "Jesus H. Christ," Atlas is saying into the receiver, "that poor bitch. Yesterday I cleaned fecal matter out of her clear up to the cervix. Why don't we stitch her up entirely? What use has she got for a vagina? The damn thing's hanging out on the sheets."

"I can't figure the anatomy of that," I say to him after he hangs up.

"That woman was quite a lady once," he says. "Owned her own string of stables, had a couple of winners in the Kentucky Derby." There's a queer iciness to doctors dealing with medicine just as there's a queer iciness to philosophers with propositions; it's just professionalism, of course it is, but it sure as hell grates on the nonprofessional ear, especially when the owner of the ear—us—is the subject in question. "I remember when she first came to me," Atlas goes on. "This was, oh, four, five years ago—and I said in the course of the examination, 'When was the last time you had sexual intercourse?' And she said, 'Young man'—I was well over seventy at the time—'Young man, I can answer that precisely: October the fifth, nineteen hundred and thirty-two.'"

But Jonathan prayed for his own special plague, and years later it amused him to think that just like Moses he had called down the plague that devastated the Stokes. Moses said to Pharaoh, "If thou refuse to let my people go, behold, tomorrow will I bring the locusts into thy coast." In September of the year after the wooden house was built, just as the har-

vest began, the daylight dimmed one sunny afternoon. The
tobacco plants stopped blowing. The Stokes and Jonathan
dropped their tools and stared. At first sight a swarm of locusts
is a glittering cloud. Locusts aren't tiny things as I'd always
thought; they're sometimes as big as hummingbirds. When
they're near, their wings rustle, which is queer because it's a
loud sound and a rustle shouldn't be loud. The largest count
of anything in the Old Testament is thirty thousand, but there
can be as many as eighty billion locusts in a swarm; Moses
had no way of describing what he'd brought down on Egypt.
Nor did Jonathan. Locusts dropped out of the sky like giant
hailstones.

They fell into the necks of shirts and pinafores, crawled
up the legs of pants and skirts, clung to faces, hair, fingers,
ears. Everybody—all six of them at once—broke into a run.
Inside the wooden house, they listened to locusts thudding
down on the roof. But they couldn't stay there. They went
back out. They had to. They hitched the insect-covered mare
to an insect-covered wagon and loaded insect-covered hay into
it. Between the tobacco hills they set hay piles afire. By late
afternoon, locusts were four inches deep on the ground from
horizon to horizon. In a swarm there are so many locusts that
if they're pink, the entire landscape is pink; if they're gray, the
landscape is gray. There's a sort of palsy everywhere. Everything jiggles with bugs. They writhe in clumps from trees.
Potatoes, carrots, beets, beans, whole fields of sorghum and
timothy sink to the ground under their weight. When you walk
through them, they organize themselves in waves and take off
in succession—wave after wave roaring as it breaks into flight
like a squadron of bombers setting out on a mission.

By bedtime, underneath the shroud of smoke not a single
tobacco plant stood—nor did any other green thing.

All night the writhing went on, the rustle of carapace and
wings, the milling, meaningless activity. The next morning—
as abrupt as a slap in the face—it stopped. The bugs sat up-

right, all of them at once. This is the genetic clock at work, a
unity of timing we humans can only dream of: this is how
locusts lay their eggs. Then they die. Hatching doesn't come
until spring, which is to say that next year's crop was destroyed as surely as this year's, and even before the seed was
sown. Alvah went out in the wagon. When he got back he
tossed a piece of paper on the table.

"What's that?" Wify said. Alvah shook his head. "What's
it say, George?"

" 'This document says,' " George read, " 'that Alvah
Stoke and Benbow Wikin are partners in Wikin's Sweetbrier:
A Good Chew. Benbow Wikin to supply three hogsheads of
Ohio White Burley tobacco, Alvah Stoke to manufacture.
George Stoke to sell around. Signed Alvah Stoke and Benbow
Wikin.' "

George looked up. "What's that mean—'George Stoke to
sell around'?"

"Wify'll teach you," Alvah said.

The Bible doesn't say what effect Moses' plague of locusts had on Moses himself and on the Jews, who had to suffer
it just as Pharaoh and the Egyptians did, but Jonathan's ag-
onies were far greater than anyone else's. His plague brought
about a critical phase in the formal education of the future
Senator Stoke. Every evening after supper, Wify taught
George the techniques that had earned her father the title of
"Best Salesman in New Hampshire" from the Barghest Traveling Medicine Show.

"Heels first when you walk, George," she'd say. "Clomp.
Clomp. Right up to the sucker. Look him in the eye and don't
let him go." She taught him to smile with his eyebrows raised,
lean his elbow against a storekeeper's counter and open with
"Howya keeping?" She chose clothes for him from the Sears
Roebuck catalogue; he was going to ride the mare and sell
Wikin's Sweetbrier in towns up to fifty miles away. A drum-
mer needs spats and a bowler hat.

A drummer needs a frock coat.

"You got to think what a frock coat meant to people like that," Atlas said to me. We got to this part of the story in midmorning. There was a brackish mixture in his coffee cup by this time, half gin and half brandy. "Looks kinda like whiskey, wouldn't you say?" he said to me. The whiskey was gone. Claire didn't nag at him, so he said, if he drank only whiskey. "She thinks she can—what's the word she uses?—'monitor' my intake that way." Atlas's fourth wife—Claire's immediate predecessor (I'd liked number four)—had thought she could monitor his intake, too. Such self-deception is standard, I'm told. Number three drank with him. I was too little for number one, and all I remember about number two was that I didn't like her; her name was Matilda and when I was only six she laughed at my jokes, the silly cow. Even at the time— especially then—I could see what a fool she was.

"A frock coat! Jesus, these were the kind of people who usually wore nothing but homespun flax. You know what that is? Wify grew it. She reaped it, carded it, spun it, wove it, cut the cloth and sewed it. They were so fucking poor, they slept in those clothes. They wore them night and day until the goddamned things fell off their backs." Sometimes I used to catch glimpses of Clark Gable's rubbery ogle on Atlas's face and then, a moment later, a hint of my own father's pewter-polished academic manner. But talking like this, Atlas's face became his own; you could see the man he might have been. "A guy like Alvah never even dreamed of wearing a frock coat," he went on. "Preachers wore frock coats. Doctors wore them. You know, rich people—you, me—people who undressed for bed and had running water. The audacity of it. A frock coat! To hell with locusts. With a frock coat in the offing, anything can be borne."

After the locusts laid their eggs and died, no green things grew again, not even a weed. The land was a desert of dirt that cracked and split. The well went dry; what water there was came from a night-drip in the stream. There was not enough food. The Stokes' homespun hung loose on them and Wify's great bones stuck up through her flesh like the tent poles of a circus big top. All efforts went on Wikin's Sweetbrier: A Good Chew. In late winter, by the time they'd manufactured several hundred pounds of it, George's frock coat arrived.

"It was serge, black, satin-lined," my uncle Atlas said, "double-breasted, two rows of mother-of-pearl buttons. Dad described it to me once, every detail, down to the price tag."

George unfolded the coat, spread it out, surveyed it, held it up and put it on with a swing of its skirt just as Wify's father, the great salesman, might have done. Jonathan's hands went on kneading sticky tobacco into plugs, but he could not look away. George stepped over to the crate that still served the family as a dining table; he bent from the waist and rested one elbow next to Jonathan's pile of tobacco.

"Howya keeping, boughten boy?"

Jonathan said nothing.

George straightened and with his eyes on Jonathan, ran his hands down the front panels of the coat that was the promised land.

Then he winked.

12

"AN ARMY with all its physical powers, inured to privations and fatigue by exercise, like the muscles of an athlete"—these are the words of Karl von Clausewitz again, the great philosopher of war—an army like this is an army that can win battles even when the odds are very much against it.

For nearly ten years, ever since George had declared the war between them that first day in the sod hut, Jonathan's hatred had held the balance. Hatred had exercised his physical powers, inured his mind to privations and fatigue, kept his spirit in fighting trim. But this wink—this was new, altogether new. He found himself off balance. Surprise allows the surpriser, says Clausewitz, "to gain a march upon the enemy, and thereby a position, a road, a point of country."

That night Jonathan made his third attempt to run away to the town that lay below the evening star.

None of the old inhabitants remained. Not one. Even the dance hall he'd remembered had disappeared. The new people had no idea what had happened to it or its owner or the girls who had danced there. "Probably gone west," they said. The one thing they did know was that there was a reward for the return of a boughten boy; as before, a bartender waylaid him and returned him to the homestead where Alvah beat him. Alvah's patience was wearing thin; this time the beating was no ordinary beating. This time Alvah used the horsewhip. Then he chained my grandfather and set him a diet of bread and water for two weeks.

During the days of punishment, Jonathan was almost less aware of his pain and hunger than he was of the shift in battle lines. George brought him food. George! Beans and bacon plainly stolen from the cold store. Jonathan was profoundly disconcerted. George won him release a day before the two weeks were up. The swagger was gone from George's voice; he addressed Jonathan by name. My grandfather waited tensely. A month went by. Nothing happened. There was going to be hell to pay.

In April the snows melted and the prairies began to bloom. On the first hot morning in May, the locusts hatched. They're always green at first, wingless and sexless; they move like the surface of a pond, sudden ripples in sudden gusts of wind. They grow, shed a carapace, grow again, shed again, five times in all; with the fifth come wings and sex. Then one day, in as abrupt a change as came over their parents the year before, there's a hush, a wait, a changing of the tide: an army forms—no shoddy human imitation of an army, either—and begins to move, its lockstep so absolute that it marches up over anything that stands in its way, houses, fences, animals; it marches into creeks, where millions drown, and more and more march in and drown until there are so many dead ones that they make up a bridge for live ones to cross on.

West was the way everything went. Jonathan's father went west; "probably gone to California," Benbow had said. Where else would he go? Where else would anybody go? The hurdy girls and the dance hall owner: "probably gone west." Where else? The locusts were no different. When the swarm took to flight, even the wingless, the sexless, the legless—the dregs that could not fly—straggled westward on the ground until they died in their tracks. And while the devastated ground around Sweetbrier caked and cracked once more, the *Overland Sentinel* ran a special edition:

BEHOLD! WE, TOO, ARE GOING WEST!

The Future Arrives in Sweetbrier This Winter!
Work on the Railroad to Begin!

An advance workforce of the St. Joe, Hannibal & Denver
starts work in November on the westbound line that will go
straight through town and link us with California.

There were elegiac descriptions of the advantages to come, but
once the magic word "west" was in print, nobody needed them.
Even in the Stokes' wooden house there was a frisson of real
excitement. My grandfather thought of the grass that had bil-
lowed around him on his first attempt at escape, when he was
too small to see his way through it, and knew that nothing
could stop him this time.

On the back page of that same special edition of the
Overland Sentinel a small item caught Miss Emelina Mc-
Clanahan's eye:

ANNOUNCEMENT

The Everett Elias Madison Scholarship for Farm Bred
Boys from Kansas will choose its first scholar for entrance
in the freshman class of 1876 at the University of Kansas
in Lawrence. Applicants must be Kansas born and bred.
They must be from local farms, and they must have received their schooling from local teachers.

Miss Emelina never doubted that this first scholar was going
to be George. During the years she'd been teaching, she'd
gained confidence and prestige; that mound of bodice had
grown more formidable, her petticoats whiter and starchier;
she talked firmly to Alvah. As a result, George had private
lessons when he wasn't out selling.

One hot night in September, George visited Jonathan in
the sod hut. "I saw your light," he said; Jonathan had no light,
nor any means of fueling one. Despite the heat George wore

his frock coat; he carried the satchel he took with him when he was out on his rounds. "Thought I'd come calling."

Jonathan gestured noncommittally and stood aside. The roof of the soddy hung low over their heads; the turf that made up the ceiling trailed with dead weeds that dangled down over ears and into eyes. The night was the kind of night that even Middle Westerners dread, hot enough to drown in; without air-conditioning, the only way of getting to sleep is to lie under a damp sheet in the draft from the doorway. The soddy's one window didn't open; there was no draft. There had never been a bed; and as for a sheet, Jonathan knew the word from the McGuffey readers but, as he says in his diaries, he had not been able to figure out precisely what purpose such a large square of cloth was supposed to serve.

"Bought us light and drink," George said. He took a candle out of his pocket, lit it, stuck it into the soddy floor; then he took out a bottle and a couple of tin cups. "Thought we ought to drink to better times." He filled the cups and handed one to Jonathan. "Come on, drink up." He said, "Here's to you," and tossed back the contents of his own cup.

Jonathan studied the liquid, sniffed it. He'd stolen milk straight from the cow; he'd drunk water.

"Ain't going to bite you," George said. "It's a peace offering. Come on, drink up."

"Why?"

"Why what?"

"You ain't here to make peace with me."

"You afraid to drink this stuff? Huh?" It was probably 110-proof red, an evil bathtub brew of bourbon touched up with turpentine and lye, enough to take rust off metal, enough to skin cats alive. But Jonathan was only fourteen or so, and young males are among the stupidest of the stupid young, competitive where the prize is worthless and fiercely proud where pride is meaningless: he drank, shuddered, gasped, choked and recovered, eyes watering, throat aflame. "Another?" George said, refilling the cup.

"I was kind of ornery before sometimes," George went on. "Can't deny it." George was fat like Wify, powerful like her, but soft rather than chunky even so; despite his farm-boy muscle, a roll of suet, white and pulpy, showed at the meeting between shirt and pants beneath the glorious coat. But when he smiled there was charm in the curling mouth, not a familiar trait, new to Jonathan and almost as unexpected as the wink. In the candlelight, the shadows around the shiny, round eyes flickered large and small, lengthening and foreshortening over the plump cheeks, as though they were breathing vents into the dungeon that Jonathan knew lay behind them. "But I made up for it, didn't I? You still got that old McGuffey?"

"What do you care?"

"You know, I remember those pages word for word practically. Bet you do, too, huh?" Jonathan could already feel the effect of that one great gulp of alcohol; it was not unpleasing. He sipped from the cup, holding the liquor in his mouth before swallowing it, closing his throat as best he could against the burn. "But you don't learn much from that crap, do you? I mean, what good is reading about a boy goes skating, a girl plays with a hoop. What's that got to do with anything? Ain't you gonna answer me?"

"What for?"

"You got to talk to me, Jonathan. I mean it. Drink up."

"I got nothing to say to you."

"Sure you do. We're more alike than any of them others. You're the only one can read as well as me. Come on, drink with me. You're the only one anywhere near as smart."

"What do you want, George?" Jonathan said. The sweat was running down his back, yet in the heat George sat there in his frock coat, and Jonathan knew with all the passion of his soul that if the coat were his, he'd keep it on, too: to hell with heat, to hell with everything. He tore his eyes away and pinned them to the dank dirt wall beyond, where ants marched in neat, military lines, carrying on the orderly, ordinary business of life. He drank deep from the tin cup.

"I want us to be friends," George said.

"No you don't."

"I know I was a shit. Ain't I said as much?"

"I ain't arguing with you about that."

"Then argue with me about something else."

"No."

George sighed, again refilled Jonathan's cup. He leaned back then and talked about the countryside he rode through on his rounds. He told about some of the men he'd met; he was a good storyteller. He talked about weather and horses. He told a joke.

Jonathan frowned. "What do you want, George?" he said again. He felt an edge of nausea—the 110-proof red probably, but he didn't know that, and so he drank again—and realized suddenly that despite his iron control, his eyes were wandering in the direction of the coat. He turned his head away.

"It bother you much, not going to school?" George said.

"That ain't what you came for."

"Look at it this way: you learn good on your own. What do you need school for? Besides, you're a good worker and workers don't need no schooling at all. What are you looking at the wall for? Why don't you look at me? I ain't ugly."

Jonathan got to his feet, steeled himself and looked at George, at the changeable shadows around his eyes—and at the coat. "Get out," he said.

"Listen, Jonathan. Why can't we be friends? I say to myself, 'Do the kid a favor. He don't see what's going on.' I owe you. I admit it. So I want to pay you back. You got to listen to me."

"Get out of here."

"Jonathan, listen! I got lots to say to you."

"I don't want to hear it. Get out."

"Listen," George cried. "Give me a chance. Listen!"

After I'd been studying truth at Columbia for nearly four years without avail, one of my professors shouted at me, "Listen!"—to this day I have no idea what made him so angry—

"Listen to me: what I'm telling you is elementary. First-year stuff. Listen!"

"Listen!" George cried again, so anxious to tie Jonathan's attention to him and to the coat that he knocked the candle over, righted it, hot wax running down his fingers, and didn't even notice the burn. The light guttered, almost dying, then gained strength again. "Listen to me," George said. "You work hard, don't you? So tell me now, where do you think all this work's taking you? Where—"

"Get out of here, goddamn you. Get out!"

They'd said to George—the older drummers had, the ones who knew—they said, "The fight is for the sucker's attention in the first place. Don't matter how you go about getting it. Liquor him. Needle him. Flatter him. Bribe him. But get his attention. When you do, your sale's in the bag." It wasn't quite that easy—nothing ever is—so in this most important of sales (testing the sucker's reactions according to his hard-learned lessons), George slipped off his coat, threw it down, and smiled to himself to see Jonathan make the hoped-for, almost instinctive grab to rescue it from the dirt.

"You're right," George said, "we shouldn't let it get dirty. A good-looking coat, ain't it?"

"It's yours," Jonathan said. The words were out before he could stop the revulsion they betrayed.

"Want one like it?"

"No."

"Sure?"

"Get out of here, George. I'm telling you—"

"You got kind of a boring line there, Jonathan. 'Get out, George.' Can't sell nothing with a single boring line. This here's a nice coat. I like wearing it. Makes me feel good." He held the coat toward the candlelight and turned it this way and that. "We got no quarrel, Jonathan. Not you and me. Not no more. That's all over with. We ought to be friends. Come on, what do you say?"

Then George reached out and grasped Jonathan's shoulder, a gentle grasp, shook him gently, too—a friendly gesture. As far back as Jonathan could remember, the hurdy girl at the dance hall was the only person who had ever touched him like that, the only person whose touch had not been a threat or a blow. I visited my brother-in-law when he was dying right here in Atlas's town (he and Atlas had grown up together, and he died six months or so after this day of my tape recorder). We held hands for a long time, my brother-in-law and I, and a nurse said to me afterwards, "It's nice to see a family member who isn't afraid to touch them." "Them?" I said. "The dying," she said. The same is true of cripples. Atlas was one of the few people who would touch me. This has nothing to do with sex. It's just human warmth. Elementary to most people. First-year stuff, as my angry professor put it. There's no defense it cannot breach if skillfully employed, and George was skillful; he'd planned long and hard. Why am I so weak? Jonathan asks again and again in these coded diaries of his. He felt a tightness spread across his chest; the spot where George's hand had touched felt the touch still.

"Let's have another drink," George said. "Hey, kid, want to feel the material? Of this here coat? This is serge. Go ahead. Touch it. Ain't gonna bite you."

Years later Jonathan wrote that at that moment, despite the alcohol, despite the fact that he was, in fact, quite drunk, his mind was clear, painfully so, so clear that he missed nothing at all, not the creases in the skirt of the coat as George held it out to him nor the small spot on the sleeve, nor the elongated shadows from the candlelight. These very details somehow seemed to bring on an abrupt sense of misery, an uncertainty and indecision in him that grew with every word George said. Unable to stop himself he reached out, the hand at the end of his own arm seeming a foreign object, some lump of alien flesh, not his, not even related to him: with this hand, he reached out and touched the cloth, and the cloth touched his finger, real cloth from a real frock coat.

"Great, ain't it?" George said. "Look at this. See here? This is the lining. Called satin. See how the shoulder part is made? That's padding. Right? And the buttonholes, look. Want to try it on? It's okay. Try it on. Here, let me help you. That's it. Right arm." Half in a trance, Jonathan felt the coat slip over his right arm, then over his left, onto his back, serge and satin, the wonder of buttonholes and tiny stitches. George brushed the material on his shoulders as a tailor might, or a wife, then stood back to survey the effect. "Well, well, well," George said, "will you look at that? A bit big for you, ain't it?"

The coat smelled of George. Even in the reek of the sod hut, Jonathan could smell the steam-sweat of George rising from his own armpits.

George watched carefully. Then he unbuttoned his shirt and took it off. "Look at me," he said. "I'm built like a girl, ain't I? Want to feel? Come on, give me your hand. They're soft, like me, girls are. Come here. Come on—"

Jonathan hardly noticed George taking hold of his hand until he felt one of the girlish breasts beneath his fingers. The sense of physical shock was terrible; he yanked his hand back, suddenly at sea with his hatreds, awash in them, unable to find reason or direction. The skin of his cheeks went numb; his scalp shrank over his skull; he tried to expand his lungs. Nothing happened.

"You have to know, my friend," George's voice went on, "there ain't anybody but me got a frock coat in mind for you. This is your one and only chance. Now. Here. With me. My coat: mine. No girls neither. Only boy's tits. My tits. You see"—the voice went on relentlessly—"this here hole in the ground where the animals shit— It's where people keep tools and—well, things like you." Jonathan looked into the shiny black eyes. "You wouldn't get it in your head that somebody's going to buy a frock coat for this here"—George turned and slapped the cow on its hindquarters—"for this dung-maker?

Now would you? What about this ox? A night with a pretty girl?" He reached over and slapped Jonathan exactly as he'd slapped the cow. "You got to understand me. A man? Shit, you ain't even human. Never will be. Your pa sold you. My pa bought you. You're a commodity. Like a cow. Or a shipment of tobacco."

The spirit of an army—that unity that reaches its peak in the migrations of insects—is no match for sheer weight of artillery: not on the human battlefield, or on the insect battlefield, either, not even when the soldiers are the most experienced of fighters. Artillery blows soldiers to bits, and the bits, the heads, arms, legs, torsos, these themselves become cannonballs that explode on impact and kill whatever is in their path. Often the minced and scattered remains on a battlefield aren't recognizable as human. Jonathan did not remember George leaving. He had no idea how George got him out of the frock coat. He knew only that the coat was gone, that he was sitting on the ground unfrocked, alone, shivering in the heat, his face sticky with sweat—and with the certain knowledge in his heart that everything George said was true. Elementary. First-year stuff.

The cow lowed behind him.

He leapt up and flung himself at her; he beat her lumpen, hairy flesh with his fists. Then he swung around and beat the mare. Then the pigs. Then he picked up a stick and, tears streaming down his face, weeping for the first time in his life as a slave (and for the last time in his life for nearly half a century to come), he beat them all again. The animals bucked and kicked and bellowed. He went on beating at them until he fell exhausted to the ground.

Early the next morning, Cathern opened the door of the soddy as she did every morning, milking bucket in hand. She sat herself down by the cow and began to draw on the teats; the cow bellowed. Cathern sniffed the driblet of milk, frowned and ran her hand over the cow's hindquarters. She glanced at

Jonathan. Then she picked up her bucket and ran. Alvah appeared almost at once. He examined the animals quickly, picked up the stick that had done the beating, and brought it down on his boughten boy. While Jonathan lay stunned, Alvah fetched the horsewhip. By the time he finished, my grandfather lay unconscious in a pool of his own blood.

13

THE NEXT MORNING when Alvah came to check the boy's condition, Jonathan turned his face to the wall—which indicated to Alvah that the beating had been properly gauged: it had done no permanent damage. But by evening he was worried; the boy would drink nothing. Animals died when they didn't drink. The following morning was the same; Alvah tried without success to force water down him. Wify tried, too. Both failed. At about noon, when Alvah was of half a mind to fetch the druggist from Sweetbrier, the black wagon of the Peaslee Traveling Medicine Service appeared in front of the wooden house. The Peaslee man cured all ills, mental and physical, animal, human, and vegetable: cure guaranteed was part of the bargain. The lettering on the outside walls was bright red outlined in yellow. Inside were bottles with heavy glass stoppers in them, just as there had been in the wagon Wify's father drove.

"What good is this stuff to me?" Alvah growled, his mind on the boy in the sod hut.

"Why, Mr. Stoke," the Peaslee man began—nobody else

called Alvah anything but Alvah—"your horses got a hoof wound? Just put this on it." Peaslee's Iodine and Resublimated Tincture, said the label. "And a drop of this—" He added a drop from another bottle. Then he lifted his arm, bottle in hand.

"So what?" Alvah said.

A sudden burst of smoke, dense and red, formed as if by magic and floated upwards; I doubt it did anything for hoof wounds but it was certainly good for catching an ignorant farmer's attention, even Alvah's, whose father-in-law, the great salesman of the East, had been a quack of the first order himself. Alvah took the salesman to see Jonathan.

"It's his teeth, Mr. Stoke," the salesman said; he had a mustache of drooping streamers that swayed in the wind. "I've seen it happen before. They've turned septic."

"He's a lot of trouble to me. Years of trouble."

"With teeth like that he can't help it, Mr. Stoke. Ain't rightly his fault," the salesman said. The salesman could sometimes get a dollar apiece for real teeth, although the market wasn't what it had been in its heyday during the Civil War. In those days, in a single night, anybody with a pair of pliers could make enough money to last a lifetime: you waited quietly at the edge of a battlefield, any battlefield, anywhere from Pennsylvania to Texas; when the shooting stopped and the living retired to base camp, you yanked your way through every dead mouth you could get to. Competition was fierce and sometimes ended in a set of molars not strictly military in origin, but think of it! Two dollars a tooth on the London markets, where ladies and gentlemen in silk were scrambling over each other to chew with the teeth of American soldiers. The Peaslee man had moral support, too. Respectable medical journals said that natural teeth caused cancer and pleurisy; they could drive men mad. Who was a mere Peaslee man to argue with respectable journals? Alvah fetched Alyoshus and George. The four of them tackled Jonathan, knocked him out, laid him down. Alvah held his head steady while the salesman pulled out all of his teeth with a copper-plated wrench.

And so it was the teeth were pulled from the boy who was all teeth and claws like the uncrowned king of Arabia.

14

"THERE'S JUST SO MUCH of this I can take," I said to Atlas, although at the time I didn't have all the details I've put down here, simply because Atlas didn't know them all, not by any means. Jonathan's coded diaries are my primary source. Back in England, when this day at Atlas's old-age ghetto in Washington State was well over, I typed hundreds of pages of these diaries into my computer, which ground out for me letter by letter (in electronic green, accompanied by electronic bleeps) a life of nightmare that makes me feel ill just to think about it: a life decoded onto fanfold listing paper with microperforations, printer chuffing through its paces as indifferently as though it were producing a tax assessment. But why were the diaries in code? What was the point of it? As a child I'd known the crude outlines—the bounding out, the tobacco farm—although in my family the hatred of Jonathan was so great that my father seemed to lay claim to these things for himself, as though they had been lived through for the sole purpose of terrorizing him. But Jonathan was efficient. He wouldn't have wasted his energy on coding diaries just because the tale they told was ugly. It made no sense to me.

"You got to keep in mind," Atlas said, "that Alvah Stoke had his virtues as a slavemaster."

"How can you say that, Atlas? This is the most terrible—"

"It's just old-fashioned slavery. Nothing special."

"—and as for George— How much more stuff like this is there?"

"Not all that much. It gets better soon."

"Promise?"

He laughed. "See, this guy, Alvah, he wasn't cruel for no reason at all; he took good care of his animals, and the way he saw it, Dad wasn't much different from the mare and the pigs. A hell of a lot more trouble, though; and he'd have killed any animal that hurt the others. Besides, the operation seemed to work—which would have justified it entirely in any slavemaster's book."

Jonathan was sick for weeks afterwards. They kept him in the wooden house and tended him just as Atlas said, like a feeble calf in winter. The pain he suffered must have been dreadful to watch, and he drank only water. But at least he drank. When he began to get better, Alvah knew there would be no more running away—not for a while, anyhow. "In a lost battle," says Clausewitz, "it is the moral power of an army that is broken to a greater degree than the physical." Alvah said to Benbow Wikin with some satisfaction, "You get you an animal, you got to break him." For just over a year, Alvah's satisfaction remained intact.

In his autobiography, George says he went out selling tobacco during this winter of Jonathan's defeat, in Sullen Springs and Frying Pan, in Whiskey, First Chance and Cow. Miss Emelina's pressure on Alvah had got him back to school; she'd started him to work on an essay called "A Drummer Looks at Kansas," which they both hoped would win him the Farm-Boys' scholarship, written up in the *Overland Sentinel*, alongside stories about the St. Joe, Hannibal & Denver Railroad that was to run through Sweetbrier. But he says nothing about his state of mind, and what a state it must have been! How much he'd learned! Play by the rules: you lose. Hold back: you lose. Consider any consequence other than winning: you lose. But lie, scheme, cheat—break every rule you've ever been taught, cross every line that's ever been drawn—and what happens? You win. This is the secret of war. This is the secret of life. What greater secret can anybody possess? The laughter in him must have threatened to boil up out of control.

But Jonathan still had that grace, like Alvah's. This shared grace must have troubled George; he loved his father more than ever with that bloodsucking, jealous love he practiced on his intimates. In his autobiography he refers to Alvah as most public people might refer to the spirit of the country they serve. Perhaps he was right. There was much in Alvah of the basic American soul—the independence, the drive, the ruthlessness—but there was still something in the way Jonathan held his head that disturbed George's sleep. George worked harder at his lessons and his essay. When he caught sight of Jonathan, he was careful to let his eyes register no more interest than they did when he caught sight of the mare.

As for Jonathan, he kept his mind to the shape of the tobacco cubes that the Stokes produced, the landscape inside his head as baked and barren as the landscape the locusts had left behind them. Before the snow had melted Alvah was entrusting him with the weekly trips to Sweetbrier to bargain for staples in exchange for Wikin's Chewing Tobacco. Without teeth my grandfather couldn't speak properly, so he didn't speak at all. He pointed and shook his head if the price was too high. To deal with the sometimes complicated haggling, he developed those extraordinary gestures that remained with him for the rest of his life. Usually little kids are merciless to people like this (I have personal experience of such matters), but they didn't harass Jonathan. Perhaps they were afraid. I don't know what he looked like at the time—there are no photographs—but probably his face showed something of the fury that his mind denied. Whatever the reason, local children followed him down the street and into Benbow Wikin's, where most of the haggling went on, as though he were the Pied Piper; they laughed delightedly when he got across some unexpected thought, and after he'd left, they squatted outside and tried to talk to each other with their own hands.

Jonathan paid no attention to them—which may have been part of his secret—nor did he pay attention to the gang of railway workers that appeared at the eastern horizon to bed the ground and lay the track that was to skirt the Stoke homestead on its way west through Sweetbrier. He hardly noticed them working throughout the bitter winter weather. He hardly noticed them disappear over the western horizon in May at just about the time George received a letter from the University of Kansas at Lawrence telling him he'd won the scholarship for 1876.

The week after George left for the university in September, the first train was scheduled to pass through Sweetbrier. Everybody from miles around came to look. It was nighttime—one of those dark, moonless nights when the stars look garish. Beside the track, Jonathan stood a little back from the Stokes, waiting like the rest of them. Twenty years ago—or was it thirty?—I watched the first moon landing and was bored to death. We have a glut of wonders. But those people in Sweetbrier lived much as their fathers had lived and their fathers before them. No industry. No electricity. No running water. Trains didn't yet play the liquid melodies of Casey-blow-your-horn; they had a high-pitched, single-note whistle, and here out of nowhere comes this disembodied sound, like no sound these people had ever heard. You have to envy them: what joy to be struck dumb by something altogether new. First the sound, then the headlight; this, too, was altogether new, a never-before-seen break in the darkness. Then the chuff-chuff-a-chuff of steam and heavy metal wheels; then the rumble. And at last a sight of the engine itself. A steam engine is a magnificent thing even to modern eyes, but for these dirt-poor farmers it's the first man-made miracle they've ever seen. Here is a huge, clanking, shaking, hissing monstrosity out of the Apocalypse: and this time the miracle is ours—theirs—human, not divine.

If people can make trains, people can do anything they want.

Jonathan didn't sleep that night. The next morning he stole candle leavings from Wify's cupboard and a piece of seasoned wood from Alvah's store. The method came to him whole, as God-given as the great train itself. He searched out a clump of clayey earth, bit into it to make a mold of his gums and filled the mold with wax to make a template. He whittled jaws and teeth to size and joined the jaws together with leather thongs. He had to hold the upper plate with his index finger when he spoke, but he could make himself understood again.

Teeth and claws were back in business.

During the first winter George was away at college, Alvah forbade Jonathan to go down to the edge of the homestead where the railway tracks ran. Jonathan went anyway, watched the trains go by and stared after them, heart pounding. Back at the homestead, he looked straight into Alvah's eyes without a blink and even—or so it seemed to Alvah—without awareness that Alvah's eyes were eyes, too. As before, Alvah forbade him this, forbade him that, but now hesitated to beat him, was afraid somehow to beat him. Jonathan went to the train station every Saturday after he'd bargained for flour and bacon at Wikin's store. Mr. Finster, late of the Pennsylvania Railroad and builder of the house that had served as model for Alvah's house, was stationmaster, a talkative man and a warm one, with the strong feelings most of Sweetbrier's inhabitants shared about the treatment of this boughten boy. He told Jonathan about Wooten fireboxes, equalizing beams and link-and-pin couplers. He explained the signals. He talked about bridges that spanned valleys hundreds of feet deep and trains that crossed the Mississippi in winter on crossties laid right over the ice.

Trains weren't scheduled for Saturdays, but one day at the end of winter, a train came through while Jonathan was at the station. His diaries say it was an American Standard, a great, brass-bound beast by the sound of it with a balloon stack and box-shaped lights two feet square. People scurried this way and that, dogs barked, children screamed. Mr. Finster carried bags and checked tickets. Trainmen bawled out orders. The engine built up a second head of steam, the whistle blew, the massive wheels began to turn.

Despite their beauty, these trains were crude pieces of machinery: they didn't even have real brakes. Men stood astride the tops of the cars and leapt from moving car to moving car to set brakes that worked only from the outside: astonishing acrobatics of courage, foolishness and grace that made bystanders gasp. Jonathan kept his eyes on one man in particular; when this one leapt, in his heart Jonathan leapt, too—and was still leaping when the man staggered and fell between the cars. Mr. Finster broke into a run. The brakeman's body bounced beneath the wheels. A flash of arm shot out from the tracks. The body bounced again, and the head flew out to rest some twenty yards beyond the arm. For a moment Jonathan stopped breathing altogether. Then he scrambled back to Alvah's wagon, jerked the reins, and whipped the mare into a gallop.

Two miles out of town, he reined in, clung to the side of the spring wagon and held his breath until there were spots in front of his eyes. First the inertia breaks, and there's a faint sign of movement, a faint stirring of the soul. Things build slowly, then a little quicker, then quicker still. Hear that beat? It builds and builds, spurred on by some hidden, internal rhythm. There's a hidden, internal trigger, too, its mechanism many times witnessed but not at all well understood: at some moment known only to the nuclei themselves, at this precise moment—bang!—the atomic pile goes critical all at once. "Jonathan's going west," my grandfather cried to the open fields all around him, where the grass blew gently in the wind as it had blown for centuries before. "Going west—no, not Jonathan—Johnny. Johnny the brakeman. I'll buy me a frock coat—Johnny's frock coat—and I'll ride and ride and never stop, go on forever, never stop. Never, never!"

For the next few weeks, while he and the family stripped, flavored, kneaded, prized and wrapped tobacco, he watched, body taut with concentration, to see just how upper teeth fit onto lower teeth. His next set was to be carved out of bone.

15

POWER IS GAINED and maintained by violence. This is as true of individuals as it is of nations. Both are born in violence, relate to others through violence, and die in violence. This is not cynicism. Nobody who has witnessed a birth can ever forget the tearing of the flesh and the screams. As to our relationships with other people, we play at manners and morals, but we only play, just as states do; the veneer is dangerously thin and what lurks beneath is murderous. As to death, it is the ultimate violation, so it's by nature violent, no matter how it looks on the surface. People who deny such truths are foolish or dangerous or both, and yet the only thinkers who speak about such things without hypocrisy or sentimentality are the philosophers of war.

Jonathan completed this second set of teeth before George was due home from the university in Lawrence for the summer. Alvah sent him to the station to pick George up; he waited there, artillery well concealed for the ambush to come, and from the once-again-impregnable fortress of hatred, he watched George climb down the steps of the railroad car.

At eighteen George's face had developed genuine attractiveness. Only a week ago, at the university, he had met Georgina Shockton, and he was not unaware of the impression he'd made on her. Her father was Shockton Beef—worth a king's ransom. She'd gone to Italy the summer before; an English guide there had dragged her party from one lapidary museum to another. Somewhere in Tuscany, casting a bored eye over the stone statues, most without legs or arms, Georgina had seen one—"unidentified Roman general," the guide translated for her—to which she had turned her mind every night since. George's face, caught at an angle and in just the right light, had something of that general's force and a great deal of his rude sensuality. And George, watching Georgina watching him from across the library one afternoon, felt the decisive tide turn in him: he was going to marry her and go into politics. As he used to say in later years, "The future'll spread her legs if you grab her by the tits."

He approached the spring wagon, holding out his hand. He wore pants and a shirt; in the warm summer weather a ring of white flesh slopped out above his belt, just as it had that hot night in the soddy when he'd defeated Jonathan. "Hello, Jonathan," he said. His voice was deeper, more confident. "Nice of you to pick me up. How are you keeping?"

Jonathan scanned the soft flesh and the belly. And then— oh, how long had he planned this tantara of the victory to come—how many nights had he seen it, tasted it—

He winked.

"A surprise," Clausewitz says, "can only be effected by that party which gives the law to the other." Like Jonathan after George's wink of two years before, George now found himself off balance. What could this wink mean? What law could this slave dictate to this freeman? Where was the risk? He was George, soon to be betrothed to Shockton Beef: George, the future senator. And yet— He grew restless in the days that followed. "Why are you looking at me like that?" he said several times, seeing danger, personal danger to him, to George, Georgina's George: seeing it flicker across Jonathan's face like phosphorescence on water. Jonathan turned away without speaking.

Then one afternoon, Jonathan sought him out. He cocked his head toward the railroad tracks at the edge of the Stokes' land.

"How come you've decided to talk to me?" George said. "You got something to show me? That it?"

Jonathan nodded.

George studied him a moment. "Okay," he said. "Why not?"

When they reached the stream by the cottonwoods, Jonathan again cocked his head toward the tracks, then splashed into the stream. George followed.

"What is this that's so special—?" George began, coming closer.

Jonathan snapped his body around and threw both fists into George's genitals.

Before the French Revolution, European generals worked for whatever prince offered the best salary, much like corporate executives today. Soldiers were mercenaries, expensive to train, hard to replace; they had no stake in the outcome of their fight, often no idea even of what the campaign was about. So war was very different: death to be avoided, battles to be fought as games of maneuver, like chess. True patriotism, true hatred of the enemy—Clausewitz calls it military virtue—is a phenomenon that doesn't appear until the French Revolution. But when it does, it is as formidable an innovation as nuclear fission. Battlefields ever after have been slaughterhouses, and Jonathan had the Rights of Man spilling over in his heart as recklessly as any French Revolutionary. He beat on long after George had collapsed to the ground.

Standing victorious over the body—standing bloody, bruised, torn, panting, but victorious—he knew he should consolidate this victory: establish the defeat, establish death. He knelt down and reached out his hand, having it in mind to feel George's pulse at the neck; but when it came to it, he could not force himself to touch that flesh. Pounding at the sodden whale of George's being was one thing: touching him after the fact was different altogether. The girlish breasts showed themselves through the torn and bloody cloth of the shirt. Jonathan swallowed back disgust, wavered, reached out his hand once more, but still could not do it. George looked dead: Jonathan had seen dead animals and had some idea what death looks like. So it was that he excused himself from his duty; just this once, and to his eternal regret, he excused himself. He gave the head one final, not very enthusiastic kick: there was no sign of life whatever, no sound, not even a trickle of blood.

"There ain't no Johnnys in books." This is what George had said out in the curing shed four years earlier, just before the building on the wooden house began. Then George had said, "You just got to make up Johnnys." Ever since then, Jonathan had known just precisely what he was going to say at just precisely this minute: "From now on"—and his voice betrayed none of the unexpected weakness his flesh had shown—"from now on," he said, "it's Georges that got to be made up." Then he set off down the tracks toward Sweetbrier station.

Mr. Finster watched him come into view. "Come with me," he said. "You're covered with blood, and Mrs. Finster would never forgive me if I did not bend all efforts to make you appear respectable."

An hour later the train going west appeared. Mr. Finster said, "I'll survey the land." The land surveyed, he said, "Third car from the caboose. Charming woman. Just talk politely." He took Jonathan's hand in both of his, shook it, pulled the boy into his arms, embraced him, shook his hand again—and only then turned away. The door to the car was open. A woman stood inside cooking at her stove; a small boy clung to her dress and four small girls of various sizes sat sewing or playing at sewing in a far corner. The boxcar held furniture, the lumber to build a cabin, a cow, two pigs and a goat.

Jonathan drew in his breath. "May I ride with you, ma'am?" he said.

She had a round, ruddy face and braids wrapped up in a crown on her head. She turned to look at him. "Whatcha got to offer, boy?"

16

HOW CAN A BOY make sense of things like this? Even as bright a boy as my grandfather? Even as fiercely determined a boy—a slave no longer a slave but a Spartacus in mid-rebellion and a murderer, too? Even if they caught him, they couldn't bring George to life again. But they weren't going to catch him. How could they catch him? The faint hiss as the train pulled out of the station: was that the pistons all the way from the engine? The clanking: that was the link-and-pin coupling, wasn't it? He turned abruptly to the woman next to him, the years of control over his face momentarily lost:

triumph, delight and dread chased each other across it despite him.

She was cradling the small boy in her arms. "Runnin' away, ain't you?" she said, smiling. "How old?"

Jonathan gestured that he was about sixteen.

"Train don't stop again till afternoon," she said. "My name's Eliza Gowdy. This is Nathan Gowdy Junior—Netty. And over there"—she looked at the four little girls—"Cassa, Carma, Levada and Lynn." The little girls lowered their eyes. "They don't have much to keep them occupied," Eliza said. He sat down beside them, drew out a handful of hay from the pile that served the animals and began to twist the strands together, a few at a time. The little girls watched, peeping out at him over the small swatches of calico they held.

"It's a dolly," the littlest girl whispered.

He told them with his hands that if he could make dolls at all, he would make one for each. They giggled.

"What's your name?" the littlest whispered then.

Beyond the door, red-tinged grass surged away in billows. Jonathan reached into his mouth to hold his teeth. "Johnny," he said gently. He had a very gentle way to him sometimes. "I'm called Johnny."

PART 3

WEDNESDAY NOON: DÉTENTE

17

RAILROADS ACROSS KANSAS and Colorado head into the Rockies at right angles. For three hundred miles, looking through the boxcar door, Jonathan would have seen only the prairies he'd known all his life. But then came Denver.

I have tried to bear in mind that George's memoirs are the memoirs of a politician, that my grandfather, Jonathan, was talking about himself, and that by the time I taped my uncle Atlas telling this story, he had holes in his head from too much liquor. But all three of these men agree that Jonathan lured George down to the railroad tracks and left him there for dead. So when the train stopped in Denver and Jonathan saw the Rockies for the first time, it was as though the tumult in him—the rage that had at last conquered George— had ripped right on through the land and hurled chunks of Kansas into a heap at the edge of Colorado. It was early morning, and morning in the Rockies, they tell me, is a study in red: red sky, red clouds, red light on the granite rock faces. What wasn't possible in such a place? Was it real at all? Eliza Gowdy's train began to pull out of the station before he realized what was happening. Staring after the caboose, feeling the mountains at his back, he knew only that this was where he wanted to be.

After a time of war comes a time of peace. But peace, after all, is only war carried on by other means (I misquote Clausewitz a little, but in a good cause). Peace is a time of bread and circuses, when gladiators tear each other apart to amuse the idle and the bored. We Americans are market leaders in such things. But a circus Eden, even when you pick it yourself, can be hard to take at first. Denver was a boomtown, ugly, crass, brutal, awash with money and blood. My mother used to say that if you whispered "Money, money, money" when you saw a falling star, you would get rich. She used to add, seeing my eager eyes, that anybody who could manage to think of money when a star was falling probably would get rich in the end anyway. There were the trappers in buckskin that you'd expect from the movies, maybe a little dirtier but not much, the mountain men, the ladies of pleasure in silk, gamblers, Indians in feathered headdresses, con men, gunmen, thieves, murderers: all standard Hollywood fare, and in fact much of it was show even at the time—a nineteenth-century Disneyland laid on to entertain European aristocrats who crossed the ocean to pay out in gold for staged thrills in the mountains and at the gambling tables. The surprising thing, though, is the international flavor of a place so deeply buried in the entrails of a continent. Mexicans, Germans, French, Chinese, Englishmen, Hungarians, Russians, Poles, every nationality you can think of, all on the street at the same time and many of them in national dress. Natives spoke bits and pieces of all kinds of languages, much like the Swiss today, and much like the Swiss today, they welcomed any currency. Banks, gambling houses, even grocery stores could make change in marks or pounds or francs.

Jonathan walked and stared for hours. For a kid off the prairies like him, just the number of people and the height of the buildings were awesome. But what does a person eat in fairyland? He took in his breath and tried a store with a wooden Indian outside it. A fat man stood behind a counter of cigars. "Yep?" he said.

My grandfather asked for a job. He asked with his hands, but hand-talking, so familiar to the residents of Sweetbrier, was not one of Denver's many languages. The fat man bristled, "I ain't having no mutes working in here," he said, already out from behind the counter, fist raised. "Get out. Go. Get out!"

Jonathan tried a greengrocer's—and fared no better. He tried a hotel where there was no clerk, only a black woman on her knees scrubbing at the raw wooden floor. "There ain't many jobs in town"—she lifted her eyes just far enough from her work to see his bare feet—"leastways not for the likes of you. If you was a girl now—" She sighed, and Jonathan turned to leave. "Hey," she called after him. "I hear they can use a yardman down at the Hannibal and Denver. I heard the yardmaster—"

He ran all the way back to the station and threw open the door to the yardmaster's office much as eight years before he'd thrown open the door to the saloon in the town that lay beneath the evening star.

The yardmaster's legs were propped up on his desk. He had only one foot. He glanced at Jonathan, squirted a stream of tobacco juice at a sawdust-filled box across the room, hit it square in the middle and let out a roar of pleasure. "Pretty good, eh, kid?" he said. "Whaddya want?"

"Yardman's job," Jonathan said, finger in mouth to hold his teeth.

"G'wan. Come back when you're weaned off thumb suckin'." Jonathan glared. "Where'd you get them god-awful choppers? Can you chew with a set of teeth like that?"

"I made them."

"No kiddin'?" The yardmaster stopped chewing. "Listen, kid, I can't put you to work. Y'ain't old enough. How old are you?"

"Seventeen."

"Yeah—seventeen going on fifteen. Christ. And no teeth to boot. Know what a yardman does? See this?" He lifted up the footless leg. "Switchman's foot—that's what they call it.

Hey, somebody been beating up on you? You look like shit. What makes you think you got the balls for this job?"

Jonathan opened his mouth to answer; his teeth slipped and clacked together.

"Ah, sweet Jesus!" The yardmaster took his legs off his desk. "What's your name?"

"Johnny Carrick."

"Carrick? You don't say. Your pa wasn't a reb, was he? Well, I'll be goddamned. I knew practically every goddamned Irish bastard in the whole goddamned Union Army. I knew your pa—probably did, anyhow. Died, did he? Well, I'll be goddamned." He chewed noisily. "Know the signals, kid?"

Some of them, Jonathan gestured.

"Here, catch!" The yardmaster picked up an ink bottle and threw it at the door; Jonathan leaped, arm outstretched. Ink splattered his face and the wall behind him, but he caught the bottle. "You got good reflexes," the yardmaster said, throwing his legs back on the desk. "Well, what the hell, come around Monday morning. I'll put your name on the board."

The story's fantastic. Of course it is. Yokels didn't get jobs like that, not even Irish yokels. I think to myself, Is my grandfather lying? In those mysteriously coded diaries of his? To me? And yet— There's a picture taken of him not long after this. I've never seen a picture like it, or a face like his, anywhere else. He did look young—that's true—but the anger in him was luminous, it really was, and even in that photograph, even all these years later, it glows, shifts, glistens—not a face that smiles often, though it must have lit up then. The yardmaster laughed.

"Hey, kid—" He took fifty cents out of his pocket and tossed it over. "Go around to Mother O'Neill. Fifteenth Street. Tell her Frank Fleming sent you. She'll give you a bed and sommat to eat."

Across town, Mother O'Neill peered nearsightedly at the coin in Jonathan's hand: a small, round woman, round blue eyes, little round mouth, little round nose, sixtyish maybe, soft flesh at the jowls jiggling with indignation, hair pulled fiercely away from her face and fastened in a tiny black bun at the top of her head. "Frank give you that, did he? He's a damn fool. Don't know what he said to you, but that'll only take care of one night, and I don't take no transients."

"I got a job," Jonathan cried. (He was, after all, still only a boy.)

She stuck her face into his. "You? Down the railroad? Yardman?" Their noses were almost touching. He held his ground. "You an Irish boy? Well, that's different, ain't it? Follow me." She handed him a boiled potato. "I'm gonna have to use kerosene on your hair—can't have lice in my kitchen." She led him to the side of the house. "Take off your clothes; water's hot from the washing. How old are you? Sixteen? Tell Frank eighteen. Take out those teeth. I'll wash them with the plates. What's your name? Carrick? I got people in Carrick, I been told." She scrubbed Jonathan with a laundry brush in a tin bath. She washed his hair with kerosene and fed him another potato. "You can't put on those clothes. I'll burn them. Wear these instead. Belonged to a yardman—got squashed yesterday. That's how come you got a job, know that? Here's his shoes. Hole in his chest you could throw a frying pan through."

18

MY UNCLE ATLAS'S WIFE CLAIRE had begun preparations for her French dinner party days before. The pace had been frantic from the beginning, so Atlas told me, and was frantic still. Just before lunch, she ran out of oven cleaner; we were sent to fetch some more. Out in the garage, various pieces of yellow oven interior lay spread out on newspapers. "What the hell are you doing, Claire?" Atlas said as he folded me into the car.

"I won't have those women saying I keep a dirty house," she said.

"Tonight? Ah, Jesus— Youngballs's dopey wife? What's she going to peep in your oven for?"

I took my tape recorder with us. In the car, Atlas is saying, "Now you tell me, how do you explain getting a job in a railroad yard to a woman like Claire? Or a bath in a tin tub: scrubbed by an old hag? How can you explain what magical and terrifying experiences these were? And afterwards: a bed to sleep on, sheets, shoes, clothes—"

"And you're different from Claire, are you?"

"Don't bitch at me," he says. "I'm no kid of privilege like you. I don't know how the hell Dad slept at all those first few nights. In fact I'll bet he didn't."

Liquor turned out to be only two aisles from oven cleaners. Outside in the parking lot, Atlas tucked a half bottle of whiskey into each of his back pockets, well hidden by the hang of his coat. This was plainly standard procedure—though it says something for his delicacy that he didn't suggest by so

much as a gesture that I might smuggle a bottle past Claire
for him. "But what the hell," he went on then, "I guess you
got a point. Slavery was just a bedtime story to me when I
was little. So was emancipation. You can't understand something like that unless you've been through it yourself. I remember—" He broke off.

"What?" I pressed.

"Oh, I don't know. I guess it's not relevant."

"Tell me anyway."

"There was this black guy—I couldn't have been more
than six or seven at the time. I don't know how he got to
Hannaville. We had Swedes and Norwegians all over the
place, but nobody black. Not then. Anyhow, this guy—his
name was Nero—he had a wife and several children, and they
all just appeared one day out of nowhere. Nobody knew what
to do with them. They had no money. Nothing at all. A couple
of kindhearted locals hired him for small jobs, but he didn't
seem to be able to do anything right and he was so slow at
what he did do that nobody could bear it. So the question
was, what do you do with them? Run them out of town? There
was a meeting about it—all the town worthies—and Dad took
me with him. I don't remember why. The argument got pretty
heated and then out of the blue Dad said, 'I'll hire him. Where
is he?'

"Jesus, we didn't have enough to keep ourselves, much
less a family of six or so on top. Everybody knew that. They
all said the guy was so stupid he ought to be locked up. All
you had to do was look at the way he rolled his eyes, they
said. Dad wouldn't budge. So they sent for the guy. They kind
of roughed him along and brought him up to Dad, and Dad
said, as polite as if he was talking to the mayor, 'Will you
work for me, Nero?'

"Nero wasn't young. Must have been ten, fifteen years
older than Dad—the wife was much younger—grizzled old
guy. He said, 'Sure enough, boss.'

"Dad said, 'Not "boss." My name's Johnny.'

"We all went in the buggy together right there and then—Nero, Nero's wife and kids and Dad and me. Nero kept eyeing Dad, gape-mouthed, and finally Dad said, 'You want to know why I'm doing this, don't you?'

"Nero said, 'Yeah, boss, if'n you want to tell me.' His voice was a monotone, no inflection at all.

"Dad said, 'We're brothers, you and I.'

"Nero rolled his eyes some and said, 'Yeah, boss.'

"Dad drove on a mile or so, then he said, 'They paid fifteen bucks flat for me. I was about four years old. Tobacco farm. Ran away when I was sixteen. I bet you cost more.'

" 'What you all telling me, boss?'

" 'I was'—Dad seemed to have trouble getting the word out—'a slave. Just like you. We are the same.'

" 'Well, I'll be,' Nero said in that monotone of his.

" 'The education came later. Much later.'

"Nero didn't look like he took it in, much less believed it. He said, 'Yeah, boss,' again.

" 'I slept in the barn. With the animals.'

"That seemed to surprise Nero some, but he didn't say anything. Then I'll be damned if Dad didn't rein in the horse, and right there in front of Nero and his wife and me, he got down, took off his coat, folded it, laid it on the seat. Then he took off his shirt. Everybody else—all the other farmers—stripped down in hot weather. Not Dad. He always wore a shirt, always wore the sleeves rolled down. I'd never seen his back or arms bare—not that I ever thought about it much—but all over them was a crisscross of long, white scars. Even I could see he'd been beaten bad at some time in his life. Maybe lots of times. That was the first hint I got of what had really happened to him. Then he put his shirt on again, still not a word, put on his coat, climbed into the wagon and off we went. Nero still didn't say anything, so Dad said, 'Nero is the name of an emperor. It's a proud name.'

"Another mile went by, and suddenly Nero laughed out

loud. 'Where I come from they call dogs Nero,' he said. I turned to look at him because the voice wasn't a monotone anymore; it was sharp and sort of musical. And—Jesus, I'll never forget it—he just wasn't the same man. He'd shed the stupidity somehow. The mouth was shut; the eyes weren't rolling around, and there was some real shrewdness in them. 'No, sirree, Johnny,' he said then. 'I didn't cost nobody a penny. I was born to the trade. They got me for free.'

"And Dad laughed. You can't imagine how odd that was: Dad laughing. I could hardly believe it: this was the only time I ever saw him laugh in all my life. He and Nero laughed and laughed. I thought they'd gone nuts—the two of them—laughing like that. They built a house together for Nero to live in with his wife and his children, and Nero worked for nothing when nothing came in, and for whatever Dad could afford when there was a little profit. He worked harder and better than anybody except Dad himself. Whenever Dad wasn't around, Nero went back to rolling his eyes, and whenever they were together there was this ease to Dad; he wasn't so demanding; he seemed to tolerate us better—almost to enjoy us like a normal father. It was never like that before, and after Nero died—he didn't live all that long: somebody in town set his house alight, and his whole family burned to death—after Nero died, it was never like that again."

But despite Atlas, Jonathan's diaries say he did sleep the first few nights in Denver; Jonathan says he slept the deep, dreamless sleep of an anesthetized patient for whom time simply doesn't exist; each morning he awoke to this queer fairyland around him with a sense of bubbling, almost uncontrollable exhilaration. Mountain air isn't like prairie air. In the summer, air in the Middle West steams and lowers: at the base of the Rockies it's zesty like the water. There's an excitement just to breathing, and there's a glint to the sun and the way it lights things that Middle Westerners see only in winter. Then there are the magnificent, soaring piles of rock, a beauty so intense it's oppressive: oppression, exhilaration, oppression, exhilaration, a masturbation of soul that makes reasoned behavior difficult for any beginner—and far, far more than that for somebody like Jonathan, whose whole life was as new to him as the landscape. The dreamless sleep didn't last. On the fourth night he awoke in a state of abject terror— he didn't know from what—and lay there all night, shaking with fear, drenched in sweat, unable to sleep at all.

This night was Sunday night. Monday morning he showed up at Frank Fleming's office to be taken out to the tangle of tracks that made up the St. Joe, Hannibal & Denver railroad yard beneath the mountains. Here, in the early morning light, he began his life on the trains—the man-made miracles of steel and steam, the huge, panting engines, the cars full of zinc, gold, longhorns, hides of buffalo and lion—these glorious instruments of his own freedom that ran along lines that drive onward and shift, drive onward and cross, drive onward and meet, mate up and lead to God knows where: to wonders beyond the reach of imagination.

Frank introduced him to one of the men in the yard.

"This here's College," Frank said. "Ask him anything, but he'll talk the bleedin' bejesus out of you."

"Talk the bleedin' bejesus out of you" was right. This is College's opening speech to my grandfather: to Jonathan Carrick, boughten boy, whom Alvah had instructed for years on end with grunts and shoves. "The soul of a railroad car is a sad, broken thing," said College, "just like the soul of a man. Here's all this power lying powerless, man alone, aimless, meaningless. Then out of the dark—lo and behold—a god appears. And with him: aim, meaning, power."

He was no beauty, College, pug nose and pockmarked skin; but the romance of the railroads pervaded everything and everyone, and College was the only man for miles around who knew how to manipulate his thoughts about it into words. Jonathan stared at this flesh-and-blood miracle in this place of miracles and was more awed than by all the others put together; he had no idea what the words might mean or even if they had meaning, but the sound of them had the sound of fate. As for College, in the circus that was Denver he played his circus trick with a clown's delight. He had a clown's perverse vanity, too; he worked to make his usual audience of silent, dour men laugh out loud and figured that later on, when half-asleep at night, at least one of them was going to fret inwardly at the edge behind the clowning—and yet as everybody knows, it's only the clown who gives his act a second thought. None of College's audiences had ever seemed so wholly captivated as this thin recruit, whom he'd watched crossing the yard only moments before with real dismay: so young, so underfed, so unbelievably raw. He laughed, delighted at his own surprise as well as at the boy's enchanted response. "Link and pin must match like husband and wife," he went on, swinging on the words now, soaring with them, as though he'd climbed off the floor of the big top and taken to the high wires above. "There's no room for careless promiscuity here. As always, it's the gods—in this case, you and I—who will pay the price."

Twenty years afterwards, Jonathan recorded this speech in his diaries word for word for my computer to grind out, not a single word forgotten in all that time. And catching the words "link and pin" out of this extraordinary medley, he formed link and pin with his hands and rehearsed for College the switchman's job of coupling one railroad car to another, a technique Mr. Finster had demonstrated to him and which he had rehearsed alone night after night with his hands in the darkness of the sod hut, dreaming of this very day but never, not in his wildest imaginings, not ever dreaming of it in such glory as this.

College could hardly believe his luck, too: not only an audience, but a fellow performer at that. He laughed again and clapped his hand on the raw recruit's shoulder. "You're a great man," he said to Jonathan, who had never before in his life had a compliment of any sort. "Now I'll do what I can to teach you: to teach you is to protect you, because the very first lesson of all is that this is dangerous work. When it rains or when the mists come off the mountains in the early morning, one slip of the foot and you're down beneath the wheels."

The link-and-pin coupling was an absurd system, as absurd as outside brakes, even more so maybe, cumbersome, unreliable, not just dangerous—College was undercutting it—but ferociously dangerous, stupidly, insanely dangerous. Too many unknowns figure in the equation, just as too many unknowns figure in what's expected of a newly freed slave. There were forty different species of couplers—species, not varieties; the varieties were endless. Pins were bent, straight, skewed, all weights, thicknesses, lengths, angles. The fit depended on the load of the train, the grade of the track, the relationship between the two cars—never of the same manufacture, never the same design—an intensely mathematical problem to be solved at breakneck speed without any tools but experience and intuition.

The similarity between his new life and his new job was so pointed that Jonathan remarks on it again and again in his diaries, half intrigued, half repelled by it. Choose your pin, step between the cars, set the pin in the link, cock it, signal the engineer. There's silence for a moment. A hiss of steam. Then slowly, slowly the huge, immeasurably heavy wheels begin to turn. The cars inch together, touch, shudder—and the pin shakes into place. Often it didn't work, though. Of course it didn't. The slightest miscalculation and the man had to pound the pin in with his hammer; if his calculations were further off than the tolerances allowed—and all too often they were—and if he wasn't fast enough getting out of the way, he got smashed between the cars or crushed beneath them. There were designs for universal couplers, lots of them, but they cost money. The romance of the railways (just like the romance of freedom), this will-o'-the-wisp of power all muddled up with death: this romance that College expressed so well to the delight of so many (many of whom had already died because of it and many more who would): this same romance refurbished the ranks of switchmen so fast that the railroad barons, at war with one another as we all love to be, were free to invest their huge fortunes elsewhere while wives of switchmen kept aside one special linen sheet, embroidered, clean, ironed, folded, ready at a moment's notice to wrap up the mangled remains for burial.

At six o'clock the day's work was over. College clapped Jonathan on the shoulder just as he had at the beginning of the day, with all the warmth of a long-lost brother, of a fellow professional discovered by accident in a desertland of amateurs, and arranged to meet him in a saloon for a drink after supper. And Jonathan, my grandfather, turned and ran across the railroad yard, jumping the tracks as he came to them.

19

THE SALOON was the Home Rule Bar, named for the Irish Republican movement—for home rule in Ireland—and so as Irish as everything else around the railroads. It was plainly a wicked place: night inside, even with the sun still shining in the streets—night inside because the windows were plastered over with WANTED posters. Jonathan's heart fluttered in his chest. There were layer upon layer of WANTED posters on the windows, year after year of them. Why hadn't he had the sense to call himself Kelly? or Brady? Anybody but Carrick, the murderer.

One of the modern-day hostages—one of the men held in Lebanon—wrote that the life of a hostage is a kind of quarter life. A hostage, like any prisoner, is a species of slave: "The mind forming and informing itself in patterns of maniacal exuberance and mind-wrenching despair: the hostage is a convoluted man, a man pushed so far and so deep into himself that he can do little but experience a kind of mental narcosis like a diver in rarefied air." Then comes release: the sudden freedom, the multiplicity of it, the dazzling, dizzying disorder of it. And when the maelstrom settles a little, when there's time to draw in a breath, the ex-hostage finds himself left with what others who delve too deep are left with: this pretty but brittle surface of ours, cheap, artificial, irrelevant. What once fit—what once was life itself—no longer fits, could never be made to fit again. Normality becomes another kind of bondage.

The comparison with what Jonathan says in his diaries is striking. But Lebanon's Western hostages were men with pasts—men who had something to try to fit back into, men whose old lives welcomed them home rapturously when they returned—while Jonathan— Well, here's somebody who had no past. Free at last, he faced a nihilist's dream at a nightmare's extremity: no foundation, no family, no friends, nobody at all to welcome him, no hometown, no background, no education, not even a childhood he could call his own— nothing to return to. Like God Himself, he had to build his world from scratch.

He says in his diaries that he spent his first weeks in Denver in a strange, heightened state. Sudden noises caused sudden spasms of anxiety in his chest. There were sudden memories so vivid and so painful that they took his breath away. His body had a robotic feel, remote, alien, controlled, or so it seemed to him, by knobs and levers operated in some distant place; his head felt watery on top of his neck as though it were afloat in an amniotic sac. The new things seemed to glut him—the goose force-fed so its liver will fetch a higher price on the market—and having glutted him, kept coming.

He hesitated just outside the door to the Home Rule Bar, considered making a dash for it, realized there was no place to go (and besides it was probably too soon after the event for a WANTED poster to have been printed in Denver), so steeled himself and entered, half in a dream.

Heavy smoke, kerosene lamps, brass, mahogany, mirrors, bottles: so far, pure Hollywood again. But the people, these heroes of the railroad, and heroes most assuredly if you run to that sort of thing—these weren't Hollywood at all, an unwashed, unkempt, hoglike lot who drank so hard, so fast and so sloppy that mustaches, beards, vests, eyebrows, dragglelocks of hair on their heads or straggle-ringed bald plates: all glistened with whiskey and bubbled with suds from their beer. Towels hung along the bar to wipe away any splashings that got sucked up their noses or slopped down their backs; it was a matter of pride to wipe away with the towel nearest no matter how filthy the towel was, and filthy meant filthy: nobody washed the towels. They hung on their hooks until they rotted off and fell to the floor to mix with the tobacco-spit and dog shit that made up a permanent slurry there.

Honky-tonk thumped at full volume. Dogs barked. Men shouted; they vied with each other—who could shout loudest? who longest?—they guffawed, snorted, choked on the fierce brew the Home Rule served, stamped, pounded the bar, clanked their spurs if they had them and their icons from the railway if they had those—brakeman's light, switchman's hammer, fireman's stoke, whatever.

College stood at the bar, a bottle and glasses in front of him. "Pour yourself a drink, Johnny," he shouted. Speaking in a normal voice was out of the question.

Jonathan had not drunk a single drink of alcohol in his

life except for that terrible night in the sod hut when he put on George's frock coat; he knew the effect of the whiskey on him had contributed to what happened then, and he had—or had developed—rigidities of spirit that wouldn't always serve him well as a freeman (however well they'd served him as a slave). Furthermore, he felt surrounded, under threat. Some of the threats were vague, as ill-defined as shadows; others were right out in front: the WANTED posters, for example, that just might rip him away from this world of things so fresh that even the air he breathed was different. But the lure of eating out the heart of a defeated enemy was the strongest element of all—of drinking his drink while he lies dead—so Jonathan my grandfather lifted his glass, remembering to hold the stuff, which if anything was wickeder than George's 110-proof red, in his mouth for a while, remembering to close his throat before swallowing; and so he showed a sophistication that College, who was watching him with the glee of the already initiated at a particularly fierce initiation, most certainly had not expected.

"Well, I'll be goddamned," College said, "you are indeed a great man. Where'd a wild-eyed savage like you learn to drink this brew?"

The men in the bar had developed a special version of half-shout, half-speak that penetrated the din while adding to it. Jonathan would have liked to explain a little to this fascinating person who had worked with him all day without a single word of abuse and seemed to take pleasure in what Jonathan already knew as well as pleasure in telling him what he didn't; but despite bone and a new design, the teeth hadn't really succeeded; speaking was difficult and shouting impossible. He made a self-deprecatory gesture instead.

College tried to imitate but gave up almost immediately and launched instead into a discussion of railroad lore while Jonathan wrestled with the anxieties, the promises, the threats—as well as the noise, the commotion, the smoke, the smell—that surrounded him and so missed some connection that he might otherwise have caught.

". . . the simplicity of it that fills the soul with pleasure," College was shouting, "simple as a goose girl—goose girl, maybe chicken girl. Why did the chicken cross the road? Am I making myself clear?" He searched Jonathan's face. "You must know that rare old joke. Don't you? Yes? No? Ah, glory be to God, what an opportunity. I'll educate you. Why did the chicken cross the road? Will you make a guess, sir? No? To get to the other side." College laughed merrily. "Don't you see? The chicken crossed the road to get to the other side."

The phosphorescence in Jonathan's head shimmered. All that crossed his mind on the subject of chickens was that he hated them. The Stokes had a cock that serviced all the hens twice a day, even the dead ones. The live ones used to run like hell to get away.

"You're supposed to laugh," College said, affronted; and it suddenly occurred to him that the boy had in fact not spoken a single word, not one, not even when they'd been introduced to each other. "Do you ever laugh?" College asked, irritable now. "Look, Johnny, I don't want to make trouble or any-thing—" He shifted uneasily at the bar. "Johnny, old boy, I'd really like to hear you say something. Speak to me of the rain, of winter, of summer on the oceans. Tell me about your dreams. Tell me about anything at all."

What was Jonathan to do? He was painfully aware of the change in atmosphere. But control it? make a shift in it? He was half drowning, half scorching in it. Even so, even in his desperation, he did say something, but he spoke gently as the teeth dictated; a crash of honky-tonk drowned him out and College saw only that the lips moved and no sound came.

"Oh, shit," College said then. "You did seem too good to be true. I speak. All other people on the railroad speak, albeit none of them so beautifully as I. Everybody who can speak, speaks at least sometimes. You do not speak. Ergo, you cannot speak." His voice now had an unvarnished edge; Jonathan opened his mouth to protest, but the teeth clattered down and while he struggled to right them College rushed on, aware only that the charge had not been denied. "This is not what Frank Fleming said to me. Which is to say that Frank tidied up the truth a little. You said nothing, but then how could you? Look, old friend, I know this is a weakness in me, but I cannot help it. I mean no offense. I'm sorry, but I cannot work with you."

Jonathan's rage was as full-blown as it was abrupt. There was a moment of quiet in the room, as though the din itself were shocked by the intensity of this one young customer at the bar. He set down his glass and said in a measured tone, "I got no money for the drink." Then he turned to leave: the silence collapsed back into clamor.

"Well, will the saints be blessed," College shouted after him. "Don't go away. Come back! Don't get mad. Hey!"

Jonathan stopped but did not turn.

"Look, you're the smartest kid I've run across yet," College went on. "You're a natural: a joy—Come back, goddammit. It's just that I thought— Talking's all I care about. Why the hell didn't you—?" Broken sentences from College sounded so odd that Jonathan turned. There was warmth and a child-like uncertainty; he was touched despite his anger and despite the fact that he'd rarely been touched in his life. "I couldn't work with a mute. I just— I'm sorry. I didn't want to offend you, but— Have another drink. Why don't we sit down somewhere? No? Why don't you speak? Is there a reason? I mean, if you can speak, why don't you?"

"You mean this? Or what you said before?" Jonathan said, checking now for exposed flanks, for tricks and traps, like the untamed creature he was on what was yet another piece of ground new to him: a small flurry, but a flurry apparently won, and won—apparently—out in front for all to see. This also was new. Radically new.

"I mean this," College said. "Of course I mean it. It's just—"

"Sure?"

"Of course I'm sure. It's just— Just answer me from time to time. Silence scares the shit out of me. I can't— Why don't you talk?"

Across the bar, one man grabbed another by the beard. Glasses smashed on the floor. Beer flew. Dogs scrambled to get out of the way. The bearded man had a high, penetrating voice and a fine line in swear words. "Fungus prick! Draw-balled cream-pisser!" he screamed.

"Teeth," Jonathan said.

"Goose turd! Slug-fucker! Bottle-assed—"

"What?" College shouted. "What did you say?"

"Piddle-prong!" And the beard was free.

"Teeth," Jonathan repeated. The anger left him; an abrupt exhaustion replaced it, and he took hold of the bar, body trembling.

"Teeth? Is that all? Who cares about teeth? Well, I guess the answer to that question is that I care. And plainly you care. Wouldn't you like to speak? Of course you would. Those teeth of yours really are god-awful. Frank says you made them. Remarkable to make a set of teeth, incredible, an amazing feat. I never knew anybody who— But you can't speak because of them? What about without them?"

Jonathan gestured that without them he couldn't speak at all.

"Why not go to a dentist? Denver's loaded with them. You can't work on the railroads like this. Really you can't."

Jonathan pulled his pockets inside out: no money.

College sighed. "Yeah, and you're going to need thirty-five bucks at least. Have another drink. It's on me. Of course it is. My grandmother has a pair of false teeth, made out of porcelain and gold. They glint when the sun catches them."

He sighed again. "Buy a piggy bank this month instead. Where are you from anyhow?"

A movement of the hand: east and far away.

College frowned. "This the first time you've been away from home?"

A noncommittal shift of the shoulders.

College slammed his glass down on the bar. "Goddammit, Johnny, you may be able to put up with silence but I can't. This I mean, and mean for sure. Silence scares the— I've already said that, haven't I? Never could stand it. So was it when I was a boy, so is it now—I hate it, dread it. I have nightmares about it: it swallows me up. Or I think it will. What's it threatening me for if its intentions are honorable?" He rifled in his pockets and thrust a wad of notes at Jonathan. "Take it. Fifty dollars. That'll get you a decent set of teeth." Jonathan shook his head, the unreality of the situation so great that he could barely keep College in focus much less understand what he was saying. "Now, look here, kid, how can I tell if you've heard me when my back is turned? You might get killed. Take this money or I really will tell Frank I can't work with you anymore."

Jonathan's dentist wore a mustache waxed into tusks that wobbled when he spoke. "Real teeth? They come very high and they rot, dear boy. Ivory rots, too, of course, but it's quite reasonable. Porcelain's best, but expensive. I wear porcelain myself. See?" The dentist slid his own teeth out into his palm. "Springs may be old-fashioned, but the father of our country wore them. How about ivory teeth in a vulcanite base? With springs? Wonderful stuff, vulcanite. What do you say to forty-five dollars?"

Jonathan agreed at once.

"Oh, dear boy, you haven't been off the farm long, have you? We'll make it forty."

Two weeks later the dentures were in Jonathan's mouth. "There!" the dentist said, adjusting them. He swung the chair around so that it faced the mirror.

Once, years ago, I caught sight of my own face in a
mirror and for a split second I saw in myself somebody that—
Well, it wasn't me at all. It was somebody wholly alien, fine-
featured, laughing—somebody who knew nothing of the
sewage that runs through my veins instead of blood. I fell in
love at once. It was the same for Jonathan. I'm sure of it.

20

THERE IS A RANDOM, episodic feel to most young lives—the
childhood pattern dispensed with, the adult pattern not yet
established—which has a peculiar charm all its own. But not
to Jonathan. As soon as he sensed it, he hated and feared it.
With no childhood and no family, with his roots ripped out of
him much as his teeth had been, there was no foundation to
anchor him, nothing except rage and bitterness to give meaning to a youthful floating free. Replacing the teeth was easy
and from the evidence of photographs, wholly successful. The
roots of a life, though: these are a different matter. Despite
himself he hungered after the uncompromising ferocity, the
raw passions of slavery, and found only vagaries, uncertain-
ties, passing fancies. He worked in the Denver yards. In an
exacting trade he got the reputation—which was the ultimate
accolade—of a kid with the makings of a good railroadman.
Two years passed. During all this time, no picture of him
appeared on a WANTED poster in the Home Rule Bar or anywhere else around Denver. Of course it didn't, but how was
he to know why not?

He toyed with the idea that George had never existed,

that he Jonathan had simply invented George. "From now on, it's Georges that got to be made up": he'd said it himself over the prostrate figure that had seemed to him to be George's dead body. Perhaps there had never been a prostrate figure. Perhaps there had never been a battle. Perhaps he had been born on the railways and had dreamed his terrible past. Or perhaps he was dreaming now. If there was anything at all to any of this, however little, then his claim to murder, and to victory, too, was as empty as his grasp of why College's chicken crossed the road. Maybe Mr. Finster had covered for him. It was possible. Maybe they thought he'd died himself, of exposure perhaps, and been savaged by animals.

He slept badly in his bed with sheets. It was a rare night that went by without a nightmare; one in particular frightened him more than all the rest. The first night he had it, he'd gone to sleep with his mind on a number 104 Consolidation, a thirty-eight-ton behemoth of an engine with four pairs of driver wheels. He'd watched it ease its great mass into the yard, pause, and then reverse, steam rising, back onto a siding. All that power so delicately moved left with him with an oppressive calm that hung on into the night. This comes from his coded diaries. Nobody knows about it but Jonathan and me.

He saw Cathern come to milk the cow again, just as she used to. He collected the little death machine he'd made out of wood and leather, just as he used to and—just as he used to—he went out to the tobacco fields. I've always been fascinated by borderlands. Just when does one thing become another? At just precisely what point in my life did I become a cripple? When the tumor began to grow? When I first sat in this chair? When does a freeman become a slave? When the money changes hands? When the spirit breaks? When does truth become falsehood? The precise moment goes by so fast we can't catch it; it's always blurred, always subject to lies, ritual, elaborate evasion. For Jonathan, that most vegetable of things, a tobacco field, becomes suddenly, unaccountably

an animal being with mouths that eat away at its own innards:
there is the world of pure terror, and then the desperate fight
of the little death machine to restore integrity. At just what
point is a battle irrevocably lost? or won?

Coming awake with a start Jonathan found his hands
moving methodically on the sheets and over the blankets,
plucking at worms, picking, squashing, doing what he'd done
for all the summer Wednesdays of his childhood.

"I signed on for brakeman," he shouted at College the
next evening over the din in the Home Rule in the half-shout,
half-speak that he'd mastered along with link-and-pin couplings and such rare delicacies as how to purchase socks and
a shoeshine.

"You what?" There were no jobs on the rolling stock of
the St. Joe & Hannibal.

"Can't stick around any longer."

"Did you talk to Frank?"

Jonathan nodded. He'd been to the Home Rule Bar more
times than he could remember now. After a few months of
tense watching and waiting, even the WANTED posters had
come to seem friendly to him, and there had been a glowing
period not long after his arrival when it had seemed that life
just might make sense to him, when he thought he'd like to
spend the rest of it in this noisy, smelly room. No longer. After
two years, the Home Rule epitomized the sham of Denver; he
wanted to run from it, run now, run fast, run so hard that
nothing could ever catch him. At least running was real.

"Where?" College asked.

"TransContinental."

"We live in restless times," College said. "The fact is,
you don't know the first thing about being a brakeman."

"Maybe the first thing," Jonathan said. He was already
a better railroadman than College, at least in the yards, and
both of them knew it.

"Well, I'll grant you that—"

"You'd better."

"—but the first thing is not the last thing, and there are many things in between. The job of a brakeman has technique, artistry—"

"I'll learn."

"Oh, will you now? Why are you so grumpy today? I'll have you know, there's no brakeman in all Colorado so brave, so deft, so quick as I am. May I offer you my services?" College made a flourish of a bow. "Private tuition on the job. Fees modest. There are mountains out there, not just these Rockies seen from the town of Denver, but the Smokies—"

Jonathan was disconcerted. "What are you talking about?"

"—the Tetons, the Ozarks, the Appalachians, great ranges that stretch from north to south, rivers running down them east and west and—" College stopped in midflight, suddenly aware that this usually quick audience really did not understand him. "Did you never have a friend when you were a boy, Johnny?" he said then.

Jonathan shut his eyes.

For all his warmth, Atlas, like his father, is a man with few friends. There have been lots of women in his life, marriages, ten-minute quickies and various stages in between—more women than he can remember—but not many friends. None of us Carricks has much talent for such things. "I worked as a gynecologist for the navy," Atlas began by way of explanation.

"How'd you wheedle your way into a job like that?" I asked.

"Oh, come on. Even servicemen have wives. And besides, there are lots of women in the navy."

"Did you like it?"

"I loved it. But at the time—"

"Why?"

"Why what?"

"How come you loved it?"

Atlas laughed. "The smell—"

"The what?"

He laughed again. "I love the way women smell. But the point is, I did some work with transsexuals on the side. It's the damnedest thing. You make them a vagina, see, but they can't keep the thing open. It's like piercing ears. If you don't wear earrings, the earlobe closes over. Because the vagina doesn't belong there, it closes over unless they wear a plug in it."

"Atlas, what *are* you trying to tell me?"

"Getting too fancy, am I?"

"In a word—"

"Hang on a minute. Hatred, anger, bitterness: these were the things that held Dad together. They were his flesh and blood, practically his genetic structure. And here he'd been transported into a world where there had to be a measure of trust and camaraderie; he couldn't function without them. What was the poor bastard to do? Well, the way I see it is this: he carved a place for human warmth in that forbidding flesh of his. Not easy. Very painful, in fact. Surgical. And once the surgery was done—this is where my fancy image comes in—he had to keep his nature prised apart much like a transsexual keeps his man's body prised apart to accommodate a vagina. The artifice of it didn't always work (doesn't always with transsexuals, either). He knew he was smart; he knew he was quick; he even knew he was a good-looking guy. But friendship? He didn't understand the first thing about it. It never occurred to him that in those two years College might actually have come to like him. See what I'm getting at?"

So when College said to him, "Did you never have a friend when you were a boy?" all my grandfather came back with was "Leave me alone."

But he was by no means always unlucky: College was not so easily put off. "My dear Carrick," he said, "it would be a pleasure for me to go where you go. Maybe not for good, but for a while anyway. Would you be agreeable?"

Jonathan frowned, started to say something, looked at College, frowned again. With infinite care, he put down his glass. "Excuse me," he said—or at least he tried to say it, but the words got caught somewhere. He had learned that he could almost control the sudden spasms of anxiety that he'd suffered ever since his emancipation if he took in his breath at just precisely the right moment and held it. It was the only method he had. So he inhaled, walked out into the street, held on, coughed, inhaled again. After a few minutes, he made his way back into the bar, where he offered an almost steady hand to College and said, "Shake on it?"

TransContinental assigned its new pair of brakemen to a Mogul engine going west.

21

YEARS AGO, in Alabama at Christmas, the radio played "Holy Night," the most glorious of carols—that soaring high note (especially sung full force by a pure, clean soprano) and gooseflesh all over: it's one of the few places left where you can sense the mystery and beauty of the idea that it's possible to save mankind. Alabama radio modulated the note into a sweet meaninglessness: a remarkable feat, the melody intact but no shiver for the listener to feel, no disturbance of spirit, nothing at all. Other countries left the power of their steam engines raw. Not us, not the people who rob even Christmas carols of their intensity. The Mogul that College and Jonathan got assigned to was dressed up for this peacetime circus of Jonathan's like a circus bear in tutu and ribbons, red, orange, maroon, green paint, a different color for every section—pilot, sand box, steam chest, gilt and fretwork domes and lights—and on both sides of the cab full-color pictures of bears skulking about on the range. The conductor, as ringmaster, had come to resemble his beast: a joke of a bear himself, with a bear's shoulders, a bear's furry body, and a bear's glassy eyes. He'd conducted this Mogul—it was already outdated at the time but a beautiful thing even so beneath its paint—he'd conducted it for twenty years and he had no thought of serving or being served by anything less.

"Wait a minute," Atlas said, sending the tape recorder flying over the edge of his desk in his enthusiasm, "I got here—It's somewhere here, goddammit, I know it is." The tape recorder in its mechanical prowess (shaken but not broken by this attack) continued to record him while he dumped out the contents of one of the boxes he'd got down from the attic for me, shuffled through some of the pictures, mumbled, knocked over his coffee, swore and at last pulled out an old drawing, about half a standard typing sheet in size, pretty good condition (not counting the coffee, that is). "Aha, what did I tell you?" he said in triumph. He patted at the picture with an embroidered handkerchief, soon coffee-stained like the picture itself. "Here's an old drawing of that Mogul. See?" But if the Mogul is there at all, it isn't visible. Only the body of the train itself shows, climbing up into the Rockies after an engine that seems to be hidden behind an outcropping of rock. On one side of the track, the cars scrape the mountain face; the other side is a sheer drop. On the roof of one car stands a brakeman, arms akimbo, legs apart, while the train lurches around a bend in this uncambered stretch. "Well, what the hell, maybe it isn't the Mogul. But that just could be Dad." Atlas tilted the picture to study it from a new angle. "Who's to deny it?"

Certainly not I, I said to myself, staring down at the picture. Certainly not I.

On the trip, the Mogul carried supplies for the building of the Great Northern extension. So here's not only the illusion of freedom, power, control and friendship, but the illusion of sex, too—sex allegorical, sex theatrical—one railroad, one man-made miracle, in the very process of generating another with rhythmic, heavy clack of metal on metal and relentless surge forward toward the twin illusions of future and progress. For a day and a half the track looped and twisted up into the wall of the mountains, past craggy rock, through forests of pines, by niches of wildflowers. Jonathan leapt from car to car, setting brakes for every change in grade and every sag in the roadbed. High in the mountains the climb leveled off. Granite outcroppings appeared and erupted sideways into layers of color. The pine forests thinned. The stone became a rocky plain. Lakes glinted in the distance. The sky opened up.

Two days later they hit California.

As soon as the train berthed, Jonathan ran to the harbor. There were ships everywhere. He hadn't reckoned on ships. There was no wind; the scene was entirely still. But as he watched, the slender, elegant masts picked up the motion of a tramp ship that wove its way through the moorings. The masts swung and banked, crisscrossing, but gently, while the battered tramp almost bounced across the harbor (no doubts there at all) and entranced Jonathan every foot of its way.

"What kind is that one?" he asked an old man standing nearby.

"Hermaphrodite schooner," the old man answered at once. "See how she's rigged? Square on the foremast, fore and aft on the main? Not so good as she used to be, I can tell you that. Where you from?"

Jonathan gestured that he had just come across the mountains.

"Mountains ain't nothing," the old man said. "It's the sea

that counts. She used to be a clipper, a real clipper. Refitted her, they did." The old man snorted. "Don't take more than twenty to work her. Lost her looks, poor bitch—used to be a beauty once."

A gust of wind caught the ship's sails.

"Lost her speed, too."

They stared after her, and through the swath she left behind her Jonathan caught his first unimpeded view of the Pacific. "Where would you go to look for a man?" he said suddenly.

"I wouldn't."

Jonathan bridled. "I would," he said, voice cold.

"Would you now? What's a boy like you—"

"I didn't ask your advice on that."

The old man sighed. "How old a man?" he said.

"Forty. Maybe forty-five." All Jonathan remembered of the man he thought of as his father was a beard, a pair of tattered army boots and the callused feel of one hand. "Gone west, I suspect," Benbow Wikin had said. "California probably."

"Boardinghouses. Mining camps. Farm directories," the old man said. "People move around a lot."

"He was a soldier, a Union soldier—an Irishman—"

"Flophouses. Whorehouses. Jails. Graveyards."

Jonathan worked his way up one San Francisco street and down another. He asked his questions and as he did, he found the picture of his father taking on more detail. The beard was black. Of course it was. One of the eyes had no lashes. There had been a limp. Well, hadn't there?

"I never saw anybody like that," people said.

"I see a hundred guys like that every week," people said.

This was only the beginning of my grandfather's search. He scoured the country for his father, for my great-grandfather, for somebody to give him an anchor somewhere, in time, in bloodline, in almost anything at all—somebody

whose existence would call a halt to the random meaninglessness of his life. He failed; my great-grandfather was not to be
found. Jonathan himself is the beginning. He who had no past
is our past, our unmoved mover, our foundation stone: the one
we all rely on. But as his train pulled out of San Francisco he
stood atop the cars with the steam abillow up around him,
that salacious rhythmic pounding of wheels under him, and in
his heart, the full and certain knowledge that if he worked at
it he could reconstruct a picture of his father so complete that
finding him would be no trick at all.

22

OVER THE HILLS of California—this is how Jonathan goes—
back over the desert and the flatlands, up into the tense beauty
of the Rockies again. My own father, Rayner Carrick—
Jonathan's oldest son and my uncle Atlas's brother—used to
fly into rages. My sisters and I cowered behind our bedroom
doors while he and my mama screamed at each other. Dishes
crashed. The Rockies look to me like that. Up there you can
actually see the howling. The earth boils up, flames spurt—
Then you're across them and suddenly, abruptly, there's calm.
That's the way it was with my father, too. The land just lays
itself down and sleeps all the way across the plains where little
towns glitter at night.

My father's anger never left him entirely. In this more
than in anything else he resembled his own father, my grandfather, Jonathan Carrick. We children learned about this an-

ger the hard way. It dissipated. Then it gathered again slowly, imperceptibly, just like the grasslands of the Middle West gather together slowly, imperceptibly across Indiana and Ohio. A haze from the Great Smokies appears in the air, and then these eastern mountains— Sometimes the rages carried on into the parental bed at night. What an education for little girls then! The violence of the Smokies is lush where the Rockies are imperial. Then morning and breakfast, down again and on to the daily noise in New York City. From the freight yards Jonathan and College hitched a ride on a passenger train into the wonders of Pennsylvania Station.

College led my grandfather out onto Broadway and walked him between the walls of buildings and up to the ponds and hillocks of Central Park. Then downtown again. They hung on to the straps of a horse-drawn streetcar, bought hot chestnuts from a sidewalk vendor, watched the traffic of ships from a bench in the Battery. There were barks and barkentines, steeply raked schooner clippers designed for the gold rushes in Australia and California—even a whaler on its way back to New Bedford. Jonathan stood up and sat in abrupt movements, twisting to catch sight of the ships, and of the passers-by, too, any one of whom might be a man with a black beard and no lashes on one eye. After all, this is America. Everybody's on the move.

So here he is in New York, seeking a father never to be found and knowing himself a murderer, which he is not, when all of a sudden he sees George. Right there in the Battery. There he is—plump, dark-haired, a frock coat. Of course it's George. Jonathan makes a dash at him, grabs him by the shoulder, swings him around—

And it isn't George at all.

That night Jonathan dreamed again the nightmare that had spurred him on to run away from Denver. Again he awoke to find himself plucking imaginary tobacco worms from his covers. But three days later the multicolored Mogul pulled out of New York carrying the makings of an entire town, and as everybody knows—Jonathan better than most—when you move you can stop thinking: maybe even stop dreaming. They carried every nail with them, every scrap of timber, every can of beans: every citizen, too, schoolteacher, preacher, saloon keeper, men, women, children. Secret reports revealed stibnite in a remote area of Nevada. Out of stibnite you can make explosives. Provided you get there first, that is. A company called Metals & Minerals of New York was getting there first.

When they reached the site of the town, they christened it Mogul in the engine's honor, and a month after the raw materials were dumped in the desert, Jonathan and College passed through the area again, this time going east with redwood trunks from California chained to flatcars and bound for Chicago. Balancing on the trunks, they looked down on the population of the town—men, women, children—everybody sawing and hammering, fetching and carrying, a busyness as busy from the top of a train as a plague of locusts from the window of a wooden farmhouse. The hotel was already complete. So was the general store. So was the boardwalk. A saloon without walls was in business. Struts for a church spire rose up not far from struts that would become a train station. The foundations of a dozen houses clustered beyond the boardwalk.

Jonathan had plainly been a charming small child once, chattering nonsense and dancing around cracker barrels in Benbow Wikin's store; he'd smothered this gaiety to survive, killed it, he thought, as surely as he'd killed George. He was as wrong about the one as about the other (as most people are about the certainties in their lives). The gaiety was rare, but it shows itself in the diaries sometimes, a complete surprise when it happens, as pleasurable as dashing through a sprinkler on a hot day. "Hey," he shouted in delight to College over the roar of the engine, looking down on the doings of this boomtown-to-be. "Hey! I helped build that." What would such a place be in two years time? In ten? Could you contain it at all?

The mountains beyond were bitterly cold. The night they reached the continental divide was foggy. The Mogul rested there to prepare for descent in the morning. Lying awake in the caboose, Jonathan played with the color of his father's eyes, but he found his mind on the town of Mogul instead, his engine's town, and on himself visiting there in two years time maybe, maybe in ten: Johnny the railroadman. Suddenly the realization came to him that he had enough money to buy a frock coat.

The town of Lenssen lay at the bottom of the mountain. On the very next day, he swore, he would buy the coat right there. Tomorrow. No matter what. Serge with a silk lining—to hell with George's satin—pearl buttons, velvet collar.

At dawn, the train began to ease its way downhill. Icicles hung from the redwoods and from the chains that held them. The wind was so sharp it froze eyelashes together. A change in the locomotive's exhaust is the only warning of a break-in-two a railroadman gets. Hear that? That easing of the sound? That's your reference point. That's what measures you—tells you who you are. If you're quick you can catch the mistake before it's actually made. But nobody was quick enough on those icy redwoods in that icy, whistling wind—not Jonathan, not College, either, not the bear of a conductor himself. The train quaked. The redwoods swung in their chains. The back half of the train pulled away from the front, paused, then cannoned forward. Well, what can you expect? You've got to die sometime. Fire sprouted from the wheels: this really happens, fire from metal on metal, and it catches the brush on either side of the track as though the train itself has melted, become molten like lava that ignites whatever it touches along its path. The redwoods tore loose. Jonathan, my grandfather, inched toward the engine, setting each of his brakes as hard as he dared. The engineer, a pinch-faced Scot whose nose had been chewed off in a barroom fight, jerked his head toward the corner of the cab. The bear of a conductor sat there, eyes staring ahead, beard clotted with blood.

When the wheels hiss, a train is sliding free, and there's nothing God or man can do to stop it. In front, the foothills leveled off. The engine hurtled on toward the solid brick walls of Lenssen stationhouse. Without a backward glance at the Scot, Jonathan scrambled out of the cab window and climbed up behind the engine's brass sand dome.

And jumped.

My aunt Claire supplied bologna sandwiches and milk for Atlas, her already tiddly husband, and for his gate-crashing niece: me. She'd made them days before and frozen them, because she'd known that on this day, at just about this hour, twelve-thirty, she'd be on the point of creating an aioli for the French dinner party to come. Claire hated garlic, and making anything like an aioli caused her agony.

"Why do you do it?" I said. "Couldn't you make a soup or something?"

"It's a matter of self-discipline," she said.

Atlas and I ate the sandwiches in his office. "Dad should have been dead," Atlas said. "There was no reason at all for him to be alive—scares me every time I think about it." He poured whiskey into the milk Claire had brought him. "But he was a funny guy. He thought—he really thought he ought to be able to control things people just plain can't control. Maybe it worked sometimes just because he thought it so hard. Jesus, he wanted that coat. He wanted it as much as he'd wanted to kill George, and nothing was going to get in his way—absolutely nothing—not even death. So he lived. Just like that." But he couldn't even get to his knees. Beyond him, a hundred yards away, lay a tangled mountain of metal and logs that seethed and stank like Sunday dinner at the workhouse. He tried to get up again and managed this time, but only with the help of the stationmaster who had rushed to his side.

"Let go of me," my grandfather said.

He had the money on him. He could hardly walk, but he made his way along the Lenssen boardwalk and found a men's tailor. There was no frock coat with pearl buttons, but he found one with a silk lining. For two dollars extra, the tailor added a velvet collar. Jonathan took a room in the town's one hotel, bathed, dressed, shaved and put on the coat.

This is what revelation is all about.

23

DOWNSTAIRS, he found College leaning up against the bar, and it was only then that he even remembered his friend's existence, which the crash had rendered as unlikely as his own. He was so stricken, so shocked, by what he'd forgot and what he'd remembered that he could hardly speak; it was such an extraordinary tactical win for George, alive or dead—this buying of a coat instead of remembering a friend—that it overwhelmed everything else. Jonathan received College's embrace mechanically, tearing at himself for his own mad priorities, but tearing at himself even more so for letting George prevail on such private territory.

"Well, you are a cold bastard, bound for hell, aren't you?" College said. "How'd you get out of that mess?"

"I jumped."

"You didn't! From the cab? What about Hecox?" The bar was small, dark, tatty, but it was a family hotel—a place where the occasional man might bring his wife—so it lacked the filth and noise of most such places. Jonathan and College were, in fact, the only customers present. The bartender hovered, listening, fascinated; news of the crash dominated the town.

Hecox was the bear of a conductor. "He's dead," Jonathan said.

"The Scot, too?"

Jonathan nodded.

"The others?"

"I don't know."

"Why aren't you dead? God, I'm glad you aren't. But why aren't you? You didn't really jump, did you?"

Jonathan nodded again.

"You shouldn't have got away with that, you know."

Jonathan nodded once more. "What about you?" He still held himself rigid against George's unexpected win, and his voice showed it.

But College laughed happily, anyway, happy to be alive, happy Jonathan was alive, happy to have so fascinated an audience as the bartender. "If it wasn't the damnedest thing: when that coupling snapped, I—the bravest man on the railroad—"

"For Christ's sake, tell the truth for once!"

"I always tell the truth—"

"You say the first thing that comes into your head."

"That's always truth."

"It's never truth."

"Don't quibble, Johnny. Have another drink. Now listen: I grabbed at the brake wheel with one hand!" The bartender's ears were dangling down on the bar and College's voice soared. "One hand! I made a complete revolution with the wheel, swung all the way around, up and over. The momentum threw me clear." He paused. The bartender stood riveted to the spot. "You don't believe me, do you?"

Jonathan sighed.

"And I the only man who knows and sees all—"

"Then why don't you say something about my coat?"

"Your what?"

"My coat, dammit."

College stepped back from the bar. "Coat?" he said, puzzled, trying to focus on this thing that seemed to him to bear no relevance to anything at all. Then he bowed, seeing the object at last but not even remotely understanding what it could mean. "My dear sir, I know it might be thought an imposition between gentlemen, but would you be good enough to give me the name of your tailor—such style—such craftsmanship—such—"

Jonathan's irritation swung into anger; he turned away abruptly.

"But you are wrong," College said, at ease with my grandfather's sticky temperament. My grandfather knew his anger was dangerous to him; he fought to hide it from his enemies, but he let his allies see it—an odd way to show trust. That's what it was, though: a tribute of sorts. Not that Jonathan figured it that way. The way he saw it, he himself was only half the audience tonight; College had the bartender as well, and it was against a clown's code to bow to the ill temper of one customer when there was still another in sight. "I know all about tailors," College went on, "they are part of any gentleman's past, and I, my good sir, am a gentleman. May I introduce myself? My name (since you have always been too polite to ask) is Rayner Hogg Malloy, and I am a member of the great middle classes. The, uh, pardon me, upper-middle classes. What I don't know about frock coats is more than a clod like you— I ran away to be a railroadman when I was eighteen. Just about your age right now, I'll bet."

Jonathan shrugged.

"My father's name is Sebastian," College ran on. "Sebastian Malloy. He's just like his name—round, fat, soft in the underbelly. He was born in Devon—over in England— and he went to Peterhouse at Cambridge because his mama

wanted him to be an English gentleman like his daddy before
him. He was going to eat mutton chops and walk down country lanes in a bowler hat. But he had asthma and went to
America instead."

Jonathan had listened to College babble for two years.
Listening, he'd picked up some ease with speech himself; even
so he sensed more than heard a new strain in this oddly personal spiel—and realized that a shift had taken place, that the
interweave of tinsel had lessened, that the bartender was forgotten, that what he was hearing was meant for him alone.
His anger disappeared. "Why did you run away?" he said.
"What was the point?"

College gulped at his whiskey. "Lo and behold!" he went
on. "In the fair city of Boston, Papa Sebastian ran across
Helen Andrews Hogg. Sixteen years old, tiny, thin, lively—
she's still like that—and she wrote poems in Latin and Greek.
Ghastly poems. But poems are poems after all. And her poems
came with an independent income of two thousand dollars a
year. Imagine it: two thousand a year. Sebastian fell in love
at once. She fell in love, too. Marriage ensued, as it will. They
were going to open a lyceum and be to Boston what Aristotle
was to Athens. If you can't be a gentleman in England—well,
what the hell—a gentleman can breed a gentleman even in
Boston." College poured whiskey into his glass until the liquor
slopped out over the bar. "Troubles, troubles. They couldn't
afford Boston. Two thousand dollars a year and they couldn't
afford Boston. So they bought a piece of land off the coast of
Maine not far from a town called Ellsworth—nice town—
whitewashed clapboard buildings, streets lined with wineglass
elms, little church with spire in a grassy square. Very nice.
And there they established—"

"You ran away from there? For Christ's sake, from a
place like that?"

College beat out a fanfare on the bar with the fingers of
one hand. "Malloy's Landing! Culture for all! There they
bred me—Rayner Hogg, son of a gentleman—and enrolled

me at the tender age of twelve months. Oh, what a good boy
was I. Mama and Papa published my poems in ads in the
Boston *Globe*. Malloy's Landing grew and prospered. When
I was eighteen there were eighteen pupils to celebrate my
birthday."

The barroom was hot. "But why did you run away?"
Jonathan pressed. "Tell me why."

College swallowed down what remained of the bottle,
then dropped it onto the floor. "Better sit down," he said.
Jonathan helped him to a table. "When I was bad they
wouldn't talk to me—silence—terrible silence— You know
what, Johnny?" he interrupted himself. "I'll tell you something
important: you smell. Now don't get offended. All men smell.
I smell. It's a fact of life. Women smell. Isn't it? Fact of life.
Get me a drink, will you?"

Jonathan fetched a second bottle.

"But not at Malloy's Landing. Nobody smells at Malloy's
Landing. Nobody shits there. Nobody sweats. Nobody—
Know where I come from?" He nodded gravely at Jonathan.
"Little Rayner came out of a water lily."

"You ran away—just—just—" Jonathan stuttered. "Just
because some other people and you didn't exactly agree—?"

"What's truth, Johnny?"

"Well, it ain't"—the pause was only fractional: the two
years of fascination with College's educated syntax had taught
him so many things—"isn't floating around up in the trees like
that." There were already the beginnings of some music in the
way Jonathan spoke, but even with the grammar correct, his
words seemed to him to clatter onto the table. "Playing at
babies being water lilies—what's so awful about that? She
never meant you any harm. You got to get a lot lower down:
you got to grub where it hurts." He could see from College's
drunkenly blank face that not one word he said meant anything. "Oh, what the hell," he went on, giving up, "maybe
you were just trying to get to the other side."

College frowned. " 'Come on, pretty biscuit'—that's what

my mother called me. 'Come on, pretty biscuit, turn over on your left side so you can go to sleep.' "

"I don't mean that," Jonathan said in a gentle voice.

"I wanted to sleep on my right side. There's silence on the left side. I hate silence. I told you that, didn't I? Jesus, I thought you were mute. The would have been— I just couldn't— It's on the left side: it hangs there, cold, gray, hazy, swinging a little in the draft and always on the left—" Jonathan was shaking his head. "Well, so what side do you mean?"

"Like that chicken," Jonathan said.

"What chicken?"

"The one that crossed the road—"

"That's not funny," College said petulantly.

Jonathan helped him up the hotel stairs and put him to bed, making sure he lay on his right side, away from the left and the silence that had frightened him there once upon a time—and plainly frightened him still.

24

AFTER THE CRASH, the episodes that made up Jonathan's life grew even more disconnected, each piece less and less related to what preceded and what followed it. No pattern remained except his recurrent nightmare, which became his constant companion. He and College went west to New Mexico for six months on the Atchison, Topeka & Santa Fe. From there they went to the Great Northern Railroad for a couple of months, then eight months on the Pennsylvania Railroad, then five on the New York Central. In the winter of 1881, they were back with TransContinental, which had ferried a whole town out into the desert three years before; and TransContinental brought them to that town again, to Mogul.

From the safety of a train top, the adult town of Mogul probably did have charms hygienic enough for a modern taste; up close, it was a symphony in shit. In the years since Jonathan had seen it, horse shit around the hitching posts had grown mountainous enough to raise the level of the street by half the height of a man. In the streets, chickens strutted and shat. So did geese. Pigs rooted and shat. There's nothing so pungent as pig shit, which was, in fact, the dominant smell, overwhelming the reek of human shit, slops and rotting offal. Over all this—and as bred in the bone as the dusting of coconut on my aunt Claire's *pièce de résistance, gâteau à la noix de coco,* which she was just finishing off as Atlas began to tell me about Mogul—over all, a layer of vegetable peelings and empty tin cans labeled "Green Corn," "Pears," "Peaches," "Oysters"—Mogul was growing up with America, no sewers, no trees, no streetlights, no running water: a full-blown boomtown geared to the quick sale of everything alive or dead, worldly or divine. Walls of saloon and Methodist chapel alike advertised whiskey, shaving cream, dried beef and—without so much as a change of paint color or script style—God Himself and the virtues of cleanliness. False fronts towered above the streets, so wretchedly put together that they swayed with every gust of wind; behind them squatted cheap little buildings, jerry-built like everything else for hundreds of miles around.

Jonathan and College arrived in the evening. The landlord of the Hotel Louis Quartz was just ringing the bell to announce supper. From my grandfather's reports of it, this supper was no worthy ancestor for Claire's *gâteau* or for her pretty arrangement of chrysanthemums, either, in the cut-glass vase on the plate-glass table that was her pride (her style with flowers, as she said, owed a great deal to the Japanese): supper in Mogul cost twenty-five cents. Jonathan and College paid, fought their way to seats at a long dining table, where a scrawny youth delivered platters as fast as he could ferry them from the kitchen—everything at once, mountains of pork, huckleberry pie, bacon, lakes of gravy. Guests snatched with bare hands, fork and bowie knife; they beat away competitors with elbows, slapped booty down on plates over beans, potatoes and bread, and shoveled it into their faces so fast that the meal took only ten minutes from payment to clearing.

Afterwards, the weather broke. Rain poured down. The street outside dissolved into liquid manure; the fumes that rose up were strong enough to make the eyes water. Jonathan and College ran to a saloon and sheltered there with a bottle of bourbon.

"How old are you?" College said suddenly. "Are you twenty-one yet?"

"I don't know," Jonathan said. "Maybe—near enough, anyway."

"You don't know?"

"I am above such things," said Jonathan, whose speech patterns by this time had come to reflect not only the ease he'd learned from College but a rough elegance all his own.

"Everybody has a birthday. You can't—"

"Everybody but Johnny Carrick."

College frowned into his whiskey. "You are confounding me."

"Good. It's about time somebody did."

"There's nothing like a man with a flexible past, is there?" College drank from his glass and then said, suddenly caught off balance by the thought, "You know, I know nothing about your past, absolutely nothing—"

"That's good, too."

"I do know you ran away from somewhere. From the look of you, you had to have been a runaway: you had to be.

Frank Fleming—he was a good guy, Frank, wasn't he?—he
said—"

"Forget it."

"Forget it? Even that? Why?"

"Just forget it. Please."

"Okay, okay," College said. "Well, if you really mean
what you say—and I know you well enough to know you always do mean what you say (unlike most people)—suppose I
pronounce today your birthday? December the fifteenth? Any
objections?"

This is one of those odd coincidences that sound made-
up but that happen all the time: this is my birthday, too. We
share this day in December, my grandfather and I. I am delighted by it, entranced. As for Jonathan, he was delighted,
too, as entranced as I. He writes in his diaries that it had never
occurred to him that he might have a birthday all to himself.
I would imagine that one of those rare smiles crossed his face
because College laughed. "You really do mean it, don't you?
No birthday at all. So"—he tapped out a tattoo on the bar—
"today, December 15, 1881, is Johnny Carrick's twenty-first
birthday. And I, Rayner Hogg Malloy, will—to celebrate this
coming-of-age—" He clicked Jonathan's glass with his own.
"I'm going to give you a birthday present."

The pride of men is a remarkable thing, responsible for
much both little and large. A brakeman's light was red. Every
brakeman had his own light, and every light was as identifi-
able as a calling card. Whenever a brakeman went anywhere—but especially to a whorehouse—he left his light
outside to mark the spot: here fucks Brakeman Flynn, here
fucks Brakeman Blake. This is why a red-light district is called
a red-light district: for no other reason at all. Jonathan and
College put their lights on the boardwalk outside Olympia
LeCleve's, the largest and most solidly built whorehouse in
town.

Olympia LeCleve herself opened the door, a tall woman

in a bustled damask gown with a row of tiny buttons running from neck to waist.

"My name is Rayner Malloy, Mrs. LeCleve—"

"Miss," she said. Her tone was polite but clipped. "Miss LeCleve."

"—Miss LeCleve," College went on without a pause, "and my friend Elder French suggested I call on you next time I passed through Mogul."

"I know Elder," she said, standing aside. "Come in. Tell me your name again—and take off that dreadful fisherman's coat." Not long after Jonathan bought his frock coat, College had bought himself a fisherman's coat in New Orleans, a heavy, bulky, oilskin affair; he'd bought it to provoke Jonathan's disdain, which it did and which amused him endlessly. The power of icons is too often underrated. Besides, College had worn the coat for three years. The joke was wearing thin. "And your friend's name? Do come in."

The parlor was long and narrow, furnished like a railway passenger coach with cane-covered chairs and lamps hanging from the ceiling, a common kind of decoration for a whorehouse—a celebration of these most romantic of customers, these railroadmen, astronauts of their day, more exalted than war heroes: men from the future who dared where none of the rest of us dared and who lived every day with secrets the rest of us could only guess at. A scarred player piano stood at one end of the room; a spray of cut daisies drooped in a large vase on top of it. Jonathan and College sat down, separated by a spittoon. Olympia sat opposite them. Her hair was bright orange. Pendants dangled from her ears down to her shoulders— a proper Hollywood whore of olden times.

"Would you gentlemen like a drink?" she asked. Without waiting for a reply, she called out, "Fritzi! Two whiskeys!"

A girl of fifteen or sixteen appeared with a tray. She was plump and pink-cheeked, fair. She wore a white dress with a ruffled bodice such as farm girls wore to Sunday school. No

Hollywood here, but even a hero fancies what he fancied as a boy and couldn't get. Jonathan watched Fritzi with fascination and Olympia watched him. "You've never been to a place like this before, have you?"

Jonathan shook his head. College had disappeared from time to time during their years of roaming around together; he'd never told Jonathan where he was going, though Jonathan had known he was going whoring and figured, older brother like, that Jonathan was too young for such entertainments. Jonathan had given in to the protectiveness because the idea of being physically close to somebody, a living person, touching the living flesh, a whore's flesh or any woman's flesh—or any man's—terrified him. It brought to mind George's girlish breasts, and not only that (in which there was an undeniable element of sex) but also the terrible weakness he had found in himself when George had touched him, which wasn't sex at all but just human contact—that most elementary of contacts, that avenue into the heart nobody understands and everybody fears, even while hungering after it.

"It's his twenty-first birthday," College said. "On my twenty-first birthday I got drunk. What were you doing on your twenty-first birthday, Miss LeCleve?" Olympia raised her eyebrows. "Oh, you must have been lovely at twenty-one," College rushed on. "A red peony: *Paeonia lactiflora*, 'Bower of Roses': my mother grew them." He tilted his head to one side. "No, not a peony. Do you know the blooms on a golden chain tree? You must have glowed like a whole grove of them in June." Dimples showed in his pockmarked cheeks and chin. "Golden chains are marvelous in July, too— Look, Johnny, see how she handles her shoulders. Were you a dancer?"

Olympia laughed. "I was a whore," she said. College laughed with her, but Jonathan's eyes lingered on the door through which Fritzi had disappeared. "You like my Fritzi, don't you?" Olympia asked, turning to him. "Tell you what, I'll give you a dollar off with her since it's your birthday." She laughed again. "Fritzi, come back." Fritzi appeared and sat on the arm of Jonathan's chair. All of this is documented in his diaries. I make up nothing. I doubt Atlas knew anything about it, though; like Jonathan's dream, his love of whores was a secret he kept from his children. Fritzi smiled at him. There was a gap between her front teeth. He tried to smile back, taking too long to do so, and her smile deepened.

"And for you," she said, turning to College. "How about Lucretia? She can work the player best. It's kind of moody."

Lucretia had black hair in ringlets; she wore a white Sunday school dress, too. "Do you like Mogul?" she said to College. "I hate it. Shall I play for you? Do you sing? What do you want to sing?"

She inserted the roll for "Careless Love" into the opening of the piano and pumped at the pedals. What else would a whore play for a railroadman, for a hero of the age? College launched into the opening stanza, elbow perched on her shoulder:

> "It's on this railroad bank I stand,
> It's on this railroad bank I stand,
> It's on this railroad bank I stand,
> All for the love of a railroad man."

College stopped abruptly. "Sing, Johnny," he said.

Jonathan flushed and they all laughed.

"Get him to sing, Fritzi," College said.

Fritzi slid down the arm of the chair into Jonathan's lap; she took his hand in hers and placed it on her bodice. Jonathan took in his breath and sang; he had a full, strong singing voice, resonant if not pure. He was hardly aware of being led upstairs.

My father Rayner—you can see now that he was named for College—said sex had the power to blot out everything else. Perhaps it was his age: he was old for a beginner: twenty-two, a year older than his father, Jonathan, who was old for a beginner at twenty-one (if indeed he was twenty-one). Stallions mount mares and pump away, jerk, jerk, jerk, half standing, sweating, faces expressionless, weight thrust forward as though they were working a recalcitrant treadle. Bulls mount cows and pump away. Dogs mount and pump, so do cats, pigs, whales, humans, even turtles, for Christ's sake—even turtles—same stance, same movement every time: jerk, jerk, jerk. Some animals have shells, some have fur, some have hair, some don't: you could shift one beast for another and never notice any difference in rhythm: jerk, jerk, jerk. It's even sillier in a whorehouse, especially before the turn of the century. Nobody knew what to do about the clap, but anybody who had any sense was scared. So here in the midst of all these profound fears about life, humanity, human relationships, touching the flesh, George: in the midst of all this and for the sake of this queer pleasure that engrosses humans just as totally as it does dogs and pigs, the whore gives the guy's prick a deft twist, inspects it as though it were a suspect pudding spoon, washes it with disinfectant from a cracked china bowl with a ring of dirt around the edge. Then she lies down on the bed, spreads her stockinged legs—her still-booted feet wide apart—and throws up her petticoats.

Well, there are enlightenments and enlightenments. People who seek patterns in life are likely to find them from time to time. What young American isn't in a state of grace when he realizes he can fuck his way across the continent? Fritzi was up and busy again. She pulled a half-full chamber pot out from under the bed. Jonathan, my grandfather, who had loved whores long before he knew what they were for, rolled onto his elbow and watched her squat over it, petticoats raised to reveal the tips of her naked buttocks, enchanted with himself, enchanted with her, enchanted with whores all over again. Could this be why the diaries are in code? My grandfather writes about Fritzi without any whitewash at all. It's likely, I guess. They were prudish times. Fritzi fetched the bowl of disinfectant, washed them both once more (to his further enchantment) and began to pull her Sunday school dress over her head.

"Is there anything else, Johnny?"

He studied her. "Again?"

On his first day in Denver Jonathan had watched a man lean over the hand of a red-gowned lady, hold the pose a moment, then straighten, eyes on the red-gowned lady's eyes. He'd thought of the scene off and on for the five years since. Fritzi had a farm girl's large hands, raw around the knuckle, but when she said once more, "Is there anything else, Johnny?"—when she said this for the second time, he took her raw hand in his without a word and bent over it, lips to her fingers just as though she were the elegant red-gowned lady of Denver.

Fritzi giggled happily and took hold of her skirt to show him. "This is real store-bought calico," she said. She was only six weeks out of a rural slum where all her life she'd shared a single-roomed mud hut with her mother and ten other kids, all of them dressed in potato sacks. She tilted her head to study the folds of this store-bought calico and whispered in awe, "Sometimes on a Friday we wear satin."

"Johnny!" College's voice came from downstairs. "Hurry it up, will you? We're shipping out tonight!"

25

THE RAIN had given way to drizzle. College wore his fisherman's coat, this icon bought to combat Jonathan's icon—this well-bred boy's cock-a-snoot at the ambitions of his friend who had grown up a slave (a subject of which he knew nothing at all, not a whit, not a hint) and whose frock coat lay carefully folded in the caboose—dressed in this coat, College alternated on the couplings with Jonathan as he always had: he did the first, Jonathan the second, then College again. The first six—stibnite from Mogul to replace canned goods and cod from Portland—went without a hitch. Jonathan took the seventh. The pin wouldn't drop. He bent over it, rain seeping through his shirt and trickling down the middle of his back.

College said, "In the interests of keeping dry, might you lower yourself to don this workingman's coat while the workingman himself gets on with the next coupling?" He held out the skirt of the coat as he spoke, much as Fritzi had held out the skirt of her Sunday school dress.

"Shut up," Jonathan said.

College shifted his shoulders under the oilskin. "Sure?"

Jonathan gestures irritably to indicate that the pin is in fact dropped and turns toward the caboose. College steps between the next cars. The gap is nearly a foot. College chooses what they called a gooseneck pin, fits it, cocks it and signals the engineer. The train slacks. The cars touch. The pin bends in the link. All of this is in Jonathan's diaries—staccato phrases, present tense and all—just the facts, no emotion. The slots are too far apart. College signals the engineer again. The train draws away a little. He maneuvers his body between the cars once more, brakeman's light (pride at the whorehouse) in the crook of his arm. While this happens, Jonathan is walking toward the rear of the train; he comes slowly to realize that the cars are creeping forward toward the engine.

"College!" he shouts, breaking into a run. "Slack running!"

College makes a leap toward safety.

In the moonlight the big coat billows out. For a moment he's suspended there, in midair. But the coat is too big: it's a parachute of a coat: its direction is down, not up, and it will snag on anything. He falls back. The cars move lazily together. "Had a hole in his chest you could throw a frying pan through": that's what Mother O'Neill said about the brakeman whose clothes Jonathan had worn on his first day in Denver, and so it was with College. His left arm dangled above his head, the wide fisherman's sleeve hooked to a bolt that stuck out above the coupling.

There are always standard signals and standard shoutings for standard accidents:

"Ease her back."

"Coupling won't give."

"That's it—slow—slow now—slow—"

A thousand tons of stibnite creeps back half an inch. More signals. The cars part. College collapses into Jonathan's arms, and in the red light of the lantern—a trick of the spectrum that in another mood gives us rainbows—the blood that pumped out of him was black. They carried him to the nearby caboose. A tired little doctor from Mogul peered down through a lorgnette.

"Morphine," the doctor said and slipped a needle under College's skin. ("I'll bet you didn't know we could inject morphine all those years ago," Atlas said.) "Take this bottle," the doctor went on to Jonathan. "If it gets bad, pour a little on your bandana and place it over his mouth and nose." The doctor's lorgnette was made of shell with gold trim. The conductor wired for right-of-way to Cheyenne.

The train bumped and jiggled as gently as possible at only fifteen miles an hour: this, too, was standard procedure. In the caboose, his body wrapped in Jonathan's frock coat, College breathed in and out, in and out, then a pause; in and out, in and out, then a pause. Jonathan counted: "One—and—two—and—" He listened intently. "Three—and—four—and—" Twice during the trip College broke into a high-pitched scream. Terrified by what such an inhuman sound had to mean, Jonathan pressed his dampened bandana over College's nose and mouth. As they neared Cheyenne station, College opened his eyes, coughed and made a snatch at Jonathan's sleeve. "Johnny," he cried. "Is that you?"

Jonathan reached for the doctor's bottle again.

College held tight to the sleeve. "No, not that— Talk to me. Don't leave me. Is there something wrong with me? For Christ's sake, speak! I hate silence. It scares the— Oh, shit. Speak to me. It's too quiet, Johnny."

"You're going to—to be all right—just fine," Jonathan began, now as terrified by the lack of pain as he had been before by the intensity of it. "Everything will be—all right. We're taking you to the best doctor in Cheyenne, where there's a bed waiting for you, a bed with linen sheets on it, no, not linen, silk—" He listened in agony to this babble of his, this nonsense out of his own mouth, learned from College, meaningless as ever, helpless now, useless, a waste, but whenever he paused, College begged him to keep on. So he kept on.

At Cheyenne station, the train at a standstill, the trip over at last, College sighed and said, "Turn me on my left side, Johnny."

Jonathan hesitated. "Don't you mean your right side?" he asked gently. "The left—that's where the silence is. Don't you mean—"

"The left side, Johnny. Turn me on my—"

Jonathan eased him over, talking all the time.

College pulled his knees to his chest, tucked his hands beneath his chin. "Oh, do be quiet," he said then. And his breathing stopped.

26

MY GRANDFATHER could write a little. He'd scratched letters in the dirt of the Stokes' sod hut, but he had in fact never written on a piece of paper. It was one of the many secrets about himself that he'd hidden from College; it shamed him deeply, as illiteracy shames anybody who suffers from it, and he'd hidden it with all the guile and cunning of Atlas hiding from Claire how much drink he got down himself during the day. It was only with immense difficulty that Jonathan filled out the forms to authorize shipment of College's body back East. He sent on College's clothes, too, a bundle of letters and just under three hundred dollars in cash. He kept back only the pearl-handled Smith & Wesson, partly for sentimental reasons and partly because a revolver didn't fit in with his picture of life at the Malloy's Landing establishment on the coast of Maine. When the train carrying the casket left Cheyenne, he made his way to a saloon called the Bowie Jack at the edge of town.

"What fascinates me is the absolute indifference of the universe," Atlas says into my microphone. "We go around feeling special somehow—you know what I mean—more dear

to nature than the rest of creation. Dogs probably feel the
same way. Bugs, too. Even viruses, if they can feel at all. So
here you are fighting a virus—the flu maybe, or maybe something far worse—and the fact of the matter is, nature doesn't
give a damn which of you wins. You or the virus: she watches
but she calls no odds. She is completely impartial. It makes
people mad as hell—especially sick people."

"Yeah, I know," I say.

"Sure you do. When people die—when somebody close
to you dies—it's much the same, don't you think?"

"Bottle of whiskey," Jonathan said to the bartender of
the Bowie Jack.

"Howya doing, railroadman?" said the bartender.

"Just give me the bottle."

"You don't look well—"

"You want me to drink somewhere else?"

The bartender shrugged; the rudeness of railroadmen was
accepted—even expected—in those days much as the rudeness
of Hollywood stars or British aristocrats is accepted today.
Jonathan took his bottle to a table. In half an hour the bar's
walls swam. He passed out, sitting there, woke several hours
later, bought another bottle. At four in the morning the bartender carried him upstairs and tucked him into bed, reluctant
to lose the custom of any railroadman and especially of one so
ready to spend.

Jonathan woke at noon, mouth furred, stomach adrift.
He had no idea where he was, and for all he cared he might
have been in hell. He found his way down the narrow, dark
stairs to the bar.

"Feeling better?" the bartender said.

"Just give me a bottle."

He drank, passed out; awoke, drank and got carried upstairs and tucked into bed just as he had been the night before.

The next day it was well past noon before he maneuvered
his way down the narrow stairs through a haze of nausea.

Leaning on the bar for support, he saw what seemed to be clumps of something hanging from the bartender's belt. He squinted at them. "What are those things?" he said.

"These? Genuine Indian scalps," said the bartender, delighted to have at last caught the attention of so important a customer. "This here one, see"—he unbuckled the belt and flopped it up on the bar—"this here's Red Eagle. Now I run into Red Eagle—"

"Are you Bowie Jack? Guy that owns this joint?"

"Yep. That's me." His features looked as though they'd been yanked together in the middle of his face by his fishhook of a nose.

Jonathan squinted at the puckered cheeks much as he'd squinted at the scalps. "They call you that because of them?"

"Yep. I cut 'em off with my bowie—"

"How'd you do it?" Jonathan said.

"Whaddya mean?"

"How do you scalp a head?"

"Don't you want to hear how I fought—"

"No."

"But most folks—"

"No."

"Well," said Bowie Jack, bravely recovering his enthusiasm, "you slip the knife in at the back of the neck first, see?"

"Why?"

"Whaddya mean?"

Jonathan sighed irritably. "Why not at the front of the head?"

"Well, gee, 'cause it sticks, sorta—you know, like skin on lamb chop fat. The hair—"

"Give me a bottle of whiskey."

"—don't come off clean—"

"Now, goddamn you!"

Sitting at his table, my grandfather's hands shook so badly he couldn't pour the whiskey into his glass; he had to drink it from the bottle. Toward evening the bar filled up. He sat at his table alone in a sea of noise, forcing the alcohol down his throat as fast as he could. His aim was simple unconsciousness, but it seemed to be taking more effort to get there than it had in the previous two days.

He bought a second bottle and set it on the table in front of him before he'd managed to finish off the first. He concentrated hard: only an inch to go. He didn't notice when the man in Galway chokers appeared. Why should he? There were lots of men around; he paid no attention to any of them, although his stomach lurched dangerously when Bowie Jack pounded the bar. "This here's Preacher Spoonable," Bowie Jack said. "What do you say, boys? Want a little entertaining?"

The preacher wore a black linen duster, a black, wide-brimmed hat; in one hand a Bible, in the other, a horsewhip.

"You can lay your Bible there, Preacher," Bowie Jack said. "Now, boys, I ain't going to sell no liquor during a sermon. But it may run on some, so now's your chance."

There was a general rush. The preacher bought, too. Jonathan tried to get to his feet, failed and half passed out— but only half. By the time he manipulated the bar back into focus, Bowie Jack had covered it with a sheet from the upstairs bed of my grandfather's two oblivious nights, and the sermon had begun.

"Out here in Cheyenne"—the preacher's voice had the rhythmic lilt of any traveling evangelist—"a man's hardly got time to piss behind the shed. You're on the run, all of you, fast as you can go. Right? Then suddenly, right in the middle of the race—wham!—you're dead." He paused, drank from the glass of whiskey beside him and went on. "Now let's say you've been dead for a month. Funeral paid for. Buddies got new buddies—can't no longer rightly remember your name. Down you go to hell. Who cares? Nobody. Right? You got vultures yanking the skin off your balls for eternity and who gives a damn?"

"For Christ's sake," Jonathan said. He struggled again

to get himself upright, but again stumbled and fell back into his chair.

"This here young man got it in one," the preacher shouted. "It's Christ what cares. Tell you something more: I care. Me and Jesus. That's why we're going to fight for you boys. Right here. Right now. The winner's prize: all the souls in this room, you and me, brothers—all of us. Let's say we're in this book." He patted his Bible. "Now, gents, the contenders. In this corner, one backwoods preacher, kind of old and dry." He drew back his sleeve to expose a skinny arm. He took another swig of whiskey, shadow-boxed a little and hefted his whip. "You, young man who doubts the Word," he said to Jonathan, "watch me." In a single flick of his horsewhip, he snatched the nearly empty bottle off Jonathan's table and smashed it against the wall.

"Now for a costume change." He turned, drew the sheet off his altar and draped it over his shoulders. "And in this corner"—the sheet made a gown; he stood hand on hip and hip thrust out; there were guffaws from the bar—"Lucifer himself, boys. Beelzebub. Asmodeus. Mephistopheles. The Father of Lies and the Bitch of the Pit."

The stance was Fritzi and George all at once, male and female all at once. Nausea erupted at the back of Jonathan's throat; he struggled to swallow it down. Men at the bar sang out raucously: "Take it off. Take it off."

"In good time, my dear sirs," the preacher said.

The dance began.

The devil swishes his tail beneath his gown, circles toward the Bible, flirts girlishly. Off with the sheet: the preacher, as himself, a pure-hearted man of God, picks up the Bible and begins to read. On with the sheet: the devil flirts more boldly. Off with the sheet: the preacher, uninterested, turns away. On with the sheet: the devil grows bolder still; hips sway, shoulders swing and—aha! at last!—the preacher takes notice. He puts down the book; he watches despite himself, prudish at first, then a little rakish, then lustful. The sex changes come faster and faster. My grandfather, nauseated, fascinated, clung to the edge of his chair. Man into woman: woman into man: borders meaningless: animal into vegetable. How can a snake swallow its tail? How can the jaws eat the jaws? The stomach digest itself? On with the sheet: the whore wraps her legs round the preacher. A hand snakes out to take hold of the Bible. The preacher draws back in alarm, struggles to disentangle himself. The whore tears off her drape and reveals the devil's cloven hoof and tail.

The fight begins in earnest.

"Gouge him, Preacher. Gouge him!" one man cried.

"Get him in the balls," cried another.

The devil conjured. The preacher picked glasses off tables with his horsewhip. The devil withdrew in defeat. Jonathan's hands and face were wet with sweat; the audience stamped and cheered.

"And you might well ask, boys," the preacher was saying, "why a poor, backwoods preacher should come to a saloon on a Saturday night and fight the devil for your souls. What the fuck do I care? Well, I'll tell you: I fight for your souls because my friend Jesus died for them. But who fought for Him when He needed help? Huh? I'll give you the answer to that one, boys. Nobody. Fight for Him? He couldn't even get Peter to stay awake for Him.

"How do you think He felt on the night before His crucifixion? He knew they were going to drive nails in His hands and feet and let Him hang in the sun until He dried out like one of those scalps around Bowie Jack's waist. How do you think He felt? He was scared shitless, boys. Like you'd be. Like me. So what does a man do when he's scared? He goes to his friend, doesn't he? He says, 'Peter,' he says, 'I don't want to take up much of your time, but you're my friend, and I need you. Just keep me company tonight. Sit with me a little.' Well, you gotta say for Peter that he'd fished fishes and he'd fished souls all day, and a man gets tired. So he sits himself down to wait with Jesus, and—not meaning any harm by it—he nods off.

"But, goddammit, Jesus was a man like you and me, boys, and He had to die like a man. But He was a God, too. And what's going to happen to you—you, me, all of us—what's going to happen to us if even a God's earthly friends can't stay awake when He needs them?" The preacher put down his whip and extended his arms to either side, fists clenched, stretching himself out upon the cross. " 'Sleepest thou?' Jesus said to Peter. 'Couldest not thou watch one hour?' "

The preacher opened his hands. There in the middle of each palm was an open wound that dripped blood in spots down over the sheet that covered the altar.

Jonathan heaved himself onto his feet and half feeling his way, stumbled outside. The sky was overcast. There were no stars, no moon. His legs seemed too loose at the knees for a steady gait, but the inside of his head had a glacial feel to it, as cold as the wind that had frozen eyelashes together above the town of Lenssen before the break-in-two, before the change in engine sound that heralded disaster—the sound that nobody heard. He stood in the light from the saloon door for a moment, gathering balance. He'd planned to go to the edge of town. In his drunkenness the edge of town seemed the proper place, but when he reached the crossroads, he could wait no longer. He took College's Smith & Wesson out of his pocket, cocked it, put it in his mouth and pulled the trigger.

Nothing happened.

The blast he'd imagined rang in his head. It was some moments before he could bring himself, ears still singing, to explore the nape of his neck with his fingers. In the dark he ran his fingers over the pistol. Two chambers were empty, including the one he'd fired. The pistol needed oiling. He shook his head in abrupt fury. What's a man want with a friend like College? Not around when you need him—no better than Peter, maybe not even as good, not just asleep when you needed him most, dead when you needed him—coat too big, ugly coat, too, pistol only half loaded. Jonathan aligned the chambers, aimed, pulled the trigger: a bullet cracked into the wood of the boardwalk across the street from him.

"Couldest thou not watch one hour?" he said out loud, not knowing quite what he meant but aware even so that he was addressing not College or the preacher or Christ Himself, but the shiny black eyes and curly mouth of that figure that lingered still, alive or dead, at the edge of his mind.

27

WHEN I WAS TWENTY-ONE, still more or less able-bodied (at least on the surface), I landed a half-decent part in an off-Broadway production of a Shaw play, one of those minor character roles with a funny accent and a few laughs tied in. I was good at it. I know I was. But on the first night I couldn't walk right—it was the first serious omen of what I have become—I just couldn't make my legs work. I went on anyway. I wasn't important enough to have an understudy. But the furor afterwards! They said I'd turned the character into a cripple—which, all things considered, I guess I had. My GP sent me to a psychiatrist (not as dull-witted a one as they usually are), who said, "I've never run across an obsession so physically based" and sent me to a neurologist. There were many tests, technological wonders most of them, painful, complex and like so many technological wonders, indecisive—all except for the

Babinski, that is: painless, practical Babinski. It was Babinski that condemned me. Here is the simplicity of true genius: the doctor scrapes an ordinary pen or an ordinary key from an ordinary keyring down the sole of the patient's foot. If nothing happens: no motor disorder. If the big toe curls up: motor disorder. My big toe curled up. Perhaps that was the moment, the very instant—the borderland for me—toe curling upward in a neurologist's office: maybe that was the moment this once able-bodied person became a cripple.

At least from that moment on I was tainted. Not that the able-bodied don't ever feel tainted, I don't mean that. Everybody comes to it in the end, and a lot of them well before the end. Even Claire. After lunch and bologna sandwiches Atlas got called out on an emergency. He had to leave too fast for wheelchairs, so I stayed behind in his office. He hadn't been gone more than a minute or two when she came in.

"I'm glad I've got the chance to talk to you," she said. "I was afraid— I want you to do something for me. I want you to talk to him."

"Sure," I said. "What about?"

"His drinking. What else?"

I shifted uncomfortably. "Uh—" I began and shifted again. "I don't see—"

"He wet his pants in the theater last week. We went to see— It's a silly play, *Barefoot in the Park,* I don't know why we went at all. It was a local production, not any good really. He just sat there and— I smelled it. That's how I knew. I was so ashamed."

"Oh, Lord, I'm sorry—"

"He wouldn't even look at me. We didn't know whether to stay sitting there or run or what." She laughed a little wildly. "What is the etiquette for wetting your pants during *Barefoot in the Park?*"

"Probably nobody noticed," I said, not knowing what to say.

Well, what can I say? Benign tumors don't run in the family, but suicide does. If fifty years of whiskey was Atlas's approach to it, he wasn't going to win any prizes among us Carricks. There is etiquette (to use Claire's word) even to suicide: whiskey just isn't up to snuff. On top of the two attempts Jonathan's already made, he has one and a half to go, and while the half-attempt is not too impressive, the remaining full attempt is very much so—which is to say that Atlas comes into this legacy legitimately, even if he doesn't show the family panache. My father Rayner did better. He swallowed five hundred Nembutals; he did it because my mother found an unfamiliar condom under the bed in his study, one of those raspberry-scented ones, and they had one of their wild fights over it. God help us, what a thing to die for: a raspberry-scented condom. In fact he didn't die right away, though; the barbiturates destroyed his kidneys and raised his blood pressure: it was a stroke that got him in the end. There is no aim, no meaning, no purpose in life—no pattern, no divine plan. This is truth, but the healthy rarely bother with it. "The trouble with depressives," as Atlas says, "is that they're right."

The stakes are so high, though, that in the afterfog of an unsuccessful attempt, life sometimes reveals a simpleminded, day-to-day charm, a patternless pattern that went unnoticed before. So it was with Jonathan, my grandfather, who thought he could see a way to be happy in just such a simpleminded, day-to-day fashion. He took a train to Billings, Montana, signed on as a brakeman for the Northern Pacific run between Billings and Duluth and when he received his first paycheck, opened a savings account at the First National Bank in Duluth. He grew a mustache, a rich black affair that hung down a little to either side of his mouth and made him look older. The railroad promoted him to baggageman. For another six months, he drank nothing, lived cheaply and worked as many extra hours as he could persuade the railroad to hire him for. What time he had left over he spent as he'd spent leftover time since that day in San Francisco, searching for the father he was never to find. The moment his bank balance stood at $1,200 he quit and took a train to the East Coast.

He arrived in Ellsworth, Maine, just before dawn on a June morning. It was a smaller town than he'd expected, neater: stores and houses clustered side by side, paved paths to walk on instead of boardwalks, cobbled streets, no smell of pig shit over the horse shit. But the wineglass elms lining the streets were precisely what he'd had in mind and so was the white clapboard church in the town square surrounded by flower beds. He caught up with a lamplighter snuffing out streetlights and asked the way; Malloy's Landing turned out to be fifteen miles to the east. He left his trunk at the station and set out on foot.

The road out of Ellsworth was overhung with maple trees and the smell of pine. Cocks were crowing. Thinking about College, he found himself thinking about the chicken story again, too. He ran his eye over the worsted of his trousers. The frock coat he wore had come from the best tailor in Chicago. His bag had a change of linen in it and a hairbrush with a pearl handle. The chicken was probably scared half to death as it set out, he thought—never mind how many roads it had crossed before—wings beating, feathers flying, all that squawking. Several miles out of Ellsworth, the trail-like road emerged from the trees for a few hundred yards. The Atlantic Ocean stretched out in shades of blue to the horizon; waves broke against an outcropping of rock a hundred feet below him. He wiped his palms on his trouser legs. The trouble, he thought irritably, was that when you got to the other side you more than likely made a goddamned fool of yourself—man or chicken—and what was funny about that?

It was nearly noon when he saw the house, a large structure made of three barns ballooning out from the rear of a tiny, two-story farmhouse. He circled it twice before he decided to try what looked like the front door. Nobody answered. Nobody answered at the first of the barn doors he tried either. Caught between relief and disappointment, he tried another door and heard footsteps inside. The door opened. A small, thin woman in bloomers peered out at him. Over her shoulders she wore a colorful scarf with a fringe that hung down past her waist, and her face was as pockmarked as College's had been.

"Yes?" she said. Her fingers scurried to her temple and plucked a tuft of hair from the bun at the nape of her neck. Other tufts stuck out here and there all over her head like random feathers.

"My name is Carrick, I—"

"Carrick?" She thrust her head toward him. "Carrick? Not Johnny Carrick by any chance?"

"Yes, I—"

"You are Johnny? Rayner's Johnny?" She turned away from him abruptly and shouted into the rooms beyond. "Seb! Seb! Come quick! It's Johnny! He's come to see us. Johnny's here." She turned back and took him by the hand. "Oh, how good to see you, Johnny. How are—?" she began, and then started on a second question before she'd got the first out: "Are you here for a—?" Then on a third before the second was out: "How did you—?" Broken sentences like the ones College had fallen into sometimes when he was upset.

The room she drew him into was the whole ground floor of one of the barns; one end was the kitchen, where two aproned women stood beyond a high worktable attending to the stove. Eight people sat at the dining table that occupied most of the middle section of the room. At the end of the table a fat man fought to free himself from his chair. "Don't run on so, Helen," the fat man said, pushing at the chair, which fell backward and crashed to the floor. "A man can't answer so many questions at one go. Besides, you haven't actually asked them. Well, well, well. So this is Johnny: Johnny at last. I'm Sebastian."

Jonathan shook the outstretched hand and searched the large head and ruddy face for some familiar trait but saw none—no dimples, no elfish smile—only a waddle on splayfeet and a meshwork of tiny veins that made the nose purple.

"Welcome, welcome, welcome. Detta, set a place for Johnny. You move along, Peewee," he said to a lanky figure folded into the chair beside his own. "Go. Away. Johnny's going to sit here today. Detta, knives and forks. A plate." He turned to Jonathan. "Sit. Sit. Sit," he said. "A glass of wine? Meat? Potatoes? Helen, why haven't you eaten anything?" One of the aproned women put a plate in front of Jonathan, piled with food, and a tulip-shaped glass of red wine. Sebastian righted his chair and sat, too. "Now, Johnny," he said in the elegant English accent College had imitated so often, "how long can you stay? Let me introduce you to everybody." He smiled benignly around the table. "This is Peewee—" He stopped, cast an eye over Helen's plate and speared a piece of potato with his fork. "Why do I have to eat your food, Helen?" he said, chewing the potato and reaching over again. "You really ought to eat it yourself."

Peewee wore an old army jacket with a sergeant's stripes on the sleeve. There were two old men, twins, who spoke in unison: a remarkable, disconcerting feat that made Jonathan edgier than he felt already. There was a middle-aged lady in a severe shirt with stripes and a cravat, a heavily freckled young woman with red hair, and a black-haired boy with angry eyes and the skin and cheekbones of an Indian.

"This is Josh," Sebastian said, gesturing at the boy. "He's my star pupil, ready for university. Wonderful mind, haven't you, Josh? Wonderful. But they won't let Indians in American universities, did you know that? I can't imagine why." Josh stopped chewing and looked Jonathan up and down. There'd been a dog on one of Jonathan's runs, a tiny, fierce-eyed poodle, white and fluffy. Baggagemen hated dogs. Dogs fought and bit, and a baggageman got no more for carrying one than

for carrying a saddle. Jonathan had tied the poodle not far
from a bucket of lubricating oil; the train hit a sag; the dog
fell in the bucket. For fifty miles Jonathan had scrubbed with
a gunny sack while the dog got blacker and shinier and its
eyes glittered more and more fiercely. The resemblance to Josh
was startling.

"Josh is just going on fifteen," Seb said indulgently. "A
difficult age. Now, Johnny, tell us about yourself."

"I'm a railroadman," Jonathan said.

"Yes, yes, of course," Sebastian laughed. "Everybody
here knows that. Everybody knows Ray's Johnny and the railroads. Everybody."

"Seb," said Helen, her fingers fluttering over the tines
of her fork, "he doesn't— He couldn't know that we— Don't
you see?"

"Oh," Sebastian said. "Yes. There were many letters,
Johnny. Ray wrote often, you know. Often. He wrote us about
railroads and mountains and oceans and—about you."

"I didn't know. He didn't tell me."

Josh pushed his plate away from him. "He wrote about
filth and violence as well," he said. Jonathan looked up. The
Indians he'd seen spoke pidgin English; Josh's accent was as
British as Sebastian's. "And prejudice."

"Down, Injun," Peewee said from the other end of the
table.

Josh's eyes glittered like the poodle's. "Your servant,
Lieutenant," he said.

Sebastian slapped the table and laughed again. "So why
has it taken so long for you to come to us? Eh, Johnny? Are
you on holiday? Perhaps you're billeted here? That would be
good fortune for us. Eh?"

Jonathan looked at the faces around the table. "I never
went to school," he said.

"Really? Where were you brought up? Kansas? No
schools nearby? So you've come to study? Is that it?"

"If you will accept me," Jonathan said.

"If we will accept— How can you even ask? We're entranced, my boy, entranced. You're almost related to us. We've known you for years, you know, years. Ah, Johnny, what a feast awaits you. Shakespeare, Milton, Dante, Cervantes. Detta, is there any more of that pudding? Americans, too. Wonderful Americans:

> 'Ah, distinctly I remember, it was in the bleak
> December,
> And each separate dying ember wrought its ghost upon
> the—' "

Detta put a second bowl in front of Sebastian; he stopped reciting instantly. "It's not quite right, you know, Detta," he went on, mouth full, shaking his head. "Butter—always use butter if you want a good pudding—and those windfall apples. But Johnny, Kansas is stuffed with subscription schools. Did your parents belong to one of these sects—you know—Helen, what do I mean? Mormons? Amish? They might have been Social Contract people, I suppose. Is that it? Or maybe Emersonians—"

There, Jonathan thought, feeling a sudden warmth inside him that made him unsure how he was going to make his jaws chew or his throat swallow— There in Sebastian's smooth, easy, largely meaningless babble lay the resemblance between father and son. He studied the remains of his wine. He'd never tasted anything like it before, but he was grateful for what little alcoholic support it afforded.

"Seb, really," Helen interrupted, "he plainly doesn't— I'll take Johnny to—" She scrambled out of her chair, plucking at Jonathan's arm, and ushered him out of the room.

She led him up some stairs and along a corridor to her study, a small, untidy, book-lined room, tucked up under the eaves of one of the barns. The moment she opened the door

Jonathan could see that it was more than just a room, though as he thought of it he guessed the same could be said for the room he'd just left. He wasn't sure why; maybe it was that somebody had plainly spent thought on the details of life. Looking around himself, he felt a homesickness for the railroads so abrupt and intense that he missed Helen's first words.

". . . find out just precisely where we want to . . ." she was saying, taking a book off the shelf behind her. She opened the book and handed it to him. "Will you—?" Jonathan looked at her in terror. "Don't be shy."

He ran his hand over the words, closed the book and handed it back to her.

"Too hard?" she said.

He shook his head. " 'A is for ax,' " he said. " 'B is for box.' 'Do you not love to play a game of ball?' "

They started partway through the McGuffey Third Reader, at just the point the Stoke children had reached when the plague of grasshoppers descended on the homestead and Benbow Wikin had struck his bargain with Alvah for the production of Wikin's Sweetbrier: "Alvah Stoke to manufacture. George Stoke to sell around."

28

THIS FIRST READING LESSON in Helen's study left my
grandfather drenched with sweat. After it she led him to a
second-floor room in one of the barns. On the door outside
there was a plaque that said STUDY-BEDROOM NO. 7, where
everything smelled of wax polish, clean linen and of the pine
trees outside the window. The bed had an embroidered coverlet over it. He peeked in the bureau drawers, discovered a
lavender sachet, sniffed it, replaced it. He opened the closet
door, took off his frock coat, hung it on a wooden hanger,
stood back to survey it: the best tailor in Chicago. He folded
down the coverlet on the bed, then the cover, the sheets, the
underblanket; he'd seen such materials before only in the frocks
of lady passengers. He took his coat off the hanger, put it on
again, picked up the reader, read a sentence: so it was that he
caught his own eye in this mirror in this house where College
had been brought up and educated, well educated, properly
educated: so it was that he caught himself frock-coated and in
the very act of his own education.

Later that evening, at dinner, he puzzled over the two
forks that lay beside each place and the napkin next to them.
He hadn't even noticed these things at noon. The men went
to the library afterwards; books lined the walls, floor to ceiling,
and Sebastian poured port from a crystal decanter. After dinner, Jonathan sought out what Helen had called the "bathroom." This turned out to have a magnificent porcelain water
closet in it with a pattern of roses and leaves. He tried it im-

mediately, but he'd never worked a flush mechanism before, and the abrupt torrent of water left him trembling. There was a bathtub with two large taps—hot and cold water both, he decided, bending down to study the lion's-paw feet underneath.

A gong at six the next morning announced breakfast. At eight Jonathan had a lesson in Helen's study. At four he had another. After the first day he added twenty words to his vocabulary cards each time he saw her. Back in his room he studied the cards, drew circles and loops on the writing pad and wrote out letters until his fingers refused to open or shut around the pen. He worked late into the night, and during the third month his head began to buzz from the inside as though he were drunk. He had not slept easily or well since his emancipation nearly seven years before, but now sleep often escaped him entirely. He seemed to float through a furious haze of words, words in formation, words in chaos, words brilliantly colored, words blackened. If he did manage sleep, he dreamed his tobacco-worm nightmare with such intensity that his hands tore at the delicate material of the sheets when he woke; so he tied his hands together—which made sleeping more difficult still. During the fourth month his back began to ache in ways it had never ached on the railroad or even at the Stoke homestead; his eyes smarted. He sat at his desk, picked up his reader, and found himself five minutes later staring through the window, out over fields, over the splashy colors of October foliage to a bank of pines and the tidal land beyond, where sometimes there was ocean and sometimes a sodden mud waste.

On the last night of November, a cold hard sleet forced its way down through the snow. He undressed and blew out the candle. In the dark someone took hold of his wrist.

He jerked his arm back. Heart pounding, he relit the candle and squinted into the corners of the room. It had been a gentle touch, more of a caress than a grasp, but he had no doubt that it was real. He got out of bed, searched under his desk, behind the chest of drawers, in the closet; he couldn't find even a small night animal sheltering from the weather. He leaned out the window. Nobody. Nothing. Only when the candle began to gutter did he get back into bed. He sat up the rest of the night, back firm against the wall behind him, staring into the dark until a grizzling, wintery gray moved in over the tidal land outside.

A few nights later as he lay under his embroidered coverlet watching, he felt the touch again, and this time, eyes open, searching the room, the window, the desk, the mirror, he knew there was nothing at all to be seen. He waited tensely for several nights more. When the third touch came it was lighter than before and accompanied by the sense—he swore to it in his diaries, though he thought it insane himself by the time he wrote about it—accompanied by the sense of a spectral presence. This presence—the word is his, not mine—had shape, form, mass, integrity, and yet there was nothing to be seen and after those first few nights, nothing to be felt. The next time, a week or so later, he could not say what told him the presence was there. It moved toward him and stood beside him, no more than a foot away from his bed. He coiled his body against attack. But the presence was already gone.

After that, it became a regular visitor. Jonathan never saw a shape, not even a shadow, never felt its touch again, nothing at all to give it the physical substance he felt in it. He found himself thinking of the locusts, how after they'd laid their eggs—after the sun had beat down for weeks and the ground was caked, cracked and brown—how the rain had come and how, on the morning after, a fine green haze had appeared over the whole landscape. He could almost smell the freshness inside him. But the locusts had rehatched. Devastation followed. His mood shifted up and down during the day, even during the hour. His ability to memorize seemed to jam somewhere. Then he was sick one night and, leaning over the beautiful toilet basin, felt the words he had fought so hard to cram into his head vomit out of him into that captive pool of water to be flushed away and lost forever.

29

ATLAS AND I didn't agree about what happened next. Oh, not the facts. It's the heart of the matter, the truth, you might call it. But who can trust Atlas? Doctors spend so much time playing God themselves that they make lousy witnesses when it comes to the heart of things. Atlas wasn't even a very good doctor; he told me himself that he had to pay ten thousand dollars for his license to practice in Washington because he failed the exam. "I'm a yard bird," he said, back from his emergency call. "If it's lying there, I'll pick it up. If not, to hell with it.

"People like Dad, people with backgrounds like that, slavery, violence of one kind or another," he went on, "these people usually have minds as brute-like as their pasts. Usually they're inarticulate, confused, slow to everything but blows. That's what's amazing about Dad. How could anybody so enraged accept a God? Or any other abstract concept?" My attempts to explain away Jonathan's conversion to Christianity annoyed Atlas. "Truth? Don't give me that crap. He didn't want truth. He wanted judgment: revenge. Just like you. What'd you major in philosophy for? A waste of time, if you ask me. You should have gone into law. You belong on the bench of the Inquisition—"

"Let's get back to Jonathan," I said, annoyed myself.

"Okay. Okay. Now, look, his conversion embarrasses you. Why? One way or another it was almost inevitable. Slavery destroys the soul. It's a narcotic: it does what narcotic addiction does, kills pride, subtlety, initiative—"

"Yes, yes," I said, still annoyed.

"So here's a guy who never had anything that belonged to him, no home, no mother, father sold him—a piece of human shit—not even his own socks. Think of him there in that goddamned place, doilies and fish forks and roses on the crapper—Christ almighty, how does a slave go about learning to live on equal terms with people like that? What right has he even to attempt such a thing? The effrontery—Jesus, the arrogance of it. That's what's marvelous. Not the dull detail of a conversion. Anyhow, he wants to do this impossible thing—more than that—he's *going* to do this impossible thing, and obviously he can't do it all on his own. So he finds himself a God to help him. It's as simple as that."

This is how it happened:

In the middle of one frozen February night Jonathan, my grandfather, woke abruptly. "Sleepest thou?" a voice said to him. "Couldest thou not watch one hour?"

Hearing these words come to him out of the darkness, he did not for one minute doubt that the voice he heard was the voice of Jesus Christ Himself.

30

IT WILL probably turn out in the end—when the cosmologists finish and the computers grind to a halt—that nobody can find a beginning for this disorder around us, for this universe that refuses to behave, simply because it has no beginning. We probably live inside some cosmic snake that has swallowed its tail, some tobacco worm that has eaten out its own insides just like Jonathan's nightmare. Not a nice thought. God is so much tidier. Things begin. Things end. There's peace of mind, an end to aimlessness, no need for tinsel and sham. Control is possible in such a life. So is meaning. Despite Atlas's interpretation, this is what lies behind my grandfather's enchantment with divinity. I'm sure of it. With God, he escaped the tobacco worms; he says so himself: with his conversion, his recurrent nightmare stopped.

His father? He had a heavenly father. He gave up searching for an earthly one. George? George was the routed enemy of his youth, now dead, now past. Within a year Jonathan read well. In three more years, he took and passed examinations in philosophy, mathematics and Greek; he became assistant to the Reverend Garson Walter Grayberg of Ellsworth, Maine. A difficult time.

The Reverend Grayberg was not anybody's image of an East Coast parson: short, irascible, coarse-textured: soup slopped on his shirtfront, gravy on his trousers. He shouted and wept when he preached; he stamped, thumped, shook his fists; he ranted on against the depraved elegance he saw around him—and managed to flatter it at the same time. To Jonathan he said, "Of course I ain't educated so fancy as you." And he said, "I learned me my trade on the hard side of life: what a kid like you don't know from fuck about." Jonathan prayed for Christian forbearance (a virtue God was stingy with in his case), and his heart sang when, at twenty-eight, he took examinations on *Wesley's Explanatory Notes and the Forty-four Sermons,* entered the Moody Bible Institute in Chicago and escaped.

Today's PR material for Moody shows dull eyes and foolishness in the faces of staff and students alike. And the courses they study! Hermeneutics and Homiletics, Techniques of Evangelism, Apologetics, Church History, Old and New Testaments, Principles of Discipleship: you can see the dull eyes grow duller as you read the list. But in Jonathan's day, God was still lively enough to give a fizz to the air. In the excitement of it all, he began to do a little writing of his own. He even wrote a few verses.

When he was thirty-two, the district synod granted him permission to set up a tabernacle in the wilderness on the south side of the Columbia River, not too far from Cathlamet, Washington. I find charm in this, that I sought truth at Columbia University while my grandfather sought it on the Columbia River. My father Rayner used to sing

> "Hail Columbia, happy land:
> Baby shit in papa's hand."

Surely this conjunction of Columbias means something.

With several other probationer ministers (a carpenter, a stonemason, a mathematician among them) my grandfather homesteaded fourteen acres there. They built a house for themselves. They built a chapel. They prayed, studied, farmed, exchanged techniques; they shared out among them the probationers' circuit on the other side of the river and four years later were ordained together in Portland, Oregon, by the laying on of hands. After that they returned to Cathlamet, and the only change they made in their lives was to wear black broadcloth and dog collars when they went for supplies on the other side of the Columbia. When my grandfather was thirty-six years old and only two months into his ordination—he'd never even administered the Sacraments—this part of his life came to an end. Ever afterwards, he referred to it with grim contempt as "the idyll."

A trip across the Columbia to Cathlamet, the standard trip except that he was alone this time: the grocer in Cathlamet (who wrapped the groceries in an old newspaper), the story (wrapped around his bacon, staring up at him): this is how it happened—the first word of George since he'd left him for dead beside the railroad tracks a lifetime ago. My grandfather saw the story—no more than an item—just as he took the last bite of the bread he was eating for his lunch. It was a misty mid-fall day. Almost before the meaning of the words registered on him, he felt the blood rush from his face. He stopped chewing and reread:

SEN. STOKE SPEAKS TO FARM WORKERS

There is reassurance for agrarian and urban workers from Senator George Stoke (Dem. Kan.) in a speech yesterday to the Farm Workers Union. Referring to next year's presidential election and the Republican fight for a gold standard, Sen. Stoke said, "Not even an Eastern banker can eat gold. He eats wheat and labor like everybody else. And for that he needs silver, just like you do. Join us. If you do, we'll win. This I swear to you."

Jonathan spat out his bread to keep himself from choking.

In a daze he cast off. In a daze he rowed his small boat back out into the river. He was lucky to make it almost to the south shore before the fog closed in. One moment he could see the trees lining the bank; the next moment they were gone and there was nothing but featureless gray on all sides of him. Even the tips of his oars disappeared into it. The river lapped at the wooden boat like the water of a pond, all points of reference gone. A log rushed past and disappeared into the murk without a trace. When Pilate said, "What is truth?," why didn't Jesus answer? Was it because He didn't know?

Jonathan had hardly been able to contain his excitement when he'd run across this question in the Bible, the first time in print, the first time since College had asked it that night in Lenssen. He'd been sitting at his desk in his pretty, pine-smelling study at Malloy's Landing, reading calmly, a man at ease with his God: and there it was: no warning, either. His heart raced; his hands trembled; and the intensity of his disappointment at Jesus's silence had been so great that he'd thrown his Bible into the corner of the room and broken its back. He stared into the gray mist of the present and sought for some sense of justice in things—some meaning—something—

Stoke is not all that uncommon a name. That was a dead man—boy—that he'd left by the side of the railroad tracks. He'd certainly looked dead. He didn't seem— Why weaken at that critical moment? Why fail to establish for certain that he was dead? Could he have been alive after all? Was it just carelessness? Is that why there had never been a WANTED poster? A clump of twigs swept past, this time going bow to stern; the boat had swung back to front since the log had gone by a few minutes before. Heaven is a concept for people who die young: if you live long enough you want no part of it. I need to be dead, Jonathan said. He tried to pray. He kneeled down, the boat swaying and rocking, and tried. But he could not. "Oh, You Bastard," he whispered urgently to the figure who had refused to answer Pilate about truth. He squinted into the gray that surrounded him, face tingling.

"Okay, goddamn you!" he shouted then. "You win this one! Hands down! Do you hear me? George?"

"Hallo! Hallo!" came the answering call from the shore beyond.

It's always the absurdity of things that gets you. Marching to your own execution, you slip on a banana peel and break your neck. Laughter surged through Jonathan, the man who never laughed.

"Hello! Hello! Call again! Hello!"

What difference does it make? he thought, pulling on the oars. You hear a cry and you row toward it, isn't that enough? Who are you to demand answers anyway? Of God or George—

But that night for the first time in thirteen years, for the first time since his conversion had supplied him with the clean borders of an orderly universe with orderly beginnings and endings, where a thing and its opposite stayed properly separated: for the first time he woke to find his hands plucking imaginary tobacco worms from the covers of the bed he lay in. He knew what the dream meant: he knew his God was dead and buried—the idyll over—and he was again as forsaken as he'd been that night so long ago when he'd tried to shoot himself outside Bowie Jack's in Cheyenne, as forsaken as Jesus in the Garden of Gethsemane.

PART 4

WEDNESDAY AFTERNOON AND EVENING: REARMAMENT

31

UNDERTAKERS MAKE regular calls on geriatricians like Atlas. I don't really know why; I wasn't allowed to accompany
him into the living room for his talk with them. Morticians:
what an inane word. I did meet them, though; Claire brought
them to Atlas's office when they first arrived: two plump young
men, very young men—painfully young—aglow with health
and money.

"Hi," they said.

"Are they old enough to be doing that sort of thing?" I
asked Atlas after the secret talk was over. It was midafter-
noon. Claire brought us tea, convinced that because I lived in
England I couldn't get through the afternoon without a tea
bag. She did not set the tray down graciously; I feared I was
in for a rough French dinner party to come. She made a second reference to seven being a difficult number around a table.

"I don't know," Atlas said. "All of them are young. They
look like they suck blood out of the corpses, don't they? There
aren't any old ones anymore. Maybe they eat the old ones."

"What do they want?"

"Business." And then he goes back to his father's religious passion as though the bridge from undertakers to epis-
temology were perfectly natural. Nobody can trust a man like
this. "Politics, music, drugs, mathematics, God," he says,
"what's the difference? They all come to the same thing in the
end. People think math is dull because they've never experi-

enced what hooks mathematicians. Get the generality, get the pattern right and it's like orgasm—like what happens when you inject heroin—like when Mozart gets just the right mix of keys."

The joke of it is that Atlas knew nothing about his father's loss of faith. Nor did my father—or any of Jonathan's other children. All assumed he was a profound believer throughout his life. Which is to say they didn't know him at all. My information comes direct from the diaries, and it fits. Without it, nothing that follows makes sense. Pulling out of Portland my grandfather felt only outrage. What right did God have to go and die on him like that? Who did He think He was anyway? A neighborhood dog? To be run down by the first dirty driver that comes along? Karl von Clausewitz says of an army that if it is a peacetime affair, inexperienced in battle, held together merely by the glue of service regulations, it may look impressive but "as with a glass too quickly cooled, a single crack breaks the whole mass." So it was with Jonathan's God. South on the California & Oregon, past the great cedars, past—who cares? Into California. Over the hills. Plot the route with care, negotiate it meticulously and even so— bang!—the world it is the old world yet and nothing he'd done meant anything at all. There was nothing he wanted from this world anymore or could ever see himself wanting. In San Francisco he booked a ticket on the Western Pacific to Salt Lake City, the route that ran through Mogul. But Mogul was no longer listed as a stop. It was a sign, he thought, wearily now, but then so was everything else. The train jostled its way across the desert until it met a westbound goods carrier on the single line of track that spanned this reach of the continent. The two trains faced each other cowcatcher to cowcatcher. Jonathan's crept forward, the other crept back, and so they inched into Mogul's station to pass one another on the siding there.

From the train window Mogul was as aggressively dead now as it had been aggressively alive before. It had been six-

teen years since College got himself impaled there on a thousand tons of stibnite, and sixteen years is an eternity in the
mayfly-like lives of those old boomtowns. No buildings remained, only skeletons, naked roof struts, half-collapsed walls,
sun-bleached clapboard. Rusty tin cans scattered here and
there, escapees from the heaps of rubbish cached between
buildings. The silence was absolute—everything shrouded in
the drab gray sand made from stibnite, quartz and the pul-
verized shells of creatures that had lived here millennia before
when the area was the bed of an inland sea. Those must have
been the great days, Jonathan thought, staring out. A heavy
damp hung in the air, not right for the place or the wintery
time of year.

When the conductor announced a delay to take on water,
Jonathan stepped down onto the rotting platform and into the
streets of the town he'd helped ferry out into the desert. No
trace of Olympia LeCleve's—not even a hollow shell. All that
wild scurrying, building, buying, selling—all for nothing. Only
a few sluggish mosquitoes remained, hatched in the strange
wet weather.

He thought of suicide—third time lucky, as the saying
goes—but laid the thought aside, carefully, gingerly, like the
family heirloom it was to become. He had to know about
George first. He'd never felt any guilt for killing George. He'd
thought about it from time to time during the idyll, but com-
mandments or not, it seemed to him, as it always had, an act
of war—and a victory at that, something worthy of a brass
band and a ticker-tape parade. Besides, not many wars are
fought without God. But sitting here in the barren street of
Mogul, he felt guilt enough to drown in. His victory over
George was as much sham as Mogul's victory over the desert.
He'd botched the foundation on which all of his adult life had
been built. Reparation must be made. And because it must,
he hints at an answer to the question of why he bothered coding his diaries. What he says is that his long-range plans make

it "probably a good idea" to use "some simple code." Apparently his whoring and the prudery of the times had little to do with it.

Malaria was common in America in those days. Cases appeared as far north as the Great Lakes. In the final accounting, so my books tell me, malaria will take the credit for killing off half of the entire human race. But it wouldn't have done Jonathan much good to have identified the mosquito that bit him now; by the time he was aware of her, she'd done her biting, he'd slapped her off and was making his way back to the train. It was cold when he got as far as the mountains, late November. The snows began, and because of them there was a week's delay in Salt Lake City. Over the Wasatch Range to— It hardly matters. Another week's delay. Then the Midwest Pacific out of Denver heading into Kansas. Despite the warmth of the train, he was cold. The car's potbellied stove poured out heat; he shivered while the rest of the passengers stripped off jackets. His hands, clutching his frock coat around him, seemed loathsome and remote. Hope and faith. What a joke. Maybe chickens crossing roads aren't funny, but hope and faith— That's enough to burst your sides.

An hour out of Denver, he was shaking with cold, lips and fingernails blue, teeth chattering. An hour later, the fever hit him, and he rode most of the way to Sweetbrier aware of very little. By the time he arrived he could hardly focus his eyes. Laboriously putting one foot down in front of the other, he worked his way along streets he didn't recognize until he found himself outside a store with buckets and brooms standing on display outside. He walked in.

A figure stood behind the counter. Jonathan maneuvered toward it.

"You ain't looking so good, Reverend," the figure said, its sharp little teeth showing in a smile and its hands rubbing together as Benbow Wikin's hands had rubbed together twenty years before.

Jonathan squinted at him. Could it be? The man's body zigzagged from side to side, legs left, pouter pigeon chest right, head left again. Could this be Benbow Wikin himself? Jonathan could not bring himself to care.

"New to town, ain't you?" The man cocked his head to the right, unbalancing his zigzag body, and Jonathan staggered. "Hey, you look lousy and that's official. You better—"

"Where does Mr. Finster live?"

"Stationmaster Finster?" Jonathan nodded. "Elm Street—big house—two blocks down. Turn left. Biggest house around. You can't miss—"

Jonathan walked out.

Later, he remembered leaning against the gatepost outside a big house and suddenly finding Bessie beside him—stiff petticoats, a smell of baking and a tea towel flung over one shoulder. A girl stood beside her, a fair-skinned girl, who flushed so intense a pink at his glance that he felt a catch in his chest. What he remembered most of all was the concern on her face as she ran toward him to break his fall.

32

THE GIRL appeared many times to Jonathan as the delirium took hold of him, but her features refused to resolve themselves. When he was a child he had whittled the hooks and joints from which Alvah made reins for the horse; he had carved the teeth for his own mouth. Later, living on the Columbia River, he had whittled for pleasure, carving out bowls and plates and even likenesses of his companions. So when he found he could not make out the girl's face, he began to whittle a nose and mouth for her himself—light, arched brows, long eyelashes, freckles across the cheeks and a pert nose. He cut and carved and sanded; he hugged the work to him when George appeared at the outskirts of his mind, where chaos and uncertainty ruled.

George appeared there often. Think only about the girl, Jonathan would cry to himself. What about her hair? Blond? No, too harsh. Strawberry blond, red-blond—rich, soft—and pulled away from her forehead. Such a forehead! He worked and worked on it, and when at last he was satisfied with this lovely creature he'd made, the concern he saw on her face moved him so deeply that he fainted. In one lucid moment he reached out a hand to her; she took it and stroked it. He knew that she thought the fever still held him so he said nothing.

"Jonathan? You hear me?" Bessie said to him at last.

He nodded weakly.

"I was terrible afraid you were going to die," Bessie said. "Could you handle a little broth?"

Jonathan pulled himself up a little "Who—?" he began.

Bessie's face widened into a smile. "Why, that's my Sarah. She's taken awful good care of you."

When Jonathan was well enough to get out of bed Bessie baked a whole ham for Sunday dinner; she basted it with sugar and fruit juice so that its fat turned black outside. During the meal Mr. Finster struggled to interest Jonathan in the new Janney coupler.

"A dazzling exemplar of man's inventive genius," Mr. Finster said. Mr. Finster was much as before, round and pleased, though his muttonchops were thinner and his hands trembled. "It employs, sir, the principle that lies behind the hooked fingers of the human hand."

"How does it work?" Jonathan tried to listen, but his glance kept straying to Sarah's face, to the set of her shoulders, to her hands as she used her knife and fork, and his mind kept wandering off to that first day at the railroad yard in Denver when College had talked about link-and-pin couplers in terms of love and marriage. Jonathan carved a piece of sugary black coating from the ham on his plate. Why did College's blood look black? Why does the color of light change things so? But his attention made an abrupt leap back to Sarah's hands—not hooked at all. Enfolded? Was there a word graceful enough?

After they'd eaten, Mr. Finster left to attend a train due in at the station. Jonathan went into the parlor with Bessie and Sarah, who sat in a wing chair in the far corner of the room and worked on a sampler.

"I knew you right away, Jonathan," Bessie said. "I looked out the window and I said to Sarah here, I said, 'That preacher out there, he carries himself like Jonathan.' And then when you tried to open the gate—"

Whenever Bessie paused Jonathan found himself straining to hear Sarah breathe.

"But I couldn't rightly believe it myself," Bessie went on. "My, my, you have grown handsome again, too, ain't you?" She surveyed Jonathan with pleasure. "But you still don't smile, do you? How'd you get to be a preacher? We been right worried about you for years."

"I was afraid you might have forgot me."

"Forget you? Never. You were such a sad little mite— and so spirited—Isn't anybody in town has forgotten our Jonathan." She reached out and patted his knee. "I'm going out to those dishes. No, Sarah, you stay setting there. You don't want to leave our guest all to himself, do you? Play him something. She plays as pretty as she looks, Jonathan."

He watched Sarah spread her skirt over the piano stool. Her heavy braid fell forward as she bent over the keys and the light wool of her bodice stretched taut across the curve of her spine. "Sarah," he said. "Will you—"

She turned to face him.

"Will you—?" he repeated. But his tongue seemed to get stuck in his embarrassed thoughts, so he gestured with his hands as he had years ago: Would she please take a walk with him?

It was very cold, near to Christmas. Everything Jonathan could see from the front path of the Finster house was new to him. There hadn't been any paved streets in Sweetbrier before. Even the trees were new; there'd not been a single tree in town when he was a boy, and yet the beech in Sarah's front yard had a trunk thicker than a man's waist. Fifteen years old at least, he thought, growing uneasy. They walked down the block.

"There's an awful lot you want to know, isn't there?" she said. He didn't have any idea what she was talking about. "It's difficult to know where to begin—"

"What about at the beginning?"

A crease appeared between her brows. "But—"

"Well then, what about now?" he said.

She took in her breath. "Right now," she said, "the whole Stoke family's in Washington." Jonathan's heart lurched sideways in his chest. "Old Mr. Shockton—he's the one with all the money—he's had a stroke, and they'll probably stay there until—"

"I don't want to hear about this," he interrupted angrily. "It's nothing to do with me."

Her startled look took him as much by surprise as his anger had taken her. "Isn't that what— I'm sorry, sir. I thought—"

"Why do you call me 'sir'? Do I seem so fearfully old to you?"

"Because— What should I call you? I'll call you anything you want."

They stood irresolute for a moment. He turned away from her, sighed irritably and turned back. "Forgive me," he said. "I talked a lot, didn't I?"

"People with fevers often do. You did say some things you must have had on your mind a long time. You talked special about George Stoke, a lot."

"I don't remember," he snapped, the anger slipping out of control again. She reached out to him, almost involuntarily, or so it seemed, touched his arm, and as quickly drew her hand back. Jonathan studied the smooth skin of her cheeks, pink from the cold air. What could he say to make sense to her, or to himself, either? But her expression, the concern in her eyes, and those gentle, protective movements—maybe sense had nothing to do with what was needed. It came to him then that what he needed was precisely what she was offering him. A gust of wind blew snowflakes into her hair, and because the day was so very cold, a second gust blew them away again. Why did the chicken cross the road? he thought suddenly. To defend? To attack?

"I've lost my faith, Sarah," he said.

She bent her head over the fur muff she carried. "Everybody has doubts. A preacher has to have them, too."

"Did I babble on about this as well?"

"It's not important. What's important is that you can't really help anybody if you're too sure—"

"I can't help anybody anyway."

They walked on in silence a moment. "Why not?" she said. "Is it blind faith you want? Like an ox?"

"Loaves, fishes, bodies disappearing from caves. How can anybody believe such stupid stuff? How could I have been taken in? I? Of all people? And for years? I don't trust anybody. I've never trusted anybody. If you believe it at all, you believe it like an ox."

"I believe it."

"Well, good for you. How old are you?"

"I'm twenty in January," she said. "I doubt things, you see, things I shouldn't doubt—"

"You'll grow out of it." She didn't know whether he meant

the faith or the doubts. "You look younger than twenty," he said then. "Twenty's a good age. I liked being twenty." They were walking in the old area of town, the area that had been all of Sweetbrier when he was a child. He stopped suddenly, pointed to a small building with a picket fence in front of it, and the childlike delight that sometimes came to him, came to him now, taking her as much by surprise as his anger had only moments before. "Look, Sarah," he said, "that's the old Sook Faris house."

"They still live there."

"Do they? Really? Is that Nannie Gander's? It is, isn't it? I wanted to ask you before: Benbow Wikin still owns the grocery store, doesn't he? I did see him, didn't I?"

Sarah laughed. "Of course you did. Lots of things are the same. Are you always so changeable?"

"I never change," Jonathan said, humoring her—which she saw and which caught at her heart so painfully that she could not answer him. "Other things change," he went on. "I remain the same."

The snow picked up; it began to grow dark. They turned back toward the house, and by the time they could see the lighted windows ahead of them, it was too dark for them to see each other, too dark even to make out the road beneath their feet.

"How pretty you are under that crepe bow," he said.

She laughed. "You can't see me now—or anything else."

Out of the dark his voice said, "You're wrong, you know. It's an especially fetching hat. I can see you perfectly beneath it."

She laughed once more, fuller this time and with a gaiety he hadn't sensed in her before. "Then my hat's a proof of your faith, Reverend. You can see for yourself it's never left you at all. You can find faith if you only look for it—hats, anything at all, little things same as big."

33

THE WEDDING took place in mid-February in the Methodist church in town. Sarah wore Bessie's wedding dress with French lace on it, and tears rolled down Mr. Finster's cheeks as he gave her away. Jonathan hardly heard the ceremony; his ears rang and his heart knocked at his ribs. Benbow Wikin himself supplied the feast that followed. That night in a sagging double bed of the best room in the only hotel in Sweetbrier, Jonathan was so terrified of hurting Sarah and she was so terrified of she knew not what that they didn't even touch hands. They left town the next morning on the first leg of the trip to the Pacific Northwest, where he had got the Methodists to assign him a circuit: the lie was to be institutionalized.

It all came down to money and sex. What doesn't? The Finsters had listened respectfully to him but Bessie, always practical, ended up with, "Well, Jonathan, if you give up preaching, how are you going to support a wife? You need money for a farm." Sarah said, "We're going west. You can start again. Your faith will come back. Just wait and see. Think about my hat." But it was the curve of her back and the way her hair hung in the braid that convinced him. If preaching was what it took to get them, then preaching was what he'd do.

Before the wedding, he hired a horse and rode out through the frozen landscape to the old Stoke homestead. Nothing remained of it; it had disappeared as surely as Mogul had and even more thoroughly. Acres of cornland—dark, tilled

earth showing in scrubby patches through a largely evaporated
layer of snow—stretched from horizon to horizon: not even
the slightest change in the contour of the land indicated where
all those passions had taken place. Jonathan spent hours with
Benbow Wikin. It was in fact from Benbow that he bought
that first horsehide-bound volume, a ledger rather than a di-
ary, that sits on my desk this very day; he made up the code
(a simple rearrangement of the alphabet) as he made the purchase itself, and with the information Benbow gave him, he
wrote in the first entries about the Stokes and about himself.
"Wify and Alvah got the fever," Benbow told him. "Dead
within a week of each other. Alyoshus sold up. Went west.
Cathern married Garley Ashton. Remember him? Skinny kid.
Bookkeeper. They went west, too. Out California way—"

"Red pigtails and all?" Jonathan asked.

"Red pigtails and all," Benbow said.

Jonathan and Sarah hardly spoke to each other on their
honeymoon trip to Washington State. She stared out the window of the train as though she were afraid to look at him. At
night she slept perched on the far edge of the bed while he
held himself rigid on the opposite side. Like the old fairy tale
about the man who experienced fear only in love despite all
the terrors that had preceded it, Jonathan was afraid now—
afraid of her fear and even more afraid of the intensity of his
own feelings. He'd survived slavery. He'd survived friendship
and its betrayal by death. He'd survived George dead and
George alive again. He'd survived God, education and malaria. But this? Already—because of her—he'd committed
himself to the life of an impostor, which is to say that already—because of her—he'd given up a crucial part of his
search for whatever bedrock it is that he and I share a passion
for: truth or meaning or first causes: it doesn't matter what
you call it. Already, though he didn't know it himself, didn't
even suspect it, already an element of him hated her for these
things and for the mortal weakness of the flank she'd exposed

in him. By the time they arrived in Seattle, both of them were exhausted.

Seattle's Western Star Hotel gave them a double room that looked out to sea; they fell asleep that night because they were too tired not to. About midnight Jonathan woke abruptly to find his hands plucking at the quilt. He sat upright in the moonlight and Sarah threw her arms around him.

"It's all right, Johnny," she said. "You're awake now—you're all right." He dropped his head on her shoulder and let out his breath. "Can you tell me about it?" He shook his head. "You have this same dream often, don't you? I want to hear. Please tell me."

What happened then? Well, talk about an egg's way of producing another egg! This wholly ruthless, madly comic act: this is how our genes go about producing genes: we're no more than DNA's way of producing another string of DNA: an instinct in us as blind as the migrations of a locust or the metamorphosis of a tobacco worm—the joke heightened by an illusion of control as idiotic as the humping itself. What difference does it make whether such stuff is carried out in the marital bed or in the whorehouse? But then how would I know? It's not seemly for a cripple to dabble in sex. I do know he didn't tell her about the dream, though. The diaries are clear: he and I are the only ones who know about that. And I know that a man with looks like his can get a woman to do what he wants without her being aware of her own resistance. Even in the depths of his illness, the anger had flickered at the edges of his face like a will-o'-the-wisp in the marshes; she'd watched it, fascinated, and legend has it that people who follow the will-o'-the-wisp lose their souls. Jonathan himself in his diaries, in one of those flashes of humor, half mordant, half charming, that punctuate what you keep assuming is an unrelieved darkness of temperament: in one of those flashes he reports that he quoted to her from their marriage ceremony, saying, voice grave, demeanor profound, that "a man shall cleave unto his wife: and they shall be as one flesh."

At this, he says, she frowned, trying to understand. "This cleaving: you learned about it"—her earnestness was absolute—"when you were studying how to preach?"

He dared not risk an answer. "All right?" he said.

She nodded quickly, eyes on his eyes while he unbuttoned her gown. "I don't think I agreed to anything like this," she said. "Nobody told me—" She broke off to study the movement of his hands.

Toward morning, an hour or so before dawn, he awoke again to find her staring down at him. He could see the outline of her face in the moonlight that came through the window, but he could not make out her expression.

"Johnny"—she drew herself up into a kneeling position beside him—"this cleaving: I'm not sure I've got it right. While it's still dark, can you show me again?"

So it was that she exposed in him a second flank. And it doesn't take a student of military tactics to know that an army with two flanks exposed is going to have a rough time on the field.

Two weeks later, despite the bitter March weather, they rode by buggy to Hannaville, where the Methodists had arranged temporary living quarters for them—a room, so they understood, in the house of somebody by the name of Mrs. Chawder. The trip took three hours; Sarah talked all the way and he listened to the cadences of her voice—its stops and starts and sudden enthusiasms—trying in vain to rearm himself against her.

"Oh, Johnny, I'll make the most beautiful house for you to live in—curtains, I'll make the curtains myself—I know how—blue curtains with tassels and a draw-line—and a pelmet!"

"What's a pelmet?" he said. But his mind was on the arch of her neck and the flecked-hazel color of her eyes.

"It's a thing that goes—didn't you ever have curtains, Johnny? Of course you didn't. I'll teach you all about it. Oh, we must have curtains—the pelmet goes on top—and carpets and wallpaper, and a piano, too—and a potted Christmas cactus . . ."

When they reached Hannaville the cedar trees that encircled the town were hung with ice and snow; they glistened in the winter sunlight.

"Um," Sarah said, looking around her. "Just the place for blue curtains and a pelmet."

34

MRS. CHAWDER'S FACE was papery yellow. Her head wobbled on a scrawny neck that jutted out from her shoulders, and her braids, piled into a crown, had slipped down over one ear. She sighed, shivering under a heavy stole and leaning on the doorknob as she peered out at Jonathan and Sarah.

"You're the preacher?" she said.

"Yes, and this is my—"

"Where you been? We been holding up the wedding for two weeks now—how soon can you do it? Tomorrow?"

"What wedding?" he said. "Look, it's very cold—"

"People get married wintertime same as summer."

"Hadn't we better come inside and talk about it?"

Mrs. Chawder turned away, and the jerky, dismissive shift of her body brought to his mind the jerking of a train about to stop. "We ain't got no time to lose, Preacher." They stood in a small one-room area, the whole of the downstairs, half kitchen, half living room, partially warmed by a potbellied stove.

"May we sit down, Mrs. Chawder?" Jonathan said. "I understand—"

"You don't understand nothing," she said. "Can you do it tomorrow? You got all the right papers? You know how to do a wedding, don't you?"

"Well, I've never done one before—" Jonathan began.

"Oh, Jesus!" Mrs. Chawder leaned her body against the wall and buried her head in the crook of her elbow. "Lord God! What am I going to do?"

"Who's the bride, Mrs. Chawder?" Sarah said. "Is it your daughter?" Mrs. Chawder nodded. "What's her name?"

"Carma."

"Carma?" Jonathan said, "I knew somebody named that once before."

"God be merciful. Who cares who you knew?" Mrs. Chawder kept her head averted.

"I do," Sarah said brightly. "You never said anything about a Carma to me before, Johnny."

"She was just a little girl— Four little girls, and they had this glorious string of names: Cassa, Carma, Levada and Lynn—"

"How do you know my girls?" Mrs. Chawder swung her head around to face him.

Jonathan half rose out of his chair. "Do you remember a runaway named Johnny? I rode out to Denver with a woman named Eliza Gowdy—four little girls—a little boy, too—years and years ago—"

Mrs. Chawder's eyes narrowed. "I done you a favor, eh?"

"So you're Eliza Gowdy. After all these years—"

"So you owe me, don't you?"

"Yes," Jonathan said. "Yes, I owe you. I certainly do."

"Then do this wedding. Tomorrow. Before— Just do it.

I ain't got much time." She eased herself down into a straight chair. "I got to get Carma settled before— I'm a sick woman, Preacher. I ain't got long to live. You'll do it, won't you? Tomorrow?"

Jonathan studied her a moment. "I gather," he said as delicately as he could, "that the—uh—groom doesn't know."

"Course he knows. You can't marry off a woman 'less of which the groom knows he's marrying her. What's the matter with your head, Preacher?"

"What I'm saying, Mrs. Chawder," he said, struggling now for patience instead of delicacy, "is that I gather he doesn't know about her condition."

Eliza's face froze. "What condition?"

"When is the baby due, ma'am?"

Eliza stared at him a moment, then laughed—a thin, high sound that she cut off by slapping one hand across her own mouth. "Ain't nothing like that," she said. "My Carma's a good girl. Carma! Carma! You come on in here. Preacher's here. Wedding's tomorrow. Carma!"

Carma's hair was like her mother's had been, like Eliza Gowdy's of years and years ago on the Midwest Pacific from Kansas to Denver. It was gathered at the base of her neck in a large bun—a luxury of hair, thick, blond—and her only appealing trait. She was large-boned with huge hands and heavy features.

"Won't you sit down, Carma?" Sarah said. Carma shook her head and remained standing.

The silence began to grow oppressive. "Do you want to get married tomorrow, Carma?" Jonathan said at last.

Carma said nothing.

"She must speak for herself, Mrs. Chawder," he said.

"What for?" Eliza said. "What kind of question is that? I can see you ain't done weddings before. She's scary, that's all. She ain't met the man but once yet."

"Then how can she—?" he began.

"Now you look here, boy," Eliza said, "we ain't rich folks up here. A woman marries or goes whoring—ain't nothing else. Answered the ad in the paper, didn't she? This old man got a farm west of here and he needs a woman on it. Carma needs a husband. Tomorrow she gets one. Leastways, she does if you can learn how to do a wedding between now and then."

Jonathan spread his hands, palm up, and shook his head.

"You ain't got no right to judge us, boy."

"Carma"—Jonathan turned aside and addressed himself to her alone—"I want to know what you want. I won't conduct a wedding unless you want me to."

Carma dropped abruptly to her knees in front of him. "Oh, yes," she said, "I do— I—" Tears rolled down her face. "I got to— I mean, all the others is married—Cassa and Levada and Lynn. There's only me. And if something happens— We ain't got no money. None at all— Oh, I do. I do. I do."

Jonathan explained that she didn't really know the man, that there would be other opportunities; Carma grabbed at his hands and wept over them. The wedding was set for four o'clock the following afternoon.

There were eight families living in Hannaville; all of them pitched in to help. Eliza herself made coffee from dried carrots. Jonathan fetched the sheet from the bed he and Sarah had slept on the night before; under Eliza's direction he hung it in one corner of the downstairs room and placed a bench so the engaged couple could sit behind it until the right moment. At a quarter to four he went upstairs to dress. When he came down again, he found the eight families and their baskets of food squeezed onto a couple of makeshift pews: men, women, children, all piled atop one another, basket atop child atop adult lap. Carma's feet and the feet and the knees of Elias Johannsen, the groom, poked out from beneath the sheet. The eight families sang "Here comes the bride." Carma timidly lifted the sheet aside. Elias turned out to be a man of about seventy, bent and gray but a tough object still, and Jonathan,

moved despite himself, performed for the first time the ceremony that seemed to him—three weeks into his own marriage—the most sacred and the most terrifying of all the
ceremonies in the world.

When he had spoken the final words, the newlyweds went
out to Elias's wagon only to find that his horse had dropped a
shoe. They would have to wait until the following morning to
leave. Over Eliza's protests, Jonathan offered them his and
Sarah's tiny upstairs room for the night. There was a feast of
fried pork and plum sauce; the party lasted into the evening.
At ten the newlyweds retired upstairs. Jonathan and Sarah
made up a bed for themselves on the downstairs floor. But just
as they were wrapping themselves around each other in front
of the potbellied stove, Elias Johannsen's voice echoed
throughout the house.

"Gawddamn! You filthy— Jesus Christ! Hey, Preacher!
You get your ass up here! Get away from me, filth! Go! Scat!
Preacher!"

Jonathan leapt up from his bedclothes. Elias stood at the
doorway to his tiny room, red flannel nightgown over thin
calves, face purple in the light of the oil lamp. Carma lay
crumpled into the narrow alleyway between the bed and the
wall opposite the door, her beautiful long hair hanging loose
down over her gown.

"You can't stuff this kind of shit down my throat," Elias
screeched at him. "Think I'm a goddamned old fool, don't
you? Playing a trick like that— Well, I tell you, I ain't taking
this! I sure as hell—"

Jonathan squeezed past him and into the room. He knelt
beside Carma, who was moaning softly. "Are you all right,
Carma? What's the matter?" She rocked herself a little to one
side and then the other, still moaning, but she said nothing
and she didn't look up.

"Don't you pretend you ain't a party to this, you bastard!" Elias shouted. "The whole goddamned town—"

Jonathan wheeled on him. "Shut up and sit down!" he said. "I have no idea what the trouble is. But I certainly mean to find out."

Elias studied him a moment, then laughed. "New, ain't you? I forgot. They told me that." He laughed again. "So they took you in, too, eh? Just let me show you something. You just set yourself right here—over here—by the door a minute, eh?" Jonathan got to his feet warily. Carma pulled herself toward the corner. "I ain't gonna hurt nobody," Elias said, "just gonna show you— Come on, Preacher. You gotta let a man have his say, ain't you?"

Puzzled, Jonathan changed places in the tight space. While he was still off balance, Elias lifted Carma off the floor and threw her on the bed. Jonathan made a wild grab at him and caught hold of the sleeve of his nightgown.

"Let go, Preacher! I can't show you nothing less of which you let go."

Carma lay on her stomach with her face toward Jonathan. Her lips moved but no sound came. He bent nearer. "I always knew—" She broke off, her eyes shut tight.

"See? Even she knows, poor godforsaken beast. Only body what don't know is you. So take a step back, man. Go on. Go." Jonathan stepped back. "Turn over, girl!" She rolled over on her back and Elias threw her nightgown up above her waist, revealing heavy legs and narrow hips. He prised the legs apart. "Now take a squint there, Preacher," Elias shouted. "Enough to make a man puke, ain't it?"

From between Carma's legs, embedded in her labia, protruded a small, partially erect penis.

"There's a ladyhole back in there somewheres," Elias said indignantly, "but it ain't rightly big enough to stick a thumb in. There's even a couple of wee-bit balls." He turned his furious face to Jonathan. "Jesus Christ, the only thing what's right in this mess is the asshole."

Jonathan reached out and drew the gown down to cover

Carma. "Wait a minute," he said. "Just wait a minute. Let's think this through—"

"I been cheated—bamboozled—load of shit sold as woman. Ain't nobody gonna—"

Before he was even aware of the thought, Jonathan struck out open-handed and caught Elias full in the face. "Well, let's have a look under your gown, old man." Jonathan's voice was soft as it always was when he was angry, but there was no mistaking the menace in it. "Let's see what you got under there that's been cheated so bad." He pulled the red flannel gown up to Elias's neck; elongated, flaccid genitals sagged down between bowed thighs. "Does that thing work? Can it do anything but piss? Doesn't look like much of a tool to me. Come on. Show me. Make it work. Get it up."

"Well, it don't rightly go *up* no more," Elias said, staring down at his naked body.

"So what were you going to do with this young woman, huh? Tell me that. What excitements did you have in mind for her?"

Elias glanced down again. "I'm cold," he said.

Jonathan let the gown fall back. He sat on the bed beside Carma; the mattress squeaked as she rocked to and fro beside him.

"Now you look here, Elias," Jonathan said, inhaling carefully. "You're a farmer, and first of all a farmer needs a woman for milking. Isn't that right?"

"She ain't a woman!"

"Carma, can you milk? Carma? Answer me." A moaned assent issued from her. "So, Elias, she can milk. Can you keep chickens, Carma? Yes? You want her to keep chickens, Elias? She can do that. Can you cook? Yes? She cooks, too. You want her to keep house and do the weeding? She can do all those things."

"No! No! I want me a woman! I been cheated! I been—"

"Don't talk to me about cheating, you old fraud." Jonathan's eyes glittered. His voice was so soft now that Carma had to stop her rocking to hear. "There's no way you can say you've been cheated of anything you could rightly make use of. Where's your common sense, man? Carma needs a home and you need somebody to do the woman's work—"

"I'll be a laughingstock! Joke of the—"

"For the love of God, think, Elias, think. A hundred miles west, nobody's going to know about her. Nobody. She'll keep you warm in your bed at night. She won't mock you for not giving her children. You'll know for sure she won't be running around behind your back. If you don't ask her for what she can't give—and she doesn't ask you for what you can't give—you've got everything you came to Hannaville for. What more do you want?"

Elias shook his head. "They flimflammed me."

"And you flimflammed them."

Outside, the wind blew. The panes in the casement window shuddered, and the room was cold enough for frost to form on the inside of the glass. Elias stared out into the dark for a moment; then he searched Jonathan's face, sighed heavily and lowered himself on the bed. "She got right pretty hair," he said, reaching out a hand. She shrank away from him and his shoulders slumped. "Ain't there no limits nowhere, Preacher?" he said.

Early the next morning Carma and Elias left Hannaville; he took her elbow to help her into the wagon and the whole town saw it. They'd heard voices in the night, too, and by evening they knew every word that had been spoken in the tiny room. Within a year, by which time Sarah was heavily pregnant, Jonathan's reputation had spread for miles. You could talk to him, they said. He might hit you in the face but at least he wouldn't go tossing the Bible at you and he always spoke so beautifully and in such a gentle voice. What these things showed for sure, they said, was that he was one of the few preachers anywhere who was a true representative of God on earth.

35

JONATHAN WAS NOT an experienced man in the way we think of experience. There had been Fritzi and a few other whores while he was on the railroads (not so many as there would have been if College hadn't died), but the thirteen years of his "idyll" were years of celibacy. He was thirty-six when he met Sarah. For most of us the intensities that come with first love are well in the past by that time, something that happens at sixteen, seventeen—even younger. What you feel then is so powerful that it lays waste everything around it and, even in the midst of your transports, you come to realize that if you're going to survive you'll have to do without feelings like it. So you grow up a little. You lose your intensity. You learn to manage with dignity but with a more shadowy product altogether. In such matters Jonathan was an innocent. His emotions had lain in wait for years: the cork hits the ceiling and the captive passions bubble out all over the place, splashing on feet, floor, furniture; there's the wild laughter and the scramble for glasses; the wine goes on spilling out over everything. But Jonathan was a person who valued his control above all. Each new rapture brought with it a hangover of bile and self-hatred. He looked into Sarah's eyes and forgot where he was as all lovers do, but instead of enjoying it he feared he was going mad. He thought of the timber wolf whose cock swells after copulation so that he and the bitch are stuck together in nature's ferocious anxiety to insure the purity of the genes, both of them whimpering helplessly, at the mercy of the elements and of any enemy that might happen by.

Because it was his profession—because it was the only way he could pay for the woman who aroused in him all these conflicts (and also because it gave him another of those pleasures he so much despised)—he held prayer meetings in houses and schools. He rode horseback from town to town through the great cedar forests of the Northwest; he married, baptized, preached, buried and rode back to Sarah, held her in his arms in bed and railed against himself over the lies he told with every breath he took.

But this wasn't the sum of it. Nobody could cross the gulf of a past like his. Over everything, around everything, through everything—even Sarah's warm, eager body—lay the battlefield symbolized by the newly come-to-life George. Jonathan's mind prowled along old roads inch by inch, reeling at the stench, the never-to-be-staunched wounds, the injustices too great to be righted. There were skirmishes at outposts that made no sense to anybody, even to him: feints, parades, half and quarter thrusts, ineffectual, meaningless. A battle, says Clausewitz, resembles "a slow disturbance of equilibrium which commences almost imperceptibly and then with every moment becomes stronger and more visible." Jonathan's life after the idyll was like this. He saw himself again as Christ in the Garden of Gethsemane, alone, friendless, awaiting crucifixion. One night, looking down at Sarah (her head was turned away from him and the moonlight lit up the curve of her cheek on the pillow), he said to her very softly, " 'Sleepest thou? Couldest thou not watch one hour?' "

She opened her eyes at once. "Of course I'm awake," she said. She turned toward him and reached out to stroke his neck. "I never go to sleep before you, Johnny. I can't somehow."

They stayed on in Eliza's tiny upstairs room. There wasn't enough money to build a house and anyway, Jonathan was afraid for Sarah to be alone while she was pregnant. Eliza, somewhat to her own annoyance, didn't worsen and die as she had so often predicted. In fact, with Carma's future settled, she began to gain a little weight and something of the energy Jonathan remembered from years before.

"Call me Mother," she said to him one day.

"I don't think that's a very good idea," he said.

"You wouldn't know a good idea if it stood up and slapped your face, Preacher. You do as I say."

"Whatever happened to your baby? The little boy—what was his name? Netty? What happened to him?"

"Went west."

"You can't go west from here," he said irritably. "This is west."

"That's what I told him. 'I'm going west,' he said. Ain't seen him since. You call me Mother."

Jonathan planned to be in Hannaville for the birth itself; he'd arranged for Dr. Mundt, who lived in Walla Walla and charged five dollars a visit, to attend. Eliza disapproved. "Birthing ain't got nothing to do with men," she said. But Jonathan's word was law. Besides, he liked Burgess Mundt, a thin, stooped young man, and the only educated company for miles around. Burgess had taken a degree in philosophy before going into medical school, and he'd taken it at a time when philosophy departments still concerned themselves with the big questions, with God, free will, the meanings of things.

"What we need is a science of truth," Burgess said one afternoon over a Sunday dinner that Eliza had prepared. Eliza added strange things to her roasts—herbs and preserves that she'd potted herself. "We need some way of dividing things up so we can make sense of them—cast off some of the veils that cloud the issue, analyze them somehow. Everybody disagrees with everybody else. Why isn't there some sort of consensus? There is in medicine. Why not philosophy?" Burgess had a long upper lip and a small, round nose; he'd come west for the sea air, but he coughed even so and there were days when he confined himself to bed with poultices on his chest.

"You agree with all other doctors, do you?" Jonathan said, his sarcasm as thick as Eliza's plum jam.

"Of course I don't. Some of them are nuts. Vaccination, for example: what an absurd idea!"

"You can't analyze God, can you? Or truth?"

"Well, I don't—"

"Then all you've got left is words," Jonathan said.

Burgess sat quiet for a while. "Just because I don't know how, doesn't mean it isn't worth trying. It just doesn't add up, Johnny."

"What doesn't?"

"Life."

"Why should it?"

Burgess would have been fascinated with the pickings through higher grammar that Columbia forced down my throat in the name of philosophy; he was plainly ahead of his time. So was Jonathan, who got to the essence of Columbia's agenda without even trying. Certainly from what he reports of this conversation, I think he would have reacted to linguistic philosophy much as I did. I was stunningly bad at it. I don't mean that I got bad grades. I didn't. I made the dean's list every term. "I see your name on the dean's list," said one of my professors, a young one, one interested in the philosophy of science, where there are real excitements, rather than in the science of philosophy, which strangles all questions it can't answer as ruthlessly as farmwives strangle stray kittens. He was a very funny man, this young professor, much loved by his students for his parodies of what Columbia's philosophers spent their time on; in the end, the department fired him. "No," he said, correcting himself, "I can't quite say that. I didn't actually see your *name* on the list: I saw the letters that make up your name—"

"There must be something solid in all the transience," said Burgess, "something to hang on to."

"How can you drivel on like this?" Jonathan said. "The pieces don't add up because adding up isn't part of the plan."

"There *is* something we can get at, something we can tie down—"

"Why?"

"Because I can feel it. *You* can feel it."

"I feel nothing."

Within the past year Senator George Stoke of Kansas, known now to an entire nation as the "fighting liberal," had launched a campaign against what he called "America's lack of community." Support for him grew every day. He attacked everything from potholes in the road and nonexistent street lighting to graft and corruption in the Senate itself, and he used all the graft and corruption available to him (which was considerable) to push through the legislation he wanted pushed through. The reports made Jonathan's hands shake: he knew that what George stood for was right. These were policies he believed in himself, policies he spoke for in his sermons, policies he would have fought for on a wider stage if he'd had the power to fight for them there—if he'd been in George's place. How can such a thing be? It caused a rebellion inside him, a state of civil war within his own soul, which in turn caused a serious loss of morale in the already weakened troops massed against George. As everybody knows, civil wars are the bloodiest, the most vicious; victory is never enough: such wars don't stop until everything lies in ruins.

"Come on, Johnny, what have you got to lose?" Burgess was saying. "What's wrong with peeling off a few layers— looking for something to analyze? Maybe we'll run across some avenue into the meaning of things. Why not?"

"The universe affronts me," Jonathan said. "I do not accept it—or its meanings."

Sarah's pains began in the middle of her eighth month. Burgess was no more than two hundred yards away, attending the farrier, whose broken leg refused to mend. Sarah was peeling potatoes. She screamed when the first contraction hit her and dropped the bowl. Jonathan came running to find her crouched among shards and vegetables, eyes white all around the flecked-hazel iris, mouth agape with terror; Eliza was on her knees, stroking Sarah's back and crooning softly. "Get her upstairs," she said to him.

He carried Sarah up the first few steps, murmuring reassurances he didn't feel just as, long ago, he'd murmured assurances he didn't feel to College when College lay dying. The second contraction caught her as they reached the tiny landing; she screamed again and clutched at him so fiercely that they almost fell down the stairs together. She screamed a third time as he settled her down on the quilt.

"You're going to need Cheeba, Johnny," Eliza said. "I'm telling you true, this ain't no job for a man."

But he was already running to fetch Burgess, who picked his way along the muddy street in patent leather shoes, took off his coat, rolled up his sleeves and disappeared upstairs.

Jonathan had watched animals being born—many times. He and Alvah Stoke had both been up to their elbows in a cow, both of them covered in blood, each grappling a leg of a breech-presenting calf, and all the while the cow chewed her cud as though bored by the whole procedure—not like this. The screaming went on intermittently all afternoon and all night, punctuated by Burgess's cough. Eliza fetched water from the pump and boiled it on the potbellied stove; she fetched towel after towel, running to borrow from one neighbor after another. Jonathan watched her carry these things up the stairs; he watched her bring bowlsful of knotted linen down again, bright with blood. But she barred his way to the room. "I already got one man in that room mucking things up," she said. "I ain't having another."

And the truth of the matter was, he didn't really want to see. Instead, he raged back and forth across the small downstairs room, hands slimy with sweat, mouth dry. He raged against the straight-back chairs in his path, against the knick-knacks on the shelf above the stove, against the windows that rattled at his angry steps, against sex, against Sarah for putting him through this, against the God in whom he no longer believed.

Before morning Burgess appeared and eased himself into a chair opposite Jonathan.

"I'm sorry, Johnny," he said, "I'm really—I'll try to save the baby"—he shook his head—"but I don't think—"

"To hell with the baby," Jonathan said. "I want my wife."

"All we've got left is prayer."

Jonathan turned away and stared out at the frozen landscape. "What kind of sanctimonious crap is that?" he said. "Where's the man of science you keep telling me about? You save my wife, dammit— What do you want, Mother?" He swung around to face Eliza as she came through the door. "Or have you just come to watch the effect of the news on the sorrowing husband?"

Eliza looked him up and down. "You're a fool, boy," she said. "I told you before and I'm telling this here man doctor, too. You got to get Cheeba."

Burgess shook his head. "Let her die in Christian hands, Mrs. Chawder. There's nothing anybody can do."

Eliza didn't even look at him. "Take potatoes. She'll follow you for potatoes. Go, Johnny. Now."

Jonathan's circuit took him to the Indian reservation five miles to the south. He'd preached in the potlatch house there only once. Almost as soon as he began the sermon he realized that his audience, hidden away on their platforms behind their family totems, watched him with sullen eyes and watched him only because he brought food. Thereafter, he visited as his circuit required, but he didn't preach; he brought food, sharpened tools, helped mend anything that seemed to need mending. He was good with his hands. The Indians hadn't grown friendly.

He grabbed a twenty-pound sack of potatoes from the kitchen store and went.

On the return trip, the Indian woman Cheeba clung to

his back. Her smell of grease and rancid sweat nauseated him even in the open air, and the dark, worn hands—broken fingernails hooked over his vest—filled him with dread. By the time he arrived with her—less than an hour—Sarah's screams had stopped. He ran up the stairs behind Cheeba, who dropped to her knees beside the bed as he entered the room and laid her greased, black-haired head on Sarah's breast. Sarah's face was gray. Eliza stood in front of the window, blocking out the light, holding what looked to Jonathan like a bundle of laundry in her arms.

"How long she been like this? Still bleeding?" Cheeba said, not looking up.

"No bleeding now, but bad from the start of things," Eliza told her as she rocked the bundle, which squeaked out a cry. Jonathan looked at it with a wrenching love so tangled that the love itself seemed to him a deadly instrument, something to be feared just as the coupling that had resulted in this hell was to be feared hereafter—and what an evil thing it was, all that gasping, slippery ecstasy, that had made of Sarah's body an instrument of torture and self-destruction. But he hadn't known. He hadn't understood. For ignorance, there is forgiveness. The baby, though: the baby was different. He'd denied the baby to Burgess as surely as Peter had denied Jesus to the maid of the high priest. For this there could be no forgiveness.

"Will it live?" he whispered to Eliza.

She nodded.

Sarah swung her head restlessly from side to side on the pillow. "Now look away, Preacher," Cheeba said. She took one of Sarah's breasts in both hands and twisted it with all the strength in her muscular arms and fingers. Sarah lifted out of the bed and screamed, her eyes opening wide. Jonathan reeled back and found himself in Burgess's arms. Cheeba twisted again. The scream was louder this time, fuller.

"Jesus!" Burgess whispered.

The Indian woman sat back on her haunches and

watched. Sarah panted and gasped. Deep red weals emerged on the skin of her bare breast.

"Want water?" Cheeba said. "You get water." She turned to Jonathan. "Lots of water—with little salt in it and little bit sugar."

Jonathan ran downstairs, filled the pitcher and ran back up. Sarah's face already showed the beginnings of color. The Indian woman took water in the palm of her hand and pressed it into Sarah's mouth. The color grew. Sarah lay silent but she was breathing firmly; Jonathan kept his eyes on the barbaric figure of her savior, on the multicolored dress, the ragged braids, the rough hands and broken nails, the beads of bear teeth and the glittering stones. Her rancid smell filled the room, and the color was full in Sarah's face.

"Thank God," Jonathan sighed to himself, hardly aware of the words he spoke and wholly oblivious of their absurdity.

36

"YOU UNDERSTAND, this wasn't magic or anything," Atlas said. He poured some of the whiskey he'd bought at the supermarket earlier into the cold dregs of tea that remained in front of us, just as he'd poured gin and brandy into his morning coffee. When he breathed in my direction the air stank of sour alcohol, and he forgot from time to time that the small microphone on the table in front of him was, in fact, a microphone; its texture seemed to please him, and he rubbed his fingers along it. I took it away from him once or twice, but after a few minutes he was back fondling it again; when I listened to the tapes later, back in England, much of what he said came through only roughly beyond the static he'd created. "When the Indian woman twisted Mother's breast, it was as though she'd injected adrenaline. That's what pain does: jolt of adrenaline. Very modern practice for people in shock. They didn't have artificial adrenaline then, and even if they had had it— But how an Indian woman knew about it—just couldn't tell you—or how she knew to put salt and sugar in the water. Dad swore it was true."

"Do you believe him?" I asked.

"Why not? Whatever else he was or wasn't, he was a painfully honest guy. There aren't many places I'd doubt him. Can't see any reason to doubt him in a thing like this."

Whatever you have threatens you because you can lose it. Sarah was so much younger than Jonathan that he had never considered the possibility of her dying before him—and so it was that she opened up yet another flank in the battered army of his spirit. Defeat was so close he could smell it; the time for serious realignment had come, and he went at the job with a fearsome array of determination. Along with the diaries, I keep on my desk the Bible my grandfather kept on his. Open to Ecclesiastes, and you find he's underlined the words "And I find more bitter than death the woman whose heart is snares and nets." This was the moat that was to surround his new battlements. He forced himself to notice that Sarah was a poor cook and that the freckles on her arms were not as charming as the freckles on her nose. He swore celibacy. He'd been celibate once; he could do it again. But he did not find it easy.

From her side, Sarah fretted over his coldness, felt it was punishment for her limitations, some of which he knew, some of which he had yet to learn. Since he was no better at expressing his love for the baby than he was at expressing his love for her, she thought he probably resented the baby, too, and resented her for having borne him. But she had no idea how to mend things, and so began to mark out a few resentments of her own.

Next to money, though, sex is nothing, and the harder Jonathan worked at the profession he despised—and despised as much for the pleasure it gave him as for the imposture it forced on him—the less money there seemed to be. People paid him with chickens and vegetables for his sermons, and even with these they seemed to be more and more niggardly. When an ignorant stuffed shirt who represented the Washington District Synod came to visit, Jonathan corrected his grammar. Afterwards Sarah said, "That wasn't wise, Johnny. You mustn't let them know how smart you are. They won't like it." She was right. And this, too, he held against her.

"Dear Johnny"—the letter was postmarked Ellsworth, Maine—"I am sorry to say I have a statement on my desk from the Washington District Synod concerning you."

Jonathan bought a ticket to Ellsworth.

Grayberg's cluttered study smelled of burned porridge as it always had; dust still hung on the walls, and the chair Jonathan sat in was covered with well-remembered dog's hairs. Grayberg was unchanged, too, still the same short, irascible, potbellied, unparsonlike parson, who loved his food much and messily; on this morning, a piece of dried egg yolk clung to his upper lip and jiggled as he spoke.

"Reports in here were middling good," Grayberg said, holding up a sheaf of papers that Jonathan knew to be his personal file, "up till about eight—maybe ten months ago." Grayberg took his breath in sharply; the piece of egg yolk stood at attention. "Examination results good. Written sermons good. Delivery good. Personal conduct good." Jonathan shifted in his chair. "But now—but *now,* my young friend—"

Grayberg selected three or four papers to waggle at Jonathan, who reached out for them.

"No, sir." Grayberg drew them back. "Nope. You ain't allowed to lay eyes on these."

"Why the hell not?" Jonathan said irritably.

"Well, what do you know? Charge number one proven just like that." Grayberg shook his head (the piece of egg yolk shook with it). "Blasphemy, Reverend. I thought that was going to be the tough one. Difficult stuff, hearsay, ain't it? Not that a few barnyard words do you any harm, but cussing as such—"

"What are the other charges?" Jonathan interrupted. "Must be more than an ill-chosen word here and there."

"You fixing to listen to me, or—"

"Is charges the right word, by the way? Am I standing in the witness box?"

Grayberg shut his mouth with a snap. The piece of egg yolk dropped to the desk in front of him. "Oh me, oh my, ain't we touchy?" He poked at the fallen scrap for a minute. "Yeah," he said. "The Ministerial Session out there wrote to me. He's your boy, they said, ask him a few questions. What I hear is that these days you ain't exhorting sinners at all. Says right here you're on about, uh"—he checked the page in front of him—"universal divinity. What is that stuff anyways?"

"I haven't the faintest idea."

Grayberg leaned back in his chair and stared up at the ceiling. "Life's a bore," he said. "East, west, anywhere at all. People want to shiver a little, cry, tremble, feel their hearts thump. You and that Baptist out there are the only entertainment they got, and if your act don't pick up you're gonna lose that circuit of yours. Hear me?"

37

BEFORE GOING TO GRAYBERG'S Jonathan had arranged to rent a horse from a stable in Ellsworth. When he arrived there the horse wasn't ready, and he took out his rage at Grayberg on the stable, the horses and the stable owner, Lemon Pinnock, who scuttled around him, stuttering apologies. "I'm right s-sorry, Reverend. My help didn't sh-show up this m-morning. Don't carry on so, Reverend, you'll do yourself an injury." When Lemon turned over to him a chestnut mare called Jenny, he said, "She's a b-biter, Reverend. Don't take it p-personal. She bites everybody except the Injun what does the mucking out. Keep your hands c-clear, Reverend."

Snow covered the ground. Jenny clattered into streams and out of them, snorting and farting as horses do, hooves slipping on the stones of the banks, tail swishing. The air was cold and sea-scented. Jonathan pressed into a gallop, still railing at Grayberg and now also at the Indian who mucked out Lemon Pinnock's stable—and at anything that came to mind. He hadn't seen Helen and Sebastian since he'd left Maine for Chicago and the Moody Institute some twelve years before; he'd written regularly, though, and received regular letters in reply. By the time he arrived in Malloy's Landing it was dark; not even an outline of the rambling structure he remembered was visible.

At his knock the door opened a crack, and an aged man poked his head out. "Who—?" a voice began. Skin drooped down over the bones of the man's face like sodden gauze.

"Johnny? Is that really—? Helen! Helen! Johnny's here." Sebastian pushed the door open and took hold of Jonathan's arm. "Johnny, how wonderful to— Helen!" There was nothing left of the Sebastian Jonathan had known. This new Sebastian was skeletal, bent, atremble—his sentences as fragmented as his wife's had once been.

Inside, the only light came from a fire in the fireplace. Two people sat at a table, one of them in shadow, the other a hugely fat old woman who fought to pull herself out of her chair, just as Sebastian had fought to pull himself out of his chair when Jonathan first arrived in Malloy's Landing all those years ago. When power shifts in a marriage—so my uncle Atlas says (and a man married as many times as he should know)—sometimes all the trappings of power, however queer, shift as well.

"Welcome, Johnny. Welcome," Helen said, and her voice had all the volume and authority that Sebastian's had once had. "Come in. Sit down." Her enormous belly slopped up over the edge of the table. Only her face and arms were still thin enough for him to recognize her. "Josh, find Johnny a chair."

"Let him find his own chair," Josh said, drawing out of the shadows. In the firelight his eyes were angrier than ever. Jonathan held out his hand. Josh eyed it, got up from the table and left the room without a word.

"Oh, Johnny—" Sebastian began again, "I'm so— He doesn't mean—"

"Forget it, Seb," Helen said. "Give us a kiss, Johnny. Have you come to stay awhile?" Jonathan bent over her brow. "You still look like Josh's blue-eyed twin from hell," she went on. "Married life hasn't changed you a bit. Tell us about Sarah. How's the—"

"Helen," Jonathan began.

"No, no, about you! Tell us about the baby."

"A baby's a baby," he said. "He's a little shriveled thing

with an ugly, screwed-up face—fists that pump back and forth— We named him Rayner," Jonathan said. "Is that all right? I thought College would be pleased." He stopped short; tears were running down Sebastian's crumpled cheeks. How can a field of tobacco, wholly vegetable, turn into something animal with mouths that feed on its own insides? How can one thing turn into another? One person turn into another? Helen into Sebastian? Sebastian into Helen? What happens in the end when the snake swallows its tail?

"What is all this?" Jonathan said, his throat dry, his voice catching somewhere in his chest. "Where are your pupils? You both look ill. I had no idea. Your letters are so vague."

"If it weren't for Josh—" Sebastian began.

"He stays on because of the money, Seb. Don't be such a fool. I've got dropsy, Johnny. Seb has consumption. Or something. We made Josh our heir in exchange for taking care of us. He's remarkably competent, but he hates our guts. Tell us what Sarah—"

"Helen, you must tell me what's going on here."

"There's nothing to tell."

"Plainly there is. Tell it."

"What you see is what there is, no more," Helen said.

"Helen—" Sebastian began tremulously, "can't we—? He's almost our—"

"No, Seb, we can't."

"Come and live with me." Jonathan interrupted them both. "You've never seen the Pacific, have you? You can see it from the top of the hill outside Hannaville. Hannaville's a pretty little town. I'll build you a house there myself. I'm a carpenter by inclination, if not by trade. We'll start a farm together."

Jonathan hated farming. It was the world of the Stokes. He hated it for its own sake, too: the fearful labor, the dependence on weather, pests, market forces, public whim, government fiddling. But he knew farming, and he realized as he spoke that the idea had been growing on him for some time simply because, however much he hated farms, he hated preaching more. He was a puritan at heart, and like all puritans he mistrusted pleasure. He had no background for it, didn't understand it, knew only that it loosened his grip somehow—somehow made him vulnerable where he hadn't been vulnerable before. Preaching gave him pleasure. His position in the community gave him pleasure. The sway he held over his parishioners gave him pleasure. His gift for oratory gave him pleasure. So (being a puritan at heart) he'd come to despise even the resonance of his own voice sounding as sure as sin while it spoke out what he knew were lies.

Besides, the old fool Grayberg had said it himself: the role of preacher is at best the role of entertainer, actor, barker—a shadowland even when practiced by a believer. For a nonbeliever like Jonathan it's a shadow of a shadowland. There wasn't any money in it, either. As for farms, whatever else can be said of them, they're real. All a farmer needs to set up, as my grandfather said to Helen and Sebastian (while the light of the fire weakened and the room grew chilly), is money, strength and experience. They had the money. He had the strength and the experience. The solution seemed so simple as he talked about it that he found himself dwelling on the beauty of the Northwest and the opportunities out there with an enthusiasm he hadn't felt for anything in years. "We can try for some new crop: soft fruit maybe. Why not? There's no fixed market, and a lot of the land is pure peat bog."

He slept that night in a tiny attic room. He hadn't been able to get a clear understanding of the arrangement between the Malloys and Josh, though by the end of the evening Sebastian was as open in his resentment as Helen; they were anxious to break away, go west with Jonathan, see the Pacific, buy a farm, live with him and Sarah, do something new—something never done before. Jonathan had seen enough of illness and death to know the Malloys were both seriously sick, that they wouldn't live long—couldn't live long—but he saw no reason why their last months should be eked out so sadly and so hopelessly. They gave him the name of the lawyer in Ellsworth who had drawn up the contract with Josh. Jonathan was sure he could find some common ground, some way to make his plan workable; they were sure of it, too.

He got up early the next morning to go into town and see what he could do. The barns stretched beyond the farmhouse as before but there were no beds in any of the bedrooms, no desks, no polished candlesticks, no pans in the kitchen, no books on the library shelves. Mold lined the throat of the rose-patterned water closet and one of the paws of the bathtub had broken loose. The walls were damp; the upstairs ceilings showed that the roofs had not been looked after.

Out in the animal barn, keeping a wary eye on Jenny's bared teeth, he hung a bag of oats over her face and found Josh standing beside him.

"You're poaching on my ground, white man," Josh said.

"You don't know how to take care of your ground," Jonathan said, instantly furious. "When you don't take care of things, you don't deserve to keep them." He took a brush out of the saddlebag and began to groom Jenny's flank with angry strokes. She eyed him suspiciously over her oat bag.

"Seb's on laudanum," Josh said. "Bungs up the bowels. Tell me, have you ever relieved an impacted bowel?"

"Turns you into a saint, does it?"

"I've been looking after these people for six, seven years," Josh went on. "They're dying, both of them."

"I can see that."

"They won't last until summer—"

"You're in my light. Move!"

"—and you come in and try to scoop off the cream."

Jonathan scanned the high cheekbones and immobile face. "It would be more seemly for you to wait until they're dead before you scoop off that cream of yours."

"What fine untarnished sentiments you bring, gentle pulpiteer. So where have you and your—uh—noble sentiments been hiding all these years?"

Until a week before, the stories Jonathan had read in newspapers about Senator George Stoke had been only text. In Chicago, on his way east to Maine and his interview with Grayberg, Jonathan had bought a *Tribune;* George stood there on page two, lower left, grainy black and white, smoking a cigar. Jonathan recognized him immediately; he was plump but not yet fat and sodden, not yet the grotesque he was to become; the shiny black eyes and curly mouth still resembled George the boy's shiny black eyes and curly mouth. You can believe anything you like until you see a photograph. Looking at this one, Jonathan had felt a nausea so abrupt that he'd hardly made it to the car door in time. George, the "fighting liberal," the senator adored by people of good will all over the nation, was campaigning in Washington, D.C.; he was promoting a plan to dam the waters of the Tennessee River and its tributaries and so develop the whole of the Tennessee Valley basin—a plan that many years later resulted in the Tennessee Valley Authority: a plan that Jonathan, stomach and mind in turmoil, could not stop himself thinking was a first-rate idea, as maddeningly sound as most of what George fought for. Why did he have to take Jonathan's side of the issues? Why couldn't he look out for the rich? Why couldn't he back the gold standard? the eastern bankers? the railroad barons? almost anything Jonathan abominated? Jonathan studied the cigar in the curly mouth. A Corona Corona, he'd decided at last. Expensive. Very expensive.

"Why haven't you repaired the barns?" he said furiously to Josh. "Not much of a businessman, are you? You're going to ruin your own investment." He bent down and began to brush Jenny's forelegs.

"Well, well, well. I'll try and make it easy for you, Vicar. Ready?" Josh followed the movements of the brush on Jenny's legs. "These poor bastards: they've just about mastered the art of eking out the little time that's left of them. One day, then the next, then the next. Never look forward. Never look back. And along comes a reverend gentleman to witter on about hope and future. There isn't—"

"The great scholar's taken on medicine, has he? And psychology?"

"—isn't any future for these people. None. There's no—"

"Or is it just high finance you've spent your time on?"

"—no west for them to go to. Have you no pity?"

"For Christ's sake, can't you fix the roof? Can't you do at least that?"

Without warning the mare whipped her head around to lunge at Jonathan; Josh grabbed the bridle. The horse snorted and stamped. "Hey, Jenny, hey girl," Josh crooned, reaching to stroke her nose. The mare dipped her head under his hand like a cat.

Jonathan felt a sudden unreality take hold of him. "You're working for Lemon Pinnock, aren't you? What for? You're the Indian who mucks out his stable."

Josh dropped Jenny's bridle. "You blab at them about it and I'll kill you. You hear?"

"You wouldn't know how," Jonathan said contemptuously.

Josh snorted, turned to stroke Jenny, paused, then whipped back much as she had only a moment before. "Hammer is *marteau!*" he shouted. "Nail is *clou.* Roof is *toit.* Canute was born in 995. Hume said, 'I look inside myself and find David Hume's experiences but I cannot find David Hume.' " The tendons stood out in his cheeks and neck. "You're right, you fucker, I wouldn't know how to kill you. I don't know how to mend a roof, either. Where do you think I'd have learned skills like that? At this place? *Hic, haec, hoc, huius, huius, huius—* All I'm fit for is clearing out horse shit." He stopped, shook his head and covered his face with his hands. "They don't have a dollar left. Not a dime or a nickel. Not a penny. Not a sou, not a centime—"

"Don't shit me," Jonathan said. "There was money. Lots of it. You know that, and I know it. What'd you throw it away on? Horses? Women? Gambling?"

Josh laughed. "Oh, I'd have liked that, Cardinal. Why didn't I think of it myself? Trouble is, I just didn't get the chance—"

Jonathan grabbed hold of Josh's shirt lapels and yanked him forward so that their faces almost met. "Who did, then?"

"Dear me, what a violent man of God—"

"Speak!"

Josh let himself hang loose in Jonathan's grip. "You know these good people, O pastor mine, as well as I do. A whimpering story and their hearts melt all over the floor. The money just drops out of their pockets of its own weight."

Jonathan let go of him abruptly. Then abruptly he turned, took the saddle from the rack, threw it over Jenny, settled in, fastened the cinch around her middle with an angry jerk. He wasn't good with animals. He used to say they never did what you told them to. "Which one was it this time? Bonds for the Utopia of Idaho? Shares in an orphanage in China? Pregnant cats? Stray dogs?"

"All those and dozens more," Josh said. "Sharks flocked to Malloy's Landing—covered every inch of the shore."

"Soft-bellied liberal miasma," Jonathan muttered furiously, giving the cinch another jerk. Jenny lunged at him again, but in his rage he avoided her easily. "Oozing sentimentality—rotten, pestilent— Where the hell were you while this was going on?"

Josh shrugged. "Me? The tame Injun? What good am I? Where the hell were you, white man?"

My grandfather mounted and rode off without another word, forcing Jenny into a gallop in the direction of Hannaville. But after he'd gone no more than a quarter of a mile he turned back. Josh was still standing at the door of the barn. "They think you stole the money from them," Jonathan said to him.

"They don't know what they think," Josh said. "Never needed to figure it out. They dream a little, trim a bit here, add a bit there until what they see is what they want to see—like good people everywhere."

"While living off your pay from Pinnock?"

"Why not?"

"Sure," Jonathan said. "Why not." He took twenty dollars—all he had—from his wallet and handed it to Josh, who received it without comment. "What else can I do while I'm here?"

"Mend the roof," Josh said. Then he turned and walked away.

38

JONATHAN SPENT A MONTH repairing the roofs in Malloy's Landing and watching the fearful spectacle of the Malloys' disintegration. Sebastian died the week he planned to leave. Jonathan stayed on, organized the funeral and preached the oration, which was to be—he swore it—his final sermon; when Helen died a week later, the Reverend Grayberg buried her. But why didn't Sarah write to him? This he could not understand. He spent two months in Malloy's Landing. He wrote her almost every day, but no letters came back—not one.

"I'm not a very good letter-writer" was all she said,

playing with little Rayner, who was by now eighteen months old and babbling happily on her lap—"letter-writer, writer-lighter" and suchlike—very much as Jonathan himself had babbled when he was a little boy, before Alvah Stoke bought him. It was the first evening of Jonathan's return. "I told you that before you left, didn't I? Now what's this decision you've come to?"

"I'm going to buy a farm," my grandfather said to her.

"What?" she said laughing. "You? Don't make such jokes."

The baby laughed with her. "Joke smoke," he cried.

"It's no joke."

"Oh, come on, Johnny—" She broke off when he said nothing. "This is ridiculous. You can't mean it. Don't say—"

"Mother hated farming as much as Dad did," Atlas shouted at me from the bathroom. The Youngballses and the Murphys were due for Claire's French dinner party at six; it was five already and I was beginning to feel pressed for time. I figured there was more than an hour of the story left to go, and I wasn't sure Atlas would be in any condition to tell the rest of it when the party was over. He had wheeled me into the bedroom so he could talk on while he bathed and dressed. "Hating farms was kind of a bond between them in the early days—the Stokes, George, all that unadulterated misery. Why the hell he was throwing away something he believed in for a way of life he hated, I have no idea. Never could figure it out. Money probably."

Atlas never knew about his father's atheism. He never read the diaries. He never understood what a puritan his father was, either: how fearful Jonathan was of anything that made inroads on his control. The idea of farming no longer had the Malloys' money to back it up, but Jonathan was not going to let that stop him. There had to be a way. There was no cooperative movement in the United States at the time; we've always been backward in such things. But Jonathan had read a little about Robert Owen, and he knew something about the weavers of Lancashire, the people who founded the first English cooperative in the middle of the nineteenth century. It was very successful. Jonathan figured that what worked with a textile mill just might work with a farm.

"It's no joke, Sarah," he said. "I intend to farm."

She studied his expression, then turned away. "So it's going to be forty acres and a mule after all, is it? After all the talk? How can you set your sights so low?"

Jonathan looked down at his hands. He turned them palm up, palm down; it was a gesture he had come to without knowing why. "You don't know me," he said softly. "I can go much lower than that. Twenty acres will do to start with. This is virgin land out here. It'll take a lot of working."

"Up at four, porridge with sorghum—" Her voice was abruptly shrill; little Rayner stopped babbling at once, chin atremble. "Out to milk, cows to pasture, hoe, plow, seed, reap. You're a preacher: for the love of God, Johnny, preach. Cook, wash, dig, cut wood, draw water. Is this what you want for me? For him?"

"Preacher preach," Rayner whimpered, fearful now, looking anxiously from Sarah to Jonathan and back again.

Jonathan sighed. "Nobody said it was going to be easy."

"Not enough rain," she said, "too much rain. If the weather isn't perfect, the crops fail and nothing's ever perfect."

"You exaggerate," he said.

When Helen died Jonathan had gone to the lawyer in Ellsworth who'd drawn up that queer contract between Josh and the Malloys. Josh was right. Nothing was left. The First National Bank of Maine owned it all. Jonathan had managed to cajole him onto the train to Washington; they'd traveled together in silence for more than two thousand miles. Then in the middle of Utah, in a featureless desert, the train had stopped for water. Josh had gone for a walk and never come back.

"Squirrels and rats and birds," Sarah cried, "cinch bugs, botflies, termites, mosquitoes." Rayner hugged himself to her and wailed. "The banker takes a cut. Transporters take a cut. Commodity speculators take a cut. Wholesaler in Chicago, broker in Boston, retailer in New York—"

"I hadn't realized you were so knowledgeable," Jonathan interrupted.

"Johnny, please, please, please don't do this to me."

"You're frightening that baby."

Rayner clung to her like a koala bear to a tree trunk. She looked at Jonathan's implacable face, at the anger that never left it, and her shoulders slumped in defeat; tears started down her cheeks.

"There's no reason to imagine the Northwest is Kansas," he began.

"What difference does it make?"

"Sarah—"

"Farming's farming."

"This is childish," he said.

"I could have married any one of half a dozen farmers around Sweetbrier," she wept. "But I didn't. I married a preacher—"

"You married a preacher who'd lost his vocation. And you knew it."

"But you said—" She broke off.

"I said what?"

"Before we got married, you—" She broke off again, frowned, sniffled, wiped her nose on the back of her hand. The baby held his breath.

"What are you talking about?"

"There wasn't enough money then. Remember?" She cocked her head (the baby cocked his, too). "Remember?"

"So?"

"So where are you going to get the money now? You'll need a lot of money. There, there, Rayner. There's a good boy. Where's the down payment coming from?"

"I'll get it."

"Nobody will loan you money like that." The sudden pleasure in her voice was so rich that the baby began to croon.

"I'll get it," he said again.

"No you won't. Oh, goodness, what a relief. I don't care how poor we are as long as we don't have to farm. You had me scared." She got up impetuously, kissed his nose and stroked his shoulder.

He shook her off.

"Don't be like that. Read to me, will you? Read my father's letter. Over there. On the table. It came in a week ago."

Early in Sarah's pregnancy, Jonathan had begun reading to her in bed before they turned off the gas lamp. He read her poetry sometimes, sometimes the novels of Hawthorne and Dickens, sometimes letters that came in from her mother and father. Sarah said she loved listening to him; she said reading hurt her eyes. He took the letter out of the envelope and scanned it. Then he read it again carefully, a little shaken by the speed of the victory it represented.

He looked up at her and back down at the letter. "How can you do this to me?" he said. He was a fine tactician, my grandfather.

"What do you mean? What is it?"

"Why didn't you tell me you can't read?" There was an odd combination of wonder and contempt in his voice.

"Of course I can read. I skimmed—"

"Don't lie to me."

"Look at that!" She snatched the letter out of his hand, jostling Rayner, who let out a shriek. "How can I read handwriting like that? My father can't write properly—that's all. How dare you—"

"Sarah, your mother is dead."

She froze, mouth agape, then shook her head and formed the questions with her lips. "It says so? In that letter?" She took in her breath. "I could never get the words the right way around somehow." The baby's cries almost drowned her voice;

she searched Jonathan's eyes. "I tried and tried, but the letters kept sliding away into one another. Don't blame me too much, Johnny. I really did— How long has she—?" Jonathan spread his hands. "Only that she's dead? Just like that? Nothing more?"

"Yes. There's more. There's money."

"Money?"

He nodded.

"How much?"

"Six hundred dollars," he said.

She held her breath a moment. "Enough?" she whispered then.

"Yes," he said. "Quite enough."

It was a judgment on them both. By the time Sarah arrived back from Sweetbrier with a strongbox containing thirty double eagles, he'd chosen twenty-two acres of sandy loam that ran right down to the railroad tracks, precisely as the Stoke homestead had, at precisely the same orientation to the sun, and for precisely double the price Alvah had paid. Jonathan took his wife—pretty, strawberry blond Sarah—who even though she was pretty, could read no better than Alvah Stokes's Wify had been able to: Sarah who had paid for his land with her mother's money just as Wify had paid for Alvah's land with her mother's: he took his Sarah to see his land just as Alvah Stoke had taken Wify to see his land precisely half a century before. Sarah carried Rayner, and they walked three miles through the cedar forests that still surrounded Hannaville.

There is something primal about ownership of land; Jonathan had felt it first when he was talking to the Malloys. So despite these similarities with the Stokes, all of which he saw and recorded in his diaries, he was in high spirits: the occasionally glimpsed gaiety in him is in full flight in his entries for this period. He dashed ahead, jumping fallen logs as he went just as years before, he'd jumped the railway ties in the

Denver yards on his first day in that land of miracles. He slapped a hand on a huge tree, fifteen feet in diameter, and yelled back to her that these were western red cedars, arborvitae.

"The tree of life, Sarah," he said. "Look at the slope of that trunk"—he drew a scoop-sided pyramid with his hands in imitation of it—"like a wineglass elm upside down. They've got wineglass elms in Ellsworth—did I tell you that?" He broke off a frond of scaly leaves, put it to his nose and ran back to her. "Smell it, Sarah. Isn't it wonderful? Smell, Rayner."

The little boy stuck the frond in his mouth.

The land was not yet fully logged off. Lumberjacks in pairs balanced on narrow platforms twelve feet up in the trees, sawing and swinging axes: Swedes and Norwegians, mammoth men with mammoth shoulders and mammoth hips. The beasts that dragged the timber away over stripling slips were hogs—not oxen, not horses: hogs—huge, red hogs called Durocs, as mammoth when compared to ordinary hogs as the men were compared to ordinary men. To the east was forest. To the west the land was clear; tall stumps of thousand-year-old trees stood in ragged disarray.

"The house goes there, Sarah," Jonathan said. "The strawberries there—and there—Anjou pears, I think." Sarah laughed at his enthusiasm despite herself. "Nobody out here grows soft fruit yet. There's no competition— Do you see? It's a completely new idea. We'll corner the market. How can we miss? The blackcaps go there—"

The lumberjacks left in the middle of summer; by the time they went, Jonathan had dynamited enough stumps to make room for the house. He smoothed the ground and laid cement for his own wooden house precisely as Bessie had taught him to lay it for the Stokes' wooden house when he was twelve years old. When the shell was largely finished, he took Sarah out to see what he had done. They left Rayner with Eliza for the afternoon and walked through the woods together. They sat beneath the big cedar tree; she spread out a blanket, unpacked a few tidbits to eat, and there she brought two years of celibacy to an end. She tickled his nose with a frond of sweet-smelling cedar, much as he'd tickled Rayner's when the three of them had first gone out to look at this stretch of land together; she laughed when he pulled away, then she loosened her strawberry blond hair and the delicate, cloth-covered buttons of her blouse.

He'd built a cupola for mating swallows on the roof of the house, a pretty dome atop a circle of fluted pillars; he'd whittled it in the evenings when it got too dark to work outside and put it in place only a week or so before. It stood there smiling down on them that summery day. "Have you ever seen swallows mating?" my uncle Atlas asked me. "They fly up high into the air, body to body, wings aflutter; they swoop and bank together. It's the most beautiful of all lovemaking: the coital kiss of swallows."

By the time the house was ready to move into, Sarah was pregnant for the second time.

39

MY FATHER RAYNER, with his romantic emotional spillage, is the one who keeps me. Fortunately for me, he's dead—fortunately for him, too; otherwise, neither one of us could afford the likes of me: cripples are expensive. That suicide attempt of his was high drama—police, sirens, write-ups in the papers, even an entry in California's medical history: "62.3

ounces pumped from this patient's stomach," and yet he survived. A few months later he had the stroke that should have killed him as surely as the Nembutal before it, but he was a strong man; he lingered on for a couple of years, a basket case, unable to speak or understand. In the end he died a natural death from another stroke. He'd taken out one of those policies that pay vast sums if you die young—and of natural causes. My mother got it all when he died at fifty-four, just weeks under the deadline. When she died, a year later, the lion's share of the two million dollars came to me, to the youngest sister: the one who needed it. This was twenty-five years ago; the capital has doubled since.

Whatever would Jonathan have thought if he'd known his little Rayner would leave two million dollars to his children? To anybody for that matter? Rayner of all people! There was Jonathan, working all day for the railroads for money to buy seed, working half the night, too, to plow and plant his own land by the light of the twenty-foot-high piles of cedar splinters that he'd dredged out of the soil chunk by chunk, collected together, and set fire to; they burned for months on end. By the time his daughter Gwendolyn was born, he'd planted his first two acres. Cinch bugs destroyed his first crop, just as Sarah had prophesied, and so destroyed his plan to buy her a piano, a pelmet (whatever that was) and curtains. The next harvest succeeded, but because the first had failed so disastrously, all the profit went back into the farm. Again, no pelmet; again, no piano. Not even a Christmas cactus. When their second son was born in 1905, Jonathan was working a hundred miles away for another farmer and couldn't afford to come back for the confinement. He didn't get home until spring, dirty, thin and unshaven. Gwendolyn ran out to meet him; she was a round, sturdy child, with fat, pink cheeks and a bossy manner. He asked her what the baby's name was.

Gwendolyn pulled back. "Shame on you, Papa. Baby is Nah-ham—"

Inside, he patted Rayner on the head, kissed Sarah and said he'd like to take a look at "little Naham." Sarah flounced away from him and ran upstairs. Jonathan stood there a moment, staring after her.

"You're silly," said Rayner, my father-to-be, who was to lecture on the economics of war at the University of California at Berkeley, and to leave his children two million dollars.

"Well, what is his name?" Jonathan asked.

Rayner lifted the one eyebrow that was to become the terror and the delight of his students. "Won't tell you."

"Why not?"

Rayner eyed him up and down. " 'Cause you're silly."

"So are you," Jonathan said angrily. "I'll call him Atlas. God knows, he'll need some endurance to survive around here." Thus it was that my uncle Nathaniel, the doctor, came to be known as Atlas, who—as Heine puts it—bears on his back the weight of this world of sorrows.

My father-to-be retreated up the stairs after his mother and cried "You're silly" once more from the safety of her skirts.

"Why does he dislike me so much?" Jonathan asked Sarah one night a year or so later when Rayner was six or seven years old. For all my grandfather's passionate love of his children (and of this the diaries leave no doubt whatever), he had no idea—absolutely none—of what a normal child, a child not brought up as a slave, might need or want. The children worked hard on the farm, many long hours every day, though not anywhere near as long and hard as he had worked. He built swings for them by the house; sometimes he watched them play, heart in throat, and wrote that he could not be working them too hard or too long if they had energy left over to play. "He just didn't understand," Atlas said, "that it's necessary for children to play."

"They tease Rayner at school," Sarah said to Jonathan.

He'd built the school for Hannaville with his own hands,

for no pay, for no return at all except that his kids, goddammit, were not going to be denied as he had been. "What are
you saying?" he said.

"He has patches on his clothes." Sarah was pregnant yet
again. She dropped her hands into her lap, a helpless, angry,
despairing gesture, not like her really, and shut her eyes. "I'm
so tired—"

"You're doing too much. You should get some rest."

"—and I'm afraid this time. It hurts so."

"What hurts? Where does it hurt? Show me."

"I don't know. Everywhere."

"It must hurt some places more than others."

"Why must it?"

"If something hurts," Jonathan said, "let's get Burgess—"

"Why do you always have to have a neat answer?"

"There's no point in talking to him if we can't tell him
what's the matter."

"I don't want another baby!" she cried out. "Why can't
you leave me alone?" But even as she spoke she snatched at
his hands and kissed them. "Oh, Johnny, I couldn't dig more
than two rows today. I'll never get the turnips in— Why don't
you talk to me anymore?" she wept. "You shout at the children. You hit Rayner—"

"He spat at me," Jonathan said indignantly. And indeed
he had, that very afternoon.

When I was a child, the fights I went to sleep with night
after night had the same rising and falling rhythms this one
has. My father Rayner took his opening role from his father
Jonathan; he began cool, controlled, in command; his professorial manner gave him great elegance. In his final fight with
my mother—the one that ended with the bottle of Nembutal—
a new neighbor, unused to the shouting, frightened by it,
knocked at the door. My father answered. He wore a red paisley robe that hung to the ground like a cardinal's cassock.

"Surely you can see, my friend," he said to the neighbor, "that the woman's hysterical."

Sarah pushed Jonathan away as vehemently as she'd pulled him to her. "What use is a sensitive boy to you?" she said. "All you want is field hands." She slapped her belly. "Why don't you get yourself a calf instead?"

"You don't mean what you're saying."

"Wouldn't a calf serve you as well? Wouldn't it? Say something! Why don't you answer?"

"Because you're not making sense."

"We were going to corner the market in soft fruit."

"And so we will—"

"Corner the market! Five years of solid labor and we can't even afford a team to pull the plow. We don't get a calf because babies are cheaper."

My mother and father's fights were foreplay; they built up to a verbal climax before the grappling began that was to end in its own furious bedroom excitements. This anticipatory violence was of the dish-throwing sort. One time my father threw a glass of iced tea across the room (I remember the smash it made, glass and ice all over the floor); another time— mad as hell, and strong as only farm boys are strong—he tore a telephone book in two. Jonathan was different. He showed his anger for the threat it held, much the way an army on parade shows off tanks and artillery, but he kept his control.

"I think it's time to stop this," he said, dismissing her and the squabble. "You are saying things you will regret. Next year will be better."

"Next year! What about this year? Bare walls, bare windows. Ugly, ugly, ugly. Remember the pelmet, Johnny? Remember? And the piano? I want a piano. I want—"

"Bring yourself up to the present, Sarah."

"I want curtains. I want—"

"Enough is enough."

"I want wallpaper. I want a Christmas cactus in a pot.

Remember the Christmas cactus in a pot? Do you? Remember? Even the poorest of the poor have something pretty in the house—"

"What's wrong with this house?" he said, his voice a shade icier but no more than that. "I built it with my own hands."

"This is your house. It's not mine. It has nothing to do with me. And it's ugly, ugly, ugly."

"Of course it's your house. Where else is there for you to live?"

"My money bought it, but it's not mine."

"It's the money that preoccupies you, is it?"

"Show me something pretty," Sarah demanded, flailing, determined—absolutely determined—to find some weakness in him, something—almost anything. "What's my money brought for *me?* Come on, show me something that's mine. No, there's nothing. So show me something that's at least not hideous. I want something to look at. I want a carpet. I want a pelmet. I want— What do I have? What is there for me?"

"You're beginning to sound as though you're just plain against me—"

"Against you? What's that got to do with anything?"

"—no matter what I say or do."

"Against. For. With. What does it matter? It's going to be like this forever. Look at you. You eat away at yourself—"

"Sarah!"

"You're eating yourself alive. I can see it!"

Chekhov—not a man given to overstatement—said that every day he had to make an effort to squeeze the last drops of slavery from his blood. But Chekhov hadn't been a real slave. My grandfather, who had been, couldn't measure his slavery in drops; it ran in his veins, as red and rich as the hemoglobin itself. Every day his heart and brain had to fight against the very stuff that fed them. Every night, the illusion-stripped world of the slave ruled him just as it rules Atlas's patients while they sink into mental and physical incontinence, bladder and bowel on the loose and brain incapable of anything but terror and sleep. What is old age but Jonathan's nightmare carried to its logical conclusions? What is his nightmare but the ultimate secret, the essence of life itself?

"Don't speak to me," he said to Sarah. There was a tremor in his voice, and the ice was gone. So it was that she knew something important had happened.

In my mother and father's fights there was always a break-free point like this. My father baited my mother beneath his professorial manner, much as Jonathan—albeit unawares—baited Sarah with his coldness of response, and my mother's voice climbed, veered off, slid here and there (as Sarah's voice was sliding), until at last she found the lever that would catch him, pull him into the fray with her, engage him a gear higher, where he could no longer escape the battle that he himself wanted so passionately. The famous raspberry-scented condom she charged him with was one such lever. My sisters and I cowered upstairs, each in her room alone, each at her door listening to the downstairs prelude in rage. I couldn't hear the words, but when the idiotic object itself appeared on the field, I recognized the moment of crisis as I'd recognized many such moments before. It's like the break-in-two of a train that Jonathan describes: there's a change in the sound of the engine's exhaust. No more. But after that, nothing is the same. It was only by accident that Sarah had stumbled into the land of Jonathan's nightmare, but Jonathan was atremble with the sudden humiliation of what she'd seen, as though in seeing, she'd made the degradation real. She'd let loose chaos itself around him.

"And you expect me to help you eat yourself alive!" Sarah cried.

"Don't shout at me," he said shakily.

"You're the one who's shouting," she shouted, although she knew it wasn't true. But her newfound power gave her an almost magical insight into the terrors he lived with. "Worse than that: you expect me to eat out my own insides for you. And why? Because next year, just maybe, but it's only a vain hope, hopeless really, not even vain—"

"Shut up," he said, catching at her wrists, holding them tight in his hands.

"Don't touch me! Let go of me!"

He tightened his grip.

"You're hurting me!" she screamed.

He didn't move: he didn't dare.

"We're not people anymore," she went on, still screaming and as relentless as George had been all those years ago in the Stokes' sod hut. "Let go of me! We're some kind of perverted subhuman form, some insect with only a mouth, a stomach and an asshole. Let go!" She struggled in his arms. "All that waits for us is babies and death. We're like worms or grubs or slugs, wretched, crawling, dung-covered— Tell me, Johnny, can you sink lower than this? Can anybody? Are you satisfied? Let me loose!"

When the control is let loose, it's an eerie sensation. There's a sudden white in the brain and a sudden vacuum in the chest. Jonathan heard the crack his hand made across her face before he was even aware he was going to strike her. He stared at her wildly, then ran out of the room. As he slammed the front door behind him he caught a glimpse of the small figure of Rayner, on his knees beside Sarah, who lay sobbing on the floor. When I was a child myself and Jonathan long dead, long past forgiving or being forgiven, I remember my father saying, "The old man hit her. He beat us kids. Nothing special in that, though: most kids got whipped in those days. But he shouldn't have hit my mother. For that I will never forgive him."

And yet my father hit my mother once, too—only once, just as Jonathan hit Sarah only once. It happened after the sound of battle had changed in that final, fatal engagement.

But this time was different from all other times. I knew it. Usually a wild coupling followed, grunts and whinnies from the marital bed. This time there was silence instead. Then a scream. My sisters and I opened the doors to our rooms and peeped out. My mother was naked—middle-aged flesh curdling on her thighs—barring the way to the bathroom door. As we watched, my father hit her, hard; before our very eyes the weal rose on her pale, soft cheek. He threw her down, out of his way, crossed the threshold, took the bottle out of the medicine chest and shoveled handfuls of Nembutal into his mouth, swallowing as fast as he could. With each handful, pills scattered on the floor. When he'd emptied the bottle, he stood there looking at himself in the mirror. My mother called the police; a squad car arrived, siren screaming. And still my father stood there—my father, Jonathan's eldest son—he just stood there in his red paisley robe like a cardinal's and stared into the mirror. So it was that he destroyed his kidneys, raised his blood pressure and caused the stroke that felled him: so it was that he provided me with the wherewithal to keep me in as much comfort as a person in my condition can be kept.

40

JONATHAN STAYED AWAY for two days, the first day drunk in a ditch, the second fighting a hangover in a boardinghouse in Seattle. On the third day he returned home, determined to work harder. No matter what, he would force himself to work an hour more every day. He could plant strawberries the following year. There was still hope. Sarah must have a piano. Of course she must. They must have curtains, too, and a carpet and wallpaper—even that damned pelmet. To signal that a new life was beginning, he brought a Christmas cactus in a pot.

But there was nobody in the house when he got back. He ran upstairs, opened the doors, slammed them and ran back down to the silence of the kitchen where plates stood in piles on the shelves next to preserves in rows and knives hanging from hooks. On the kitchen table lay the note in Rayner's neat, firm hand.

Dear Father:

We are going to visit Grandfather in Sweetbrier. Mother says she is going to take tests to become a teacher and maybe we will live there and you can come and see us at Grandfather's house.

Your loving son,
Rayner

Jonathan picked up the cactus and hurled it at the wall, where its pot shattered and fell to the ground in shards much like the shards he'd found Sarah crouching among, eyes agape with terror, when Rayner was about to be born.

By the time the Youngballses arrived for Claire's French dinner party, Atlas was bathed, clean-shirted, ascot-tied; he even smelled of talcum powder instead of liquor. I suppose it isn't surprising that a man who runs an old-age ghetto and calls himself Dr. Youngballs—I don't for a moment believe that anybody could have been born with such a name—should turn out to be an ascot-tie kind of man, too, and more than a little oily into the bargain. What *is* surprising—and irritating—is that I didn't dislike him. Also, his wife was not nearly as dopey as Atlas made her out to be. She kept an amused eye on him—on Atlas, that is—as he mixed drinks: short on the whiskey, long on the soda for the guests; in his own glass, whiskey topped up with gin. Claire was safely in the kitchen. The Youngballses said they didn't know the Murphys, but when the Murphys arrived Mrs. Youngballs said, "You know, I think I made a mistake, Dr. Murphy. I think I do know you. I recognize the voice."

"But not the man, eh?" Dr. Murphy said. Almost all the men Atlas entertained to dinner were doctors. Dr. Murphy had a shuffly walk and an unexpectedly sweet smile. "Can't say as I blame you," he went on. "Just the other day I was out at the mall, and I saw this poor old duffer coming toward me—he was talking to himself, can you imagine? in a shopping mall?—and I said to myself, 'Look at that fumbling old fool. He ought to be dead.' And you know what? It was me: in one of those reflecting windows." Claire came in from the kitchen, and he made a little bow in her direction. "So this is to be the famous French dinner, is it? I'm not much on foreign foods, my dear. I hope I won't disappoint you."

"The point," said Claire a little stiffly, "is educational."

"For education, a man must be educable," Dr. Murphy said. "I will try, Claire, but I promise nothing."

Sarah my grandmother was not so sophisticated: for her, mortification was guaranteed. How could a functional illiterate possibly imagine herself as a teacher? In those days, anyway? Dr. Murphy probably *was* educable, though perhaps less so than his disarming speech implied. Sarah wasn't. She just plain wasn't. She might have had a better chance today; somebody just might recognize what was doubtless dyslexia and be of some help to her. We're all a little dyslexic, we third-generation Carricks, children of her children.

Over the months that followed Jonathan pared his food to the minimum and used no heat. He worked eighteen hours a day. By Christmas he'd managed to sell his crop at a good price, plant two hundred apple trees, and the first two acres of strawberries—that most precious of crops, the crop on which died. Jonathan wrote an impassioned appeal to the district synod; and the district synod, lacking any other suitable candidate, made him the dead man's successor. Jonathan did this for the small pickings of money it would bring in; he did it for the piano and the pelmet; he did it for Sarah because he loved her and wanted to please her despite her betrayal: which is to say, he followed her betrayal of him by betraying himself.

Every day his thundery expression became more thundery and his temperament more mercurial. The atheist preacher who lives in the town that pays his bills must make his children a party to his deception. No child can be relied on to pretend, so my grandfather made the pretending real. They said grace at meals, which they had done only erratically before, whenever Sarah thought to insist. Each child learned a verse of the Bible every day, went into Papa's study and said the verse—and got a whipping if the verse was not correct. Sundays were miserable: church, Sunday school, no play, only chores and God, and whoever dared otherwise got a whipping.

Atlas assumed his father's faith was completely genuine. My father never doubted it, either; it never crossed his mind that the religion-bound household of his childhood was an exercise in play-acting. He never even knew his father's diaries existed. When he was fourteen he went out behind the barn to defy God and his old man, all in one stroke, and to pay for it with his life if that's what it came to. He said, "God, I defy you," and waited for the thunderbolt. When none came, he figured God hadn't heard and so defied Him again. Thereafter he, too, was an atheist. This rebellion pleased him immensely; it was a source of strength to him throughout his life. Yet the pity of it is that his watershed didn't amount to rebellion at all; in the end, all he was doing was joining forces with his father in the very way that would have pleased his father most.

If Jonathan my grandfather was a harder man when Sarah returned from Sweetbrier, she had grown softer. There were three more babies in the next five years, all girls; Sarah named the youngest one Hope because by then she knew there was no hope left—not for her anyway. She was too tired to play the piano Jonathan went into debt to buy for her; she was too tired to make a pelmet or curtains for a pelmet to go over. When a twenty-six-acre piece of land abutting the farm came up for sale—this was in 1914, the year World War I broke out in Europe, the onset of a wonderfully profitable few years for American farmers—when this neighboring piece of land came up for sale, it was Sarah who proposed buying it. They mortgaged the land they had to get it.

Then the next year came the bull.

Atlas told about it seated at the head of the table at Claire's French dinner. The dinner was in full swing, a pretty tense swing, too, with Claire's battle-line preparations all too reminiscent of my grandfather's war on life: two wines and three courses down: the aioli on a platter with raw vegetables around it, the soup, the fish *(filets de sole gratinés à la parisienne):* our party of seven (an awkward number) seated around Claire's plate-glass table with the iron filigree base, the Japanese arrangement of chrysanthemums in a wide cut-glass bowl in the center, the confusion of glasses: here we all sat when drunken Atlas (falling into one of those alcohol-induced holes in his head and so forgetting that our interview was suspended for the duration of the festivities)—here we sat when Atlas began the tale of the bull.

"An ugly brute," he said out of the blue, "irritable, old—near the end of his career—blind in one eye, but cheap. That's why Dad bought him."

"What was this?" I said. None of us, Claire, Murphys, Youngballses, not even I had any idea what Atlas was talking about. "An animal?"

"A bull, for Christ's sake: a bull."

"He bought a bull? Your dad?"

"Course he did. Farmers shared them out in those days. You only needed one to service the cows—all of them in the neighborhood." Mrs. Murphy giggled, more because of the bull's appearance at Claire's dinner table with its Japanese chrysanthemums, I think, than because of his work with cows. "He had a ring through his nose, connected to a twenty-foot chain."

The bull's first June was hot. Flies were rampant. Botflies lay their eggs just under the animal's skin; Atlas was explaining the details as Claire brought in the *boeuf en croûte*. Before he began to carve, wavering to his feet (whyever had Claire arranged to let this drunken oaf carve?), he poked through the pastry—carving knife a scalpel—that covered the roast to demonstrate just where a botfly might be found; steam gushed out of the roast's wound. At the other end of the table, an infuriated Claire forgot to pour out the burgundy—which left us with the white wine she'd intended only for the fish. Already the repercussions for tomorrow were terrible.

The boils ooze; they're very painful. While Jonathan inspected the bull's back, Rayner stood apart, pitchfork aimed like a bayonet. There were at least a dozen boils. Jonathan touched one with creosote. The bull reared. It's a magnificent sight—a bull rearing—a ton of anguished beef balanced on its back legs, suspended by a chain through the nose. Then the skin of the nostrils burst open. The ring snapped back against the wall of the barn. The bull tore through an open gate. Jonathan grabbed Rayner's pitchfork and ran: he cornered the animal at the far end of the field beyond.

Around the dinner table, our silver forks waited tensely in front of our mouths, *boeuf en croûte* growing cold while Atlas, an old man more frail than he let on and now seriously in his cups, but a wonderful storyteller still and just a little boy all those years ago—too tiny to do anything, too scared to run for help—Atlas stood quiet and watched the bull, and the bull stood quiet, too, there in the field, head toward the unenclosed land beyond, presenting Jonathan with his massive rump: tail switching, ponderous testicles swaying between great thighs, hump of muscle erect above his shoulders.

"Dad really was lousy with animals," Atlas said. "He said it again and again: 'The bastards just won't do what you tell them to.' Christ, the worst tool you can use with a bull is a pitchfork. He jabbed at that exposed rump: jabbed— Bull kept backing toward him: backing, swaying, backing: then with a sudden, deft flip, he tossed the pitchfork right out of Dad's hands." Carried away, demonstrating with his knife, Atlas tweaked the beef pastry that lay on his plate: it arced through the air and landed amid Claire's chrysanthemums. In the silence that followed, we the guests, and our fascination with Atlas's story, grew manic.

"His name," Dr. Youngballs croaked, "he did have a name, didn't he? this bull?"

"Yeah," Atlas said. "That was the joke of it. He was called Sir George."

The moment seemed to Jonathan, as he wrote about it in his diaries afterwards, to have been the moment in which he first caught sight of the truth stripped bare. But it went by so fast that he was flat on the ground underneath the bull's horns before he could make sense of what he saw. The bull rolled him along like a log, and the grass whipped at his face just like the Kansas grass of so long ago. He struggled to his knees. The bull knocked him down, leapt over him and rolled him from the other side all the way to the fence some forty feet beyond. Once there the bull began to play, butting Jonathan against the fence, retreating, butting again, blood from the torn nostrils pouring down over grass and man both.

Claire realized she'd forgotten the burgundy only when she was clearing the beef to make way for the salad with walnut oil—too late, way too late: there was no remedy at all.

"So what happened then?" Mrs. Youngballs asked, elbow on table, eyes glued to Atlas. "Did he die? Was he dead?"

"No. But he was hurt bad—not really conscious, Rayner crept up behind the bull to get the pitchfork, and Jesus if he didn't pick the damn thing up and stab it into the bull's neck. The bull woofed and backed away, pitchfork stuck in his neck like a bull at a bullfight—which bought Rayner the time to get hold of Dad, get him out. Don't know how much of this Dad understood. Old Mundt couldn't find an unbroken rib in the poor bastard's chest. Nothing's as painful as broken ribs: childbirth, cancer, forget it."

World War I was a year old. The newspapers carried almost as many stories about opposition to it as about the war itself. George Stoke's antiwar stand was vocal and as usual, well publicized. He had no belief whatever, he said, that war, this or any other war, was going to make the world safe for democracy. He and a number of other prominent liberals hoped the war might stimulate agitation for peace; meantime, though, it stagnated in the trenches of Europe. Jonathan, lying on his bed in agony, pushed toward death, pulled away again, pushed, pulled, pushed, pulled, just as the bull had butted him toward the fence and away again: in this state, he thought of George, knew that he agreed with what George had said—that again he agreed, again!—and the agreement pained him so greatly that it seemed to him, so he wrote in his diaries, that the walls screamed all night long, a desperate sobbing scream like a child's. How was he to know that it was not his own pain he was hearing but his youngest daughter's? Hope's pain? Hope, given her name because Sarah had no hope.

"Couldest not thou watch one hour?" he whispered to Burgess Mundt some ten days later.

Burgess frowned. "Just try to get some rest."

"Send me the boy."

Rayner stared down at him, his face expressionless except for a slight movement of one eyebrow that he seemed to be struggling to control.

"The bull?" Jonathan said, watching that eyebrow. He'd meant to thank him—wanted to thank him—but the words wouldn't come. If he could have used his hands, perhaps he could have gestured but— Why did the damn boy always have that look of contempt on his face?

"I called Mr. Wade. Like you said."

"Do you want him?" Rayner had said to the itinerant butcher who peddled meat to houses and farms around Hannaville. "Will you pay me for him?"

"Depends. We'll see."

The bull had wandered around in the field all afternoon with the pitchfork sticking out of his neck. "Toward evening Rayner went to the barn and got a pretty young heifer," Atlas said (the French dinner party, to the great relief of all its partakers, had reached the firmer ground of Roquefort and sourdough bread from San Francisco). "He put her on a leash, took her out into the field to tempt the bull. There's an irony for poor old Dad, huh? Jesus, the number of times he quoted to us: 'And I find more bitter than death the woman whose heart is traps and snares.' Anyhow, Rayner slammed the door behind them. By the time Mr. Wade arrived next morning, all was calm. Mr. Wade shot the bull, paid twenty-five dollars for him, ground him up and sold him to neighborhood housewives as hamburger."

Atlas toyed idly with a crumb of Roquefort. "They found buckshot in the rump," he said, as though puzzled by the blue veins in the cheese. "Somebody'd mistreated that animal once."

Jonathan didn't notice when Rayner left him. He just knew that the boy was gone and that he had not managed to thank him.

42

ALL WE GUESTS at Claire's dinner table put on a brave face
for the pièce de résistance, the magnificent *gâteau à la noix de
coco,* which turned out to be chocolate as well as coconut.
Claire poured out a lovely chilled Château d'Yquem to go with
it. The glasses were a wedding present from her mother, her
first marriage, not her marriage to Atlas; they had gold-leaf
rims on them. Atlas fell silent and picked idly at his cake, just
as he'd picked at his cheese, lifting and dropping forkfuls without putting them near his mouth. The conversation was des-
ultory when I noticed that Dr. Youngballs, on Atlas's left, had
wriggled so far down in his chair that only head and shoulders
showed above his plate; he had one leg stretched out, probing
under the glass table. (I am helpless, an innocent bystander:
I can't move my legs at all.) The dining room carpet was white.
Next to Atlas's foot lay a dark glob of *gâteau à la noix de
coco.* If Dr. Youngballs could get to it before Atlas lifted his
foot and ground it into the rug, perhaps all wouldn't be lost.
Success at hand (or rather at foot), and suddenly Atlas stands
up. "Got to take a piss," he says, lurching away from the
table: behind him on the carpet, a squash of *gâteau à la noix
de coco.*

   One morning in early August, two months after the bull
was dead, my grandfather maneuvered himself downstairs.
Sarah and the older children were out in the fields; he sat in
the parlor where Hope was playing with a piece of toweling.
Hope was three years old, a pretty child with her mother's
red-blond hair.

"Speak to me, Hope," he said.

She got to her feet, picked up the hem of her dress, spun around once, skirt billowing, and fell back down again.

He watched her a moment, then said, "Hasn't Hope anything to say to me?"

She slapped at the toweling but said nothing.

There are times when you know something's askew in a person, but nobody ever knows quite what to do about it. Jonathan made an abrupt move toward the little girl, to touch, to reassure. Such movements are ill-advised with broken ribs; his recoil was just as abrupt. She caught the abruptness—or so he thought—but not the concern behind it. She began to beat the towel into the floor with her fists. It occurred to him, as he battled the pain in his chest, that he hadn't heard her voice among the others for some time, and there were still no words—no crying, not even grunts. Her frenzy increased: she tore at the piece of cloth with her teeth. He watched helplessly. When Sarah came in from the fields a few minutes later, Hope was flailing the towel against the edge of the table with such violence that the table rocked back and forth and her own small frame shuddered.

Sarah dropped to her knees beside the child. She spat on her hands and rubbed saliva on the child's skin much as a stable lad might rub liniment into the joints of a horse after a race. "She started crying one night," Sarah said while she stroked, "not long after you— It was just a couple of days after we killed the bull. She cried and cried. All night long. Perhaps you didn't hear—no, how could you? You weren't hearing much of anything."

"What does Burgess say? What can he say? Is this permanent?"

"He doesn't know. A fever maybe. Maybe some kind of infection. He doesn't know."

Jonathan dragged himself into the kitchen for lunch. Sarah had burned the potatoes just as Wify had so often burned them before her. There was no meat. Nobody spoke. Across the table

Hope tore at her food just as she'd torn at the piece of toweling. She prodded potatoes into her mouth with her fingers, eyes scanning right to left and back again as though on the lookout for predators. The kitchen with its dirty stove and morning's porridge still aboil was more or less the kitchen of the Stokes' wooden house. Sarah hoisted herself up from her chair; she wasn't as heavy as Wify but she was getting there.

Jonathan grappled his way to his feet and left the kitchen, his chair falling over in his wake.

My aunt Claire's dinner party didn't end in disaster for the simple reason that the Murphys and the Youngballses left as early as they dared. Claire retired under the table with carpet cleaner and scrub brush.

"Could you talk a little more? Or are you too tired?" I asked Atlas.

"Never tired. Let's talk."

"Here?" I said, trying to be diplomatic. I didn't see how he could get himself anywhere else.

"Nope. Office." He held on to my wheelchair for balance and together we staggered away from Claire's scrubbing and toward my tape recorder, a shut door and yet another secret drink, poured out into a dosage glass from the remainder of the whiskey he'd bought that afternoon. "God knows what Dad had in mind," Atlas was saying. "He got his shotgun from the parlor: 110-gauge single-shot: carries small pellets— you use it for short range—a good little gun. He sat out there near the barn. I just kept out of range: I knew how far the thing would shoot: I was ten years old. It went on for about three hours—he just lay there up against the rail fence. Cleanest farm in the community, Dad's farm was, straightest fences—made of cedar rails. He told us to get the hell out, leave him alone, he had something to do. Jesus, we were scared. In the end it was Rayner— You know, your dad, Rayner, he had a real warmth and gentleness to him that my dad never saw. Anyhow, Rayner went out to him and about five minutes later they came back together. Don't know what happened. Nobody ever said another word about it. Lay you a bet that if you ever figure out how to read those diaries, you won't find any mention of it in them, neither."

Atlas was wrong. It's there. Jonathan had his own fierce standards. Rayner walked up to him, right through the full range of that shotgun, not flinching at all (the auto-destruct bravado that is our family legacy), and he said, "You selfish bastard. What's going to happen to Mama? What's going to happen to Hope?" And so Jonathan gave him the gun. This isn't the way Rayner told the story to me when I was little. He told only of the siege itself; and hearing it, I felt myself at the edge of whole landscapes of nightmare that lived in Jonathan and that threatened me through him. But I've never quite made out, not even now, grown up, with his diaries in front of me, precisely what it is that frightens me so much—and yet I know that somewhere here lies the secret bond between him and me.

43

FOR THE NEXT SIX YEARS (owing more to the boomtime wars bring with them than to any increase in my grandfather's Herculean efforts), strawberries moved out of the Carrick farm over the Northern Pacific Railroad eastward to elegant restaurants in Chicago where such luminaries as George Stoke ate and entertained. Strawberries paid part of Rayner's tuition at Reed and most of Gwendolyn's nursing school in Seattle;

strawberries were scheduled to pay some of Atlas's premed at the University of Washington when the time came. But there was little left over—and neither the will nor the energy to spend that little on pleasantries. The occasional stories about George that appeared in the paper—his power, his family, his good works and in one story, his "fabled love of strawberries"— penetrated my grandfather's head like whisperings from hell.

One morning in August, Sarah collapsed in the fields. "Will Gwendolyn come and stay?" Burgess Mundt said. "She's going to need a nurse, you know."

Gwendolyn had grown into a fierce-faced young woman in strong shoes and a starched uniform. She drove into Seattle and bought wallpaper, carpet and curtain materials. "Let Rayner pay all his tuition next year," she said. She hired a man to put up the wallpaper; she made and hung the curtains, spread the carpet on the floor and bought a special bed that cranked up and down. Jonathan carried Sarah downstairs and laid her on the new bed. She looked around at the room, eyes alight. "Am I dying, Johnny?" There was excitement in her voice, a delighted anticipation as though she'd been invited to a party. "Is that what it is? Is it over? Really? Oh, what a relief! What a— But there's no pelmet. I want a pelmet, Johnny—" She looked up at him, and a shadow of the old concern crossed her face. "Oh, don't take it like that," she went on. "I'm so tired—" She broke off, shut her eyes and lay back against the pillows.

Before winter she lost the weight she'd put on; in spring she shrank and grew yellow. The following June, tiny, wizened and brown, she died.

"What was his reaction?" I asked Atlas. "Did he show any?"

"I found him out in the barn," Atlas said. "He was crying. I'd never seen him cry before, so I put my arm around him, and—" Tears came to Atlas's eyes. He looked down into his drink. The tears flowed faster. He was very, very drunk.

"And what?"

"He beat the shit out of me," Atlas said.

PART 5

THURSDAY: WAR

44

JUDGING BY ATLAS'S CONDITION after the French dinner party, I wasn't at all sure he could manage the trip we'd planned for the following day all the way to Hannaville and Jonathan's grave. It was Claire who had to help me to bed—and him, too. In the morning, it was she who helped me up, she who maneuvered him out of bed at about ten, she who organized the trip, and she who sat at the wheel to begin with, while he snored, open-mouthed, drooling a little, looking not just old but ancient: eyelids papery behind fighter-pilot trifocals askew, body splayed out at the mercy of us all as vulnerably as it was splayed out across the back seat of the car. He must have taken Valium or barbiturates to make him so calmly groggy—no sign of jitters at all. He'd said at the end of the evening that he didn't really know what his father had done after his mother's death: "Something happened," he said. "Not for a year or so, but then—I don't know: something." Most of my details come from Jonathan's diaries; a few come from newspapers; the rest is guesswork. But then what's truth without out a bit of guesswork thrown in?

After Sarah's death, the only thing my grandfather did with passion was wait. At night he waited for morning to come. In the morning, he waited for noon. In the evening he waited for eight o'clock, then for nine o'clock, then— Even lifting a spoonful of porridge came to seem an intrusion. This waiting went on, as Atlas said, for a year or so: seventeen months, to be exact. What point was there in it? What point was there in anything? Why not just sink into the grave? There must be answers to questions like these that buzzed across Jonathan's mind like bluebottles in an outdoor crapper, and then buzzed back again, back and forth, back and forth, bodies thumping against the walls to mark the end of each passage: the biblical questions, the fundamental ones, the ones rejected these days by philosophy departments. His old nightmare was constant; no night went by without it. Weeds encroached on his land. His once pristine fences, made of cedar rails, once the straightest fences for miles around, bowed and sagged under the weight of snow.

Then came the story about the Methodist Congress—and at the same moment his decision to go to the source itself: to go to George, to settle the affair between them that had ruled his life and beggared his spirit. This decision changed everything: it led him beside the still waters; it restored his soul. It gave him aim, purpose, meaning. Most important, it stopped the questions and the nightmare, just as God had stopped them during the period of the idyll.

The principle that rules modern philosophy departments has always ruled in war: as Clausewitz says, war is easy. In war, if a question can't be answered, it must be ignored: a question posed is a question with an answer—exactly what linguistic philosophy teaches. What a wonderful conjunction of purpose! The philosophic and the military wedded at last, united in this neatly closed interval of thought which is the metaphysic of battle. Jonathan was ready—had been ready for years—supplies depoted, troops on standby, strategy planned, tactics worked out. The trip to Sweetbrier pleased him as nothing had pleased him in years: over the mountains, across the deserts and plains he'd crossed and recrossed so many years ago on the railroad, and straight on to Sweetbrier itself. His glimpse of George from across the lawn left him exhilarated; his talk with George's daughter brought him the kind of taut excitement known only to military professionals on the eve of action. Jonathan's generals conferred in camera; his troops massed along the border. He kept these preparations secret by spending two weeks at the Methodist Congress in Topeka where he attended lectures and meetings and where, professional that he was, he even heard his own voice speaking from time to time.

"Yes, yes, of course."

"No, no. That would never do."

"You must forgive me. I really can't venture an opinion."

He strained against the days that stood between him and George, between him and the answer, between him and truth, precisely as all those years ago he had strained against the weeks that stood between him and the moment he'd left George for dead beside the railroad and run away to the west, to Denver and a peacetime circus of a life, where the air was clean and the mountains glistened. But when he slept now, even with the tension on him, he slept the sleep of angels—quiet, unperturbed, undreaming, his nightmare as far away from him as such things are from any of us who know the justice of what we're doing, and feel easy with it.

On the last night of the conference, he excused himself from the celebratory dinner; he said he felt a touch of flu coming on.

"I will get a doctor," said the Reverend Jeffcoat, who was in charge of the celebratory dinner committee.

"That's not necessary," Jonathan said.

"But my dear fellow, you are plainly—"

Jonathan struggled to control his irritation—and failed. "Leave me alone," he said and turned his back on his tormentor, who watched him walk away, admiring his fortitude if not his manners.

At the hotel, my grandfather told the clerk he was not to be disturbed. Half an hour later, he put on his frock coat. This frock coat may have been twenty years out of date by this time, and in its way an absurdity, but then so is any cockade. How foolish they all look when looked at cold: epaulets, rows of decorations, army helmets, panaches—and yet how glorious, too. A man in a frock coat hasn't failed. Of course he hasn't. Who could possibly suggest it? Jonathan my grandfather walked quietly down the back stairs, cranked up his ancient black Saxon and rattled down the roads toward George's mansion.

On our modern-day trip to Hannaville, in Atlas's squashy bathtub of a car, Claire drove for the first hour or so. Atlas was proud of her driving. "She's as good as any man," he'd said. "She nips in and out of traffic just like me." Despite her fluffy white curls and pink pantsuit, there was no timidity, no indecision; she was fast, firm, controlled. The road she drove us along, out of Dr. Youngballs's old-age ghetto and up the Washington coast, was one of those roads that look as though they could be anywhere in the United States, East Coast just as well as West, North, South, Middle West, anywhere at all: a smooth, meaningless highway from nowhere to nowhere, heavy traffic in both directions. But it was a pretty day, clear and cool, not at all like the awful midwestern summer night Jonathan describes in his diaries: "Hot enough to drown in," he says, the very same words he used to describe that terrible night half a century before when George had come calling at the soddy door. Jonathan parked the Saxon a mile from George's mansion. He walked the rest of the way. Not until he reached the outskirts of George's land did he sense the full power of the ordered ranks around him: old hatreds and animosities in battle formation, indestructible as only blind instincts can be. He listened to the dark night as he crossed the lawn and heard echoes from the picnic of two weeks before: George's voice midstride in a platitude, the giggled whispers of children, the rustling skirts of George's pretty daughter, his own footsteps on the grass as he walked toward the big house.

45

"HERE ON THIS SPOT, in this very hour," writes Clausewitz on the eve of battle, "to conquer the enemy is the purpose in which the plan of the War with all its threads converges, in which all distant hopes, all dim glimmerings of the future meet." Jonathan's strategy followed the age-old principle: seek the simplest solution. His tactics were complex but clean-lined, classical; he managed things so that he saw George before George saw him. "Good evening, Senator," he said. His voice was mild.

George stood on his grand portico in the light from the doorway behind him, as black and featureless as his shadow which zigzagged down over the stairs; he started a little at Jonathan's voice, just a little, but just enough for Jonathan to see.

"Hey, listen at you, boy. Who'd ever think *you* could sound so fancy? Welcome, Jonathan. Welcome. Watch the step there. Not lit good from where you are, is it?"

George shifted back into the light, which threw shadows over the contours of his face much as the candlelight in the soddy fifty years ago had thrown shadows over him that lengthened and shortened as though the shiny, round eyes were breathing vents into the dungeon of a soul that lay behind them. Jonathan took the steps slowly. Midway up he could see that the cheeks were puffy now, edematous rather than plump. Near the top of the stairs, and the round eyes were dull and lashless behind round spectacles; they peered out above swells of flesh greasy with sweat. There was wariness where the contempt used to be. The lines around the mouth and beyond the smile were lines of serious pain. Jonathan had seen enough of death to know that this was a dying man, and not a man dying easily. How could he have missed something so evident? And only two weeks ago? Christ, he thought (asweat himself, now with relief as well as the suffocating heat), a month more and I'd have been too late.

George laughed. "Look at that face: just exactly the same. What are you doing in this part of the country? Huh? God, it's good to see you again."

Jonathan heard his own voice in response but could not make out the words.

"Come on in," George said. "It's cooler inside—a little, anyhow." He clapped an arm around Jonathan's shoulder and led him through the hallway into the study beyond. There are wounds to be suffered in the first encounter of any battle; that arm, full of memories and portent, lay heavy on Jonathan's shoulders. He bore stoically the nausea it brought with it— here's the virtue of well-drilled troops—but the sense of release when George removed his arm as they entered the living room was enough to make him giddy.

"Take a seat," George said, waving him toward the sofa where only two weeks before he had sat, talked to the pretty daughter and drunk a glass of water. "Sit down. Drink? Or do you Reverend guys abstain? Apple juice?"

Jonathan said something. It didn't matter what.

"You had a long drive?" George said. He poured liquid into two glasses. "Come to see me special, didn't you?"

"Of course." Since George made no response to this, Jonathan wasn't entirely sure he'd managed to get it out: perhaps he'd only thought it. The richness of the room shimmered around him—colors too strong, shapes too highly delineated. Crass, ugly, vulgar, and yet powerful even so—so much money, so much certainty—book-lined walls, marble fireplace, eaglehead candelabra, elegiac painting of the American Revolution. The painting was not quite as big as Jonathan had remembered it: he scanned the soldiers in satin coats, the flags snapping in the wind, the dead man at the center, with a pretty trickle of blood over the lace at his throat. Beads of sweat trembled on the wattles under George's chin; he had on the frock coat he'd been wearing at the picnic. Why doesn't he take it off? Jonathan thought. Velvet collar. Why don't I take off mine? But he'd known all those years ago that if he'd had a frock coat he'd have kept it on for such a fight as this with George. At the edge of his thoughts he caught sight of the town that lay beneath the evening star as he'd first seen it from the roof of the sod hut—a dozen saloons and all the promise of the future.

George handed Jonathan a drink and lowered his massive thighs into an overstuffed chair. "Course a frock coat don't look so funny on a Reverend gentleman as it does on an old senator. So—" he said, lifting his glass and smiling.

Jonathan lifted his glass, too: smiled, too, into George's smile and took a sip of the drink. What was it? Apple juice? Whiskey?

George slapped one fat leg. "My daughter says to me, this guy looks kind of peaked, so she brings you inside and she likes you. A preacher, she says. Then she shows me how you use your hands. I near to dropped dead. 'Only one guy uses his hands like that,' I say to myself, 'and that's Jonathan Carrick.' "

Jonathan tilted his head to squint at George.

"I says to her," George went on, " 'Victoria,' I says, 'this preacher of yours: was he wearing a frock coat like me?' And she says, 'Daddy, you're a genius.' "

George's laugh split in the middle, and Jonathan—noting the split and the vulnerability it implied—nodded, knew he had gained a point of country and felt calm determination edge its way through the tension of his battle lines.

"You got to know how much this means to me, Jonathan—your coming here to see me. Answer to my prayers, kind of. Jesus, when I think of that lousy hovel—"

"Which hovel?" Jonathan said. "Yours or the one I—what's the right word?—occupied?"

"What difference's it make? They both stank."

"It makes a difference to me."

George laughed. "Yeah, you're right. Of course you're right." He shifted in his chair, an awkward shift that made him wince. "Shit, I spent so many years trimming I don't hardly notice when I'm doing it anymore. How'd you get to be a preacher? Funny thing for a guy like you to do. Of all the things I'd have thought— Hey, you married? Got any children?"

A fan creaked around in the ceiling but failed to stir the sodden air.

"I have tried to do no harm," Jonathan said and was so surprised at his own words and at the anger so evident in them that he barely heard George's response.

"Yeah," George said. "What a waste."

One weekend during Jonathan's first year in Denver, College had taken him into the mountains. They spent the night up on a ridge about a hundred yards above one of those mountain springs that rush and gush through the rocks below. The next morning, about halfway down the mountain, working their way toward the stream, they saw a whistling marmot. I've never seen one of these creatures myself, but Jonathan says in his diaries that they live in rocks; they make nests there, and they call to each other from rock to rock, a moaning, sad note. Jonathan was carrying College's little single-shot .22 rifle; he aimed at the marmot, just for fun, carried away by the beauty of the place and the freedom of the mountains, never thinking of firing at it. College said, "You can't hit that thing." Jonathan said, "The hell I can't," and shot the marmot through the head.

Atlas was the only one of us Carricks who had any idea where Jonathan was buried. My father Rayner had made a point of not knowing. What few Carrick stragglers remained— other than myself, that is—did the same. After an hour or so on the road toward Hannaville, Claire stopped for coffee. She managed the wheelchair and me both; Atlas snored on in the car. We'd hardly spoken during the morning, Claire and I, but as soon as she'd fetched coffee for us and settled herself opposite me, she reached out and put her hand over mine.

"I'm sorry I was so irritable yesterday," she said. "I shouldn't have asked you to talk to Nate. It wouldn't do any good."

"I know."

"No, you don't. Nate doesn't know what day it is anymore. I mean really: Is it Tuesday? He doesn't know. Is it July? He doesn't know. He can't even remember what year it is. He loses his way when he goes out, gets fuddled on the way to the hospital, turns right when he should turn left. Sometimes he can't remember the way home."

"Really? He sounded fine all day yesterday—"

"Did he?"

"Well, not at the table," I said unhappily. "That was—But what about his practice? I can see there are some difficulties— He seems to manage pretty well still."

"There isn't too much he can do to harm these poor old folk. He reassures them. They need it; he's good at it, and most doctors don't bother. If anything important comes up, he usually has the sense to send them to someone else. Not always, though. There have been, uh, mistakes, and Dr. Youngballs is terrified of a suit. And now this cancer business—"

"What cancer business?"

"They're implanting radium seeds tomorrow: that's what the operation's about. Prostate cancer. Didn't he say?"

I shook my head. "What do radium seeds do?"

"I don't know. They set off alarm bells when you go through those metal detector things in an airport: that's what Nate says, and it's about all I know about them. I guess they buy a little time."

In George's ornate living room all those years ago, when only inventors and daredevils traveled by air, before there ever were such things as airports with metal detectors: in the steaming opulence of that room, the relentless ceiling fan creaked round and round, creak, creak, creak. It was as ineffectual as an airport alarm that reveals only radium seeds. The air hung as heavily as before.

"You really ain't changed at all, know that?" George said to Jonathan, my grandfather. "Not a bit. The voice is fancy and the way you walk and all, but the face: just the same. Inside, too, I bet. I can feel it. Well, what the hell, I can't offer you anything to eat. Wife off. Kids off. Gone to fucking Europe. Too hot to eat anyway. Servants off, too. Not a soul around."

Jonathan nodded as he had before.

"Knew that, did you? I'm glad you wanted us to be private. Well, ain't nobody here but you and me. Just us chickens. Want a cigar? Here, take one." Jonathan shook his head. "Come on, come on: they're Corona Coronas. The best." Jonathan shook his head again. The first picture he'd seen of George alive, in the Chicago *Tribune* on the way from Hannaville to Ellsworth, Maine, where he'd buried the Malloys: in that first picture George had been smoking a Corona Corona. George lit one now and grimaced as the taste hit him. How the hell can he keep it up? Jonathan thought. The pain—whatever it's from—is plainly terrible. And so goddamn fat, too. What's he on? Laudanum? Morphine?

"Ah, Johnny," George said. "Beautiful Johnny. You were my first foray into politics. Know that? Sure you do. Practically every fucking day I think to myself, Shit, I'm one of the best there is at this politics business—used to be anyhow—and

how did I learn my trade? Did my damnedest to squash you—
and you a defenseless little kid. So what happened? The defenseless little kid defended himself. Wonderful! By God, I
learned from that—"

"Have you been happy, George?" Jonathan interrupted.

George drank from his glass and grimaced at the taste of
the whiskey just as he'd grimaced at the taste of the cigar. "I
married a stupid bitch for her money, raped her a dozen times
to get kids for election purposes— I wish I could get this liquor
to taste like it used to. How come that happens, huh? You're
getting old and you feel lousy. What do you need? Liquor.
And what does the liquor do? Tastes like hog's piss. Cigars
taste like turds. There's justice for you." He put the glass back
on the table with a sigh. "I'm a whore, my old friend. I sell to
the highest bidder, and the bidding's getting lower these
days—"

"Cut the crap. You were a great senator."

"Yeah. But in politics you ain't happy 'less of which
there's a pack baying for your blood. Ain't nobody interested
like that in old George anymore." George put the cigar to his
mouth, hesitated and took it away again. "You were the first
one wanted to kill me maybe, but there was plenty after you.
And now? Nobody gives a fuck. Not a soul."

"Oh, come on, George," Jonathan said, letting his
amusement show. "You know I came here tonight to kill you.
Just in time, too, wouldn't you say?"

46

BY THE TIME Claire had maneuvered me into the car again, folded my wheelchair and got it back into the trunk, Atlas was awake. He insisted on taking the wheel, and he did not drive anywhere near as well as Claire. "Look at this country," he said, waving at the endless highway. "We're not far from Walla Walla. Beautiful, isn't it? One year when I was still in premed I worked in the wheat fields near here. And one day they let me drive an old Hayward combine. Know what that is? No? I always wanted to drive one—wonderful machine, drove a twenty-one-foot sickle, cut the wheat, shook the grains loose, blew them out to separate the chaff. It took thirty-three horses to pull the thing—"

"We go out at the next exit, isn't that right, Nate?" Claire said. "A mile further on."

"Thirty-three horses!" The car wavered a little as Atlas overrode Claire's instructions. "They used what you call a Shenandoah hitch for them. You look out over them—over the backs of them—sea of horseflesh. Six abreast, five rows, three leaders for the team. Line goes back from those three—all the way back to the guy with the reins—me—"

"You want the next junction, Nate," Claire said.

"Think of the swath you're running—you got the whole world in your hands, like the song says. You got to start a turn way ahead so the ripple effect hits the wheel horses just right—"

"This is the junction coming up." Claire's voice was sharp this time. "Five hundred yards ahead."

"The sickle swings into the wheat. Out again. See? If you're good enough, if you signal at just precisely the right moment—you can make a right-angle turn. Think of it: thirty-three horses: and a perfect right angle!"

"Now, Nate! Now," Claire shouted. But we had shot past the junction.

Atlas knew nothing—nothing at all—of this meeting between George and his father that I'm describing, nothing of the plans for it, nothing of what followed the plans. My father Rayner knew nothing about it, either. I alone know. George showed no surprise at the announcement that Jonathan had come to kill him. He picked up his glass and stared into it. "You never was like the others," he said to my grandfather. "How you going to do it?"

Jonathan opened his coat and displayed the Smith & Wesson that nestled there in a pool of sweat: College's Smith & Wesson: College who had not shot the whistling marmot, who was impaled on a railroad coupling and died with his face turned toward the silence and the dark.

"Well, I'm damned. Seems a good way for the eminent senator to go, don't it?" He stuck his fur-covered tongue into the whiskey. "Suicide's out. For me anyways. I'm a fucking federal institution and federal institutions don't— Assassination, though— That's beautiful." He put the glass down and leaned forward. "The question is why? See, like I been saying, for all this show I ain't—"

"Why what?"

"Motive, Johnny old friend. Public likes a motive for the murder of a federal institution." He laughed once more, and a shadow of the old contempt suddenly appeared in his eyes. "Holy shit, it's good to see that hatred in your face: makes a man feel alive, being hated—especially by you."

"Always wanting something more, aren't you, George?" Jonathan put his glass down on the table in front of him. "Now I know what you want, perhaps I won't oblige you after all. This apple juice is fermenting."

"You don't mean that."

"Yes, I do. I can smell it. I don't even—"

"I don't mean the goddamned apple juice. Shit! Have a whiskey instead. Then do it. I hurt like hell but I can wait through another drink." He scanned Jonathan's face. "Don't kid me, Johnny. I hurt too much for kidding—"

"What is truth?" Jonathan interrupted. "I am much interested in truth, George."

George's contempt disappeared as suddenly as it had arisen. "How the fuck would I know about something like that?" he said. "I'm a politician. Why don't you drink some whiskey?"

After my Columbia professor got so angry at me for refusing to accept truth as no more than a function on a computer: after he'd shouted at me, "Listen! What I'm telling you is first-year stuff! Elementary!" After that, he said to me wearily, "What do you want, anyway?" "Some explanation of things," I said. He sighed in disgust. "Then for Christ's sake, forget truth. Try coinage instead. You can feel it, spend it, and it sure as sweet Jesus tells you who you are."

"Why are you asking me questions like this?" George said to my grandfather.

Jonathan spread his hands.

"You want a map? Answers?"

"No. Only a theory."

"You don't work power with theories," George said. "Nor elections neither."

"I most particularly want your opinion—and on one particular theory." The heat in the room was so great that the smoke of George's cigar hung motionless as though encapsulated in steam. "According to this theory, truth itself can't be separated from a person's search for it. A process of elimination goes on. If you clear away enough of the underbrush, what's left has got to be truth. The question is, is it possible that you determine this thing not by what it is in itself but by what you discard to get at it?"

"Don't know what that means," George said. " 'By what you discard': that got a meaning?"

Claire took over the driving; it was miles before she could right Atlas's mistake—miles—and we ended up on a road neither of them knew at all. "After Mother's death," Atlas said from the back seat, "my sister Hope disappeared. Search parties went out to look for her, but it was Dad who found her, snuggled away under a bush. When he pulled her out, she snapped at him, teeth bared—like that horse Jenny that had snapped at him when he was at Malloy's Landing. There was blood caked all around her mouth. She'd bitten the flesh away from the fingers of both her hands—never heard of anything like that before or since: literally bitten it away—right down to the bone. There were ants feeding on the ragged remains of skin."

In George's splendid room, Jonathan turned his own hands palm up and then palm down in the gesture he did not understand but had become familiar with in himself; he studied the dry, work-hardened skin. "Right from the beginning you discard things," he said, "extraneous things, things that are too painful, things you haven't time for, little things, big things: what you end up with is certainly a judgment on you. The question is, is it truth? What do you think?"

"Don't know what the fuck you're talking about," George said irritably. "What I'm left with is you."

"Yes," Jonathan said. "Yes, that's it. Precisely. Thank you. Now tell me what's the matter with you."

"The matter?"

"This sickness of yours. What is it?"

George spread his massive thighs: his testicles nestled inside his left pant leg like a dead ferret, bloated and elongated, reaching down as far as his knee. "A mess, ain't it?" George said, looking down. "Christ, what I'd give to hear my pee hit

the side of a barn from three paces again. I ain't got no pleasures left. Can't eat. Can't sleep. Can't screw. Hurt all the
time. 'Discomfort,' these bastards call it. Discomfort, shit: agony— Get this over fast, will you Johnny?"

"I think I'll go now," Jonathan said, rising from his chair.
"Let you get some rest."

George started so abruptly that he knocked over his drink
and cried out from the pain of it. "You got to kill me first.
You said— Settle old wrongs. Two birds with one stone—
efficient—you were always efficient. Come on. Do it. I never
hated you, Johnny, you got to believe that. You're the one did
the hating. I never— You must of known it, too. Sometimes."

"No," Jonathan said.

"I walked around the parlor in that godforsaken little
wooden house," George rushed on, "wearing that frock coat
from Sears and Roebuck, and all I could think of was, 'Hey,
my Johnny's watching.' Always called you 'Johnny' to myself.
Know that? Shit, I used to feel your eyes on me, weighing me
up. You had beautiful eyes, Johnny. Still do—blue eyes with
black hair. Look at me: piece of meat waiting for an abattoir—
'Tonight Johnny comes,' I says to myself, 'and maybe the
whiskey will taste like whiskey again.' You must of known I
really loved you, Johnny, back then. For Christ's sake— It
was so goddamned obvious. I couldn't keep away from you.
Loved your backside and your belly and— How the fuck could
you not know?" George's eyes stayed fixed on Jonathan. "I
remember times," George said, then stopped and began again.
"Good times—"

"You'd better get some rest, George," Jonathan said
again.

"No! Don't go! No!" George tried to get up but failed.
"You can't leave me to die like this. Have another drink. We
never drank liquor together before, you and me, did we?"

"Yes," Jonathan said. "We did. Once. It was my first
taste of whiskey. You came calling at the soddy."

"Oh, Christ, yes— I didn't mean—"

"Didn't you? You let me put on your frock coat. Remember?"

"It wasn't hate, Johnny. It was love. Can't you see that? It was love!"

Jonathan said nothing.

"It was a shitty thing to do," George said, half sobbing now, plainly in such pain that he could hardly control his voice—or anything else. "I never should have— I've always regretted—"

"A bit late for apologies, isn't it?"

"The point is, that ain't got nothing to do with now. Now's different. You got to help me. You got to. Ain't you a preacher?"

"Not anymore."

"Once a preacher, always a preacher. You bastards are supposed to look after the dying."

"Not to the extent of mercy killing."

"What the hell did you come here for then?"

Jonathan who rarely smiled, smiled. "To hear you beg," he said.

The satin pants on the central figure—the dead man—in George's painting of the Revolution were the same pale cream color Jonathan had remembered. The man's eyes were shut, face in calm repose. This is not death. This is Disneyland, a soft, plastic event suited to Bugs Bunny and a traveling salesman's inflatable doll. George was real. His pants were serge; the thick ferretlike testicles were half-alive inside the cloth of the leg that darkened now with urine. "If begging's what you want, then I'll beg," George sobbed. "If that's what it takes—"

He maneuvered his massive posterior to the edge of the chair he sat in and then fell to his knees so hard that the glasses on the table slopped their contents. He let out an agonized groan at the shock.

"Get up, George," Jonathan said, standing so abruptly himself that he knocked over the chair he'd been sitting in. "Get up!"

George crawled on his knees, a clumsy, leaden crawl, toward my grandfather, who backed away but found himself trapped between George and the fallen chair. "Please, Johnny. Please, please. You're my only hope, only hope I got left. I seen guys die of this—this—"

"I have no purpose here. Get up."

"You ain't fighting fair. You always were a shit— I'm begging you, Johnny. Can't you see? I'm begging—"

Jonathan looked at him in a rage of triumph and disgust. "Aren't you going to wink at me, George?" he whispered.

George reached out and grabbed hold of Jonathan's frock coat—oh, frock coat! "How the fuck can I wink at you?" George wept. "You ain't said a fucking thing a man can get his hands on."

47

JONATHAN WAS HARDLY AWARE of the gun in his hand: George's head seemed to blossom into that shapeless red mass all of its own accord. My grandfather thought of the grapes Sarah used to hang in a muslin pouch above a bowl in the sink; the jelly that came from them was a deep red, and the dregs when she spread them on a tart were the color of what remained of George's face. The ceiling fan creak-creaked slowly round and round overhead, as helpless against the heat as ever; a grandfather clock tock-ticked off to one side. It was only when the weather broke that Jonathan moved, startled out of his trance by raindrops thudding down on the roof as locusts had thudded down on the roof of the Stokes' wooden house all those years ago. He walked out of the senator's mansion, leaving the door open behind him.

The assassination of Senator George Stoke is one of the great unsolved crimes of the century. Everybody knows this. Everybody has a theory. There were a number of arrests at the time. One of the suspects died in a way never explained and so came to the center of the stage; many were satisfied, but by no means all. I remember the precise position of my hand on the page when I read the last paragraphs of my computer-translated edition of Jonathan's diaries. So *this* is why he'd coded them. From the moment he purchased a leather-bound ledger from Benbow Wikin way back before the turn of the century he'd been planning to kill George, do what he'd failed to do as a boy, give his life the meaning it lost when he lost God and gained back George all in one fell swoop. There I sat sixty years and six thousand miles away from the murder, and watched my grandfather whom I'd feared as a child for his implacable justice and the rigidity of his adherence to moral precepts: I watched this man become the most famous murderer of his age.

He says he had little recollection of starting up the car. He set off toward Topeka, racing down the road, lurching from side to side, water running in sheets over the windshield. When he was about halfway there, he jerked the car to a stop in the middle of the road; and with the downpour making him blind, he saw that it was with him just as it is with us. He'd lost. He'd lost absolutely. Just as we have. We've harnessed the power of the sun; we can fuse atomic nuclei, and what has it brought us? Twenty-eight levels of war. Twenty-eight levels! This idea is Herman Kahn's—a brilliant man, a modern Clausewitz. At this twenty-eighth level we and our enemies end in "spasm war": total mutual annihilation. Jonathan died before I was born, when nuclear fission was only a dream, fusion not yet even that, but sitting in his Saxon in the middle of the road all those years ago, he was right up there at that twenty-eighth level, and he knew it.

"Ain't nobody here at all," George had said. "Just us chickens."

Chickens, Jonathan said to himself, thinking of College and long ago. That goddamn chicken. Then in spite of himself he began to laugh. Why did it cross the road? To get to the other side. Just to get— Why didn't I see it before? It's so obvious— He laughed until tears ran down his cheeks and his chest hurt. Just to get to the other side! No more reason than that. He held his breath to stop the laughter, failed, and laughed again.

He was back in Topeka by ten, in time for the morning's meeting on the last day of that year's congress. That evening the paper carried the headline SENATOR STOKE ASSASSI-NATED! INSANE FANATIC SOUGHT! The story mentioned a statewide alert, police searches, roadblocks, but Jonathan could not work up enough interest to finish the article. The next day he set out on the trip back to the Northwest.

As he approached the Kansas border he saw a police car across the road and slowed down.

"Roadblock. Where you going?" the officer said.

"Washington State."

"How come?"

"I live there."

"What you doing in Kansas?"

"Attending the Methodist Congress in Topeka."

"You a preacher?"

Jonathan nodded.

"Gee, I'm sorry, Reverend. You just drive on through."

"I take it you're here because of the senator's death?"

"Yeah. We'll get the guy. Don't you worry."

"And you don't think I'm responsible?" Jonathan said.

"Well," said the cop, smiling, "if you're going to get through life at all, your faith's got to start somewhere, don't it?"

Behind Jonathan lay the cornfields of Kansas, ahead of him the cornfields of Colorado, the boundary between the two marked only—and only for today and maybe tomorrow—by this solitary policeman with faith. "I don't know," Jonathan said at last. "Faith will probably serve as well as anything else. Is the road ahead clear?"

48

THE HANNAVILLE CEMETERY is simple but pleasant-looking and not badly kept. Jonathan's grave lies near one edge of it under a cedar tree; he would have liked that, I think. But we had difficulty finding it. Claire stayed in the car, and Atlas had quite a struggle pushing my wheelchair over the grass. Sarah's gravestone stood up brave and strong, a solid slab of granite with her name and dates on it and a fond, if somewhat sentimental, message.

"Where's Jonathan's grave?" I said.

"I dunno," Atlas said, peering down at the ground. "Gotta be here somewhere."

"He starved himself to death, didn't he?"

"Yeah. Old Irish custom. Awful."

There was no stone to be seen. I leaned down over my chair and ran my hands through the grass; the edge of a concrete brick showed just above the ground. I looked up at Atlas.

"Well, yeah, you see—" he began, embarrassed. Then he broke a twig off the cedar, lowered himself to the ground and began to scrape. The ground gave way after a bit, and as it did it revealed a succession of eroded letters that spelled out JONATHAN.

"Wouldn't even drink water," Atlas said, continuing to scrape. "Every couple of days I brought down four, five liters of saline and the tubing. Jesus, he looked miserable. Old Mundt didn't believe in any of it, and I was only a premed student— Damnedest thing, right at the end, Dad started plucking at the sheets. I said to Mundt, 'What's he doing?' Mundt said, 'Dying.' But I never saw anybody else pluck at the sheets like that—like he was picking up bugs off them." Atlas sighed. "But at least the poor bastard died hydrated."

Squinting from the height of my chair, I could see something on the concrete brick that might once have passed for CARRICK. No inscription, no dates.

"Good God, Atlas—" I began.

And my uncle, who had so patiently spoken into my tape machine all day the day before, who had given me the memoirs he valued so much even though he could not read them— my uncle, who had never before said a harsh word to me, suddenly grew angry.

"You think you understand everything, but you understand nothing at all," he said. "Look, I'll tell you. The human body is a wonderful thing. Just because you sit in a wheelchair doesn't change that. I'm a drunk: that doesn't change it, either. Life clings tight to its shape. Look in the mirror. Day after day, year after year, there's hardly any change at all. That's you: wrinkles, gray hair, what the hell—you can see it's you. I can see it. And yet every bone, every muscle, every patch of skin, tendon, blood vessel—every single particle—is being destroyed and replaced right as you look. Surface calm—and a mad scramble of activity underneath. So Dad suffered. But think of the performance! Incredible! The shape, the form, the pattern—all unchanged and yet not one single molecule of what was you seven years ago is part of you now. What do you want? Eternal permanence?"

"Some consistency. Some meaning."

"Oh, Jesus— Life's not like that, for Christ's sake. It's a whirlpool, a vortex. Sure it spirals downward, and when the water runs out the vortex collapses. You were born and then you die. If that's tragedy, life is tragic. But what's important is the rotating center. Where's your sense of wonder? The pattern is alive. Infinitely complex. Full of strands that weave in and out. It replenishes itself from surrounding waters again and again and again. Peel off the layers—grab at the veils— and there's nothing at all inside—not a smidgen. Well, why should there be anything? Truth's a convention, a fashion: it changes every year."

"Wheel me back to the car, Atlas."

"Look, goddamn you. You're trying so hard for a hemline that you're missing a miracle!"

We drove back to Atlas's house without speaking. When I got home to England (I've always felt like an alien; living abroad more or less institutionalizes the feeling), I wrote the Hannaville Cemetery Committee and enclosed payment for an appropriate memorial to Jonathan—granite to match Sarah's, but somewhat more tasteful, I hope. I won't ever see it myself. There's no point in going back now: Atlas died of leukemia a week ago. Radium seeds have a tendency to do that. Radium is a poorly understood, unstable atom, and the seeds of it in his belly managed to hold off his cancer only at the price of producing their own.

As Jonathan himself said, faith will serve as well as anything.

AUTHOR'S NOTE

My grandfather was a slave. This isn't an uncommon claim for an American to make if the American is black. But I'm not black. I'm white. My grandfather was white, too. And he was sold into slavery not in some barbaric third-world country: he was sold in the United States of America. A midwestern tobacco farmer bought him for fifteen dollars when he was four years old; not many people know about such sales, although they were common just after the Civil War. The slave's life my grandfather led until he ran away at sixteen so scarred him that no one who came near him afterwards could escape the effects of it; four of his seven children—including my father—ended up as suicides. My sister's therapist said to her, "You have all the hallmarks of an alcoholic's daughter." But alcohol has no part in it: it's the emotional skids and the dark anger that taint anybody, black or white, even at the distance of two generations away from slavery. *Theory of War* is an attempt to understand what my grandfather might have felt about what he'd gone through, and what we—his descendants—still have to cope with because of it.

A NOTE ON THE TYPE

This book was set in a modern adaptation of a type designed
by the first William Caslon (1692–1766), greatest of English
letter founders. The Caslon face, an artistic, easily read type,
has enjoyed two centuries of ever-increasing popularity in our
own country. It is of interest to note that the first copies of the
Declaration of Independence and the first paper currency
distributed to the citizens of the newborn nation were printed
in this typeface.

Composed by Creative Graphics,
Allentown, Pennsylvania

Printed and bound by The Haddon Craftsmen,
Scranton, Pennsylvania

Designed by Cassandra J. Pappas

BRA   Brady, Joan.

           Theory of war.

$20.50

DATE			